Blood Surrender

Also from Cecilia Tan and Blue Moon Books:

Color of Pain, Shade of Pleasure

Blood Surrender

Edited by Cecilia Tan

Blood Surrender

"Blue-Blood Moon" first appeared online at gothic.net in 1998.

"La Paloma Blanca" was first published in "The Hunter's Prey: Tales of Texas Vampires" by Diane Whiteside, Ellora's Cave Publishing, Inc. Copyright © 2001, 2002.

"The Permanent" was first published in "Big Book of Hot Women's Erotica 2004" edited by Marilyn Jaye Lewis, A Venus Book Club Exclusive, 2004.

Published by
Blue Moon Books
An Imprint of Avalon Publishing Group Incorporated
245 West 17th Street, 11th floor
New York, NY 10011-5300

ISBN 1-56201-445-5

9 8 7 6 5 4 3 2 1

Printed in Canada
Distributed by Publishers Group West

Table of Contents

Moonlight and Trouble

Thomas S. Roche

She's been waiting for me, her white nightdress blowing in the wind, lolling in and out of sleep, her dreams a beacon to my hunger. She wants it; she's heard her calling to me. Why else would she leave her window open on such a cold night as this? I perch on the windowsill. She lies awake, her eyes open but blinded by sleep; she doesn't see me yet. I watch her. Her nightdress is soft and see-through around her breasts; her nipples, hard from the cold, stand full and erect. Her blonde hair is scattered across the pillow.

There's a moon tonight, full and pregnant as a sow. Swollen. Aching. But it's been dark till now, as the clouds, also pregnant, also swollen and aching, cover the moon.

At the instant I begin to transform, a break in the clouds lights me. She sees me, a shimmering liquid bat-form outlined against the single molten beam of moonlight. She gasps.

Then the clouds shift above, the light is gone and she sees nothing. I am in darkness, and she is in trouble.

Perhaps now fear has gripped her; she opens her mouth to scream. I catch her eyes as I begin the transformation, and her scream remains strangled in her throat. Her mouth wide open, she seems to be asking for the drink she knows will transform her.

I change, my body liquid and shimmering as I become myself

again. I walk slowly to the foot of the bed, lifting my cloak and spreading it until I fill her vision.

Her body, lithe and pale under her white nightdress, invites me. I can see the cleft of her thighs under the see-through gown. Her legs are slightly spread, her pussy downed with fine blonde hair.

I'm wearing nothing—naked, except for my cloak.

She goes to scream again, wrestling against her need for me, resisting. I shake my head, and she accepts the "no," surrendering once again to my will.

I climb onto the bed and guide her into a sitting position—without touching her.

She bends down as I kneel before her. She takes my cock in her mouth and begins to suck it. She moans softly, low in her throat, as her head bobs up and down on it, her golden hair glimmering in the candlelight. She's whimpering, begging for it as her mouth works its way up and down my shaft. I grasp her hair firmly, tangling my fingers in her golden strands.

I pull gently on her hair and she lets out a desperate wail, hungry with need. Her mouth stays clamped around my shaft and she fucks her mouth down onto my cock, unstoppable. I pull more firmly, a sob choking deep in her throat as she feels me pulling her off. She resists. Her mouth slides down low enough to force the head of my cock into her throat. I feel the slight clench of her muscles as she wrestles with her own internal resistance; then her throat is open and she's taken me down, all the way, her throat filled with me.

I remove my hand and let her suck me.

Her whole body is undulating with the thrust of her mouth up and down on my shaft. She's bent forward on all fours now, her ass raised high in the air, its half-moons lovely under the ephemeral white of her nightdress. I can smell her pussy on the chill night air. She's moaning, the sound of it muffled in pizzicato by the fullness of my cock in her mouth and throat as she pumps it hungrily.

My fingers tangle again in her hair, and this time I don't let her stay. When she lets out a petulant sob and whimper, I yank, and her mouth comes off my cock, her lips parted wide, her mouth still working, her tongue lolling, drool stringing its way to the head of my cock. Her eyes full and open but glazed with sleep and lust, she begs me without a word, almost choking with sobs.

Her tongue ripples and surges, heaves and falls, seeking hungrily for my cock and my come as I hold her at bay.

She is beyond speech, her need having devoured her. I see tears running down her cheeks. They dribble, warm, onto my cock as she struggles against my grasp on her hair.

"Please," I hear her whimper. She's desperate, anxious. She has long ago been released from my spell, but this has only caused her to be consumed more than ever. The spell of her own need is the one that will destroy her.

"Please," she cries, weakly, miserably. "Please," she whispers. I see her lips moving over and over again, no sound escaping them. "Please. Please. Please. Please."

And again, her wet eyes in mine. "Please?"

I look into her shimmering green orbs, the glisten of her tears making my own hunger surge, my cock aching for release.

"There's no coming back," I tell her.

She hesitates, struggling with her need for it and her desire to remain pure, to remain in the life she knows.

She licks her lips, their red curves glistening, her tongue flickering like a serpent's.

Her tongue lolls out, cupped in supplication.

Still holding her hair firmly, I reach out with my other hand and take her wrist. I guide her hand to my cock and her fingers circle my shaft; their grip is firm, and she utters a plaintive, needy wail as she begins to stroke me.

The first stream fills the chalice of her cupped tongue; she moans, deep, low, hungry, and closes her mouth, swallowing. More come strikes her face as she opens her mouth wide; my semen covers her cheeks and dribbles down onto her chin. She whimpers sadly, trying to place her mouth on my cock, but I won't let her. She opens wide and accepts the next pulse of come, then the next, and the next, her throat wide to gulp as she savors the taste and heat on her tongue.

When I'm finished, I release her hair, and she swallows greedily, planting her mouth on my cock again, suckling my member, finding it hard, licking the remaining come as it drools out of the tip. Moaning, she sucks me again, her mouth working up and down my shaft as she swallows the tiny droplets that ooze out.

"No," I say firmly. "Now there's no turning back. It's time."

She looks up at me, her mouth wrapped tight around my cock. I can see her eyes are still moist, tears streaming down her glistening cheeks. She swallows, slowly eases my cock out of her mouth. Sadly. Her eyes riveted on it as she licks her shimmering lips. She never takes her eyes off of it as she slides onto her back, reclining, her hips lifting slightly off the bed, her breasts heaving invitingly as she moans softly.

"Please," she whimpers.

Her eyes remain on my cock, which does not go soft as men's do.

Her hands rush to her hips. She gathers her nightdress in her hands, pulling it quickly up.

"Please," she moans.

Her nightdress is bunched around her waist, her legs spread wide. She's not wearing anything underneath the nightdress. Her pussy is smoother and wetter than her waist. Pink, inviolate, untouched.

"Please," she whispers, her eyes still on my cock.

I drive forward onto her without a hint of the gentleness I've shown until now. I grasp her wrists in mine and shove them back hard against the bed. Her breath comes out of her in a rush, a gasp, a little moan of terror and desire. I land hard between her spread legs and pause only when the head of my cock spreads her pussy lips, forcing open her entrance.

I hold there, feeling her body tremble as she hovers under me, her ass lifted off the bed, her hips raised, her pelvis tilted for me to take her. Her legs spread, her feet flat on the ground. Her lips still glistening, working.

"Please," she whispers.

My thrust is hard but stops short. I force myself into her tightness perhaps an inch, and stop when I feel the press of her maidenhead. She whimpers and moans in pain, struggling against the pressure on her wrists and in her cunt. But then her hips lift further, and I smile as her eyes lock in mine, begging.

I slam into her, feeling her hymen give way with helplessness, her surrender signaled by the pressure of its rending. She chokes back another strangled moan of pain and her eyes go very wide as the breath goes out of her.

She settles underneath me as she feels that my cock has taken her. She shivers with pain and surrender and once more whispers: "Please."

Now, there is no cruelty greater than going slow. I take her gradually, pressing my mouth to hers and invading her with my tongue. She looks up into my eyes, the fear evident—she knows that this is the final moment, that never again will she know the sweet breath of living existence. Eternity will be hers, but life forever denied her, torn from her as completely as I've taken her virginity.

My lips stretch back around the sharp points and when she catches sight of them she freezes, her body thrust up against mine, her hips raising me up above her, her cunt grasping my hard organ. My fingers tangled in her blonde hair, I force her head to one side and expose the pale pulse of her throat.

I pierce her flesh with the same ease as I tore her maidenhead. The warmth of her carotid artery throbs in my mouth as I take her. The hot jet of blood shoots down my throat and I fuck her harder, faster, reaching my completion just as she explodes in climax, a scream of ecstatic release frozen in her savaged throat, exploding into my body instead. The taste of blood is sweetest of all when it fills you with an orgasm's scream—the scream of pleasure so overwhelming that the scream itself never made it. She comes again as I fill her cunt and drain her throat. I see her eyes, glassy and open, as I lift my face from her throat. Her lips work rhythmically, soundlessly. She would, I know, be whispering "Please"—if she was still able to make even the faintest sound.

I fuck her until I'm finished with her pussy, but I'm not nearly finished with the rest of her.

The strength has gone out of her, the softness of her slim body a wordless surrender. I lower my mouth to her throat again and drink deeply as I feel her hovering on the very edge of death.

I want to take her all the way. I want to devour her and leave her empty and destroyed, a husk in a blood-stained nightdress, legs spread, throat ravaged, eyes open wide, soul vanished into me.

But I don't, because there's something I want even more.

Reluctantly, I rise from her ruined throat, wiping my mouth with the back of my hand.

I sit her up and pull the nightdress over her head. I lay her back down, naked, her eyes open in death, her lips moving faintly—a prayer for me to take her? To save her? Or let her die?

Or, more likely, to fuck her again?

I bite into my wrist, squeezing out a single drop of blood. She is very close to death, now, and I must wait until the precise moment. Her lips work, her tongue lolling out, seeking the vampire's blood as if she's scented it.

The drop of blood forms, grows larger. I don't let it fall yet.

"Say 'Please,'" I tell her.

"Please," she whispers, and her eyes grow still and glassy, her lips and tongue rest immobile, tongue still extended, lips still parted to receive my elixir.

I squeeze the blood out onto her tongue. It trails down her throat and her naked body gives a start.

She begins to moan softly. I'm hard again, and as I shove my wrist violently to her mouth, I enter her ravaged pussy and take her once more. I fuck her faster as she twists and writhes under me, her moans rising in pitch as she suckles from my wrist. When I feel the sharpness of fangs against my wrist bones, I grab her hair, wrest my arm away from her, and plunge my tongue into her mouth.

The taste of blood mingles, sharp and metallic, as we kiss. I lift her legs into the air and push her hard against the bed, fucking her as we share this new taste of blood—a taste she will come to know very well in the coming months, years, centuries. When she senses I'm ready to come, her mouth works again, hungry for this elixir, as well. I pull out of her and lean back on my haunches as she bends down and takes my cock in her mouth. She eagerly sucks the come from my cock and swallows every drop.

She looks up at me, her face a mask of surrender and love, her lips slick with come and blood. We kiss, hungrily, as her naked body pulses with new life underneath me.

I carry her from the bed, wrap her in my cloak, and go to the window. The moon has broken through the thick clouds, bringing silver ghosts of moonlight to rest on the tops of the trees. I cradle my new mate's naked form curled up in my grasp, feeling her shift slightly against me, feeling her lips move soundlessly against my chest. Mouthing the word, "Please." I caress her moonlit hair with a long-nailed hand. Holding her, I leap from the window, taking wing.

SHE

CAROLINE AUBREY

I swear by the moonlight in her eyes, by the look of love in those deepened, black pools of night, that I was not looking for anyone to share my bed, no less share my loneliness and my fear. Fear of what I had become, fear of what I might have turned into, fear of the power that pulsed in my veins, searing pain in every heartbeat, every sound, every vision of death that filled me as I walked the lonely gas lamp-lit streets as music and cheer filled my head, heightening my sense of fear and longing. Heightening my loneliness and the sense that only moonlight could light what was left of my life, of never seeing the sun again and knowing only the lighted darkness of that blessed silver orb. I had grown accustomed to the sight of my skin in moonlight; where once my skin had been dark coffee lightened with sweet milk in the golden days of my youth, now my flesh was a dampened pale drowned silvery brown, like the once-golden color of honey soaked by the silver rays of the moon in the brightest, blackest night.

Ah, but I digress. The river does that to me, brings me back two hundred years to when I was first crossed-over, to where I was an angry young man afraid of the looks in the eyes of men when they looked at me too long and too hard, afraid of the affections of women in whom one snap of my teeth would kill and scatter bones without so much a thought or remorseful word. I had dreamt of the river the day before, of the dark recesses and mysteries held within its depths, that Mississippi River, one foot in the north, the other in the south, stretched long-limbed and resilient in what had become the modern world. It was this river that brought her to me, or me to her, however one would want to look at it.

In the past now, so far away yet as if the taste of yesterday were upon my lips, I would hunt the night for fresh blood. There was no theatrics involved, no cat and mouse game of it, no hunter and the hunted chase through dark streets. Simply, I was hungry, and I would feed. After stalking some unfortunate slum of the French Quarter for nearly half the night, and upon disposing of the body of my fresh kill, I would escape the noise and din of town and head to the river, basking in the reverie of a fresh feast, letting the hot blood seep through to my bones and into my muscles, filling me. I was not a bitter immortal, but a rather the bitterness I felt as a mortal had turned into a great melancholic pondering as an immortal. I would stare at the stars and marvel at how I, the child of a great quadroon beauty, lover of an African priest, educated and of great intellect, had come to cross over to the world of the blood-hunted. Stars swam in my eyes of red tears as I recounted, night after night, the warm evening in which my African aristocrat took me in his arms and showed me his fangs. I ran my tongue over those sharp, opaque points, and knew that I would at last exact my revenge upon the citizens of New Orleans who looked at my mother with viciousness, disgust, jealousy, lust, and hate. But once I had turned completely, there was no revenge as the motivation of my feeding, no great plan to rid the world of the evil as I saw it. Once my eyes were opened as a vampire, I simply saw things differently. With humor, with respect, with reverence, if you will. All of God's creation was suddenly beautiful, and the cosmic joke was that I would be around forever to enjoy it, to see it in new eyes no mortal ever could, albeit alone. And I would be destined to watch, alongside the beauty of His creation, the destruction and desolation His minions would wreck there. I would watch them destroy themselves in their hatred of "the other."

For one hundred years I had hunted the streets of my home, watching it turn from a sleepy French trading town to an American city, the best and brightest this alleged new nation had to offer, yet at the expense of its native peoples. I watched as the natives were pushed aside, along with us, the *gens de coleur libre,* free people of color, in order for the English to have their power and call their new "free state" America. To me, it was a sign of their viciousness and greed. New Orleans was the last vestige of hope in this supposed New World, and they had taken it from us, under a cloak of darkness. I was under my own cloak of darkness, taking from them what they had taken from us: blood. It sustained me in more ways than one can imagine . . . satisfied my hunger, my need for revenge, my solitude. Laughter and tears came easily to me as I fed, then followed by my solitude, the solitude of the night's stars and sounds, its beauty and vision filling me along with the blood of its children. This solitude is what led me to the river that night, to the sounds of tears and prayers in a voice more ancient than the spires of the great cathedrals of the Old World.

I was thinking of my lover, my maker, the African priest whose name I have never spoken since I had crossed over. His long, darkened hands, his hair the color of the deepest night, and the way his hair fell upon my chest in its free flowing braided cords flushed gray in moonlight; the swarm of stars as I closed my eyes on my mortal life one last time, his lips pressed to my throat . . .

It was her scent that lulled me out of my dream-like state, rooted there in the magnolia and river-scented earth. I likened most mortals' scents to the comfort foods of childhood, when the sounds of the kitchen wooed and rescued me from the rigors of my studies and the harsh edicts of my French father. My mother would stand guard in the kitchen, slim-waisted, long dark hair falling well past her ample child-bearing hips, barking orders in French to the cooks, black eyes throwing darts at anyone who questioned her. Ah, my beautiful mother. Felicity. Felicity Carriere, quadroon mistress to the great Michel Revard, mother of his four white-looking, octoroon children, well paid for her services when my father's wife was tired or not exotic enough for him. We had our own house, our own servants, and money to spend. I adored my mother, and when she died it broke my heart to see how my father stayed away from her at that time. Death had ravaged her face, and the great beauty died with her. Looking upon her face in death sent me into further retreat from the world, and in doing so I became filled with hatred of this world that judged one so magnificent by the color of their skin or by their gender. I came to understand that no matter how beautiful, how educated, and how rich my brothers and I were, we would always be Revard's colored bastards.

How I hated the way men would look at my mother, out of the backs of their eyes, when they thought their wives weren't looking; I swore I would kill them when I could, suck the thin blood out of their pale, old guard bodies and watch it flow into the river, away from Mama and away from all of us. When my lover offered me the chance to cross over, I saw my perfect, beautiful revenge taking shape. Yet when I crossed over, the scent of the old guard was like stale grapes, overripened and rotting; to this day their blood makes me sick, but then I would take them, make them ask for me, then watch as their life faded away in the river that pumped in my veins, filling me, as their hate mingled with mine and made me rage. At first I had fancied myself, with my youthful folly, a voracious hunter, a vicious killer; if I could not bring my mother and my lover back, then the rest of the living world would pay for the sins of those who sent them away from me.

She, however, changed everything for me—everything and nothing. I would bring them back. My mother and my lover. Both of them. In her.

The Africans' scent was like sweet molasses, dark and rich, melting candy in the sun. The more mixed they were, the less like pure molasses and more like deep, rich honey. But she was like no one I'd ever scented before. Her fragrance maddened me, charged me in a way I hadn't been in many years. And then I heard her voice.

I could not understand her words; she was speaking in the old language I had only heard a few times along the river, but I could recognize the hushed, tearful strain in her voice and knew she was praying. Through the trees I could see her, and still very far off I could make out the long dark hair, the sleeveless blouse with the diamond back design along the bodice, and the black skirt and shawl which covered her arms. I could scent that she was sorrowing, that she had given birth just recently, but I knew from her voice the child had died. It was at that moment I understood true grief: grief over the promise of new life stolen from under a mother's breast, grief from living through the deaths of one's children.

Her face was dark, eyes black pools of water reflecting in the moonlight. She had a long, aquiline nose and full lips parted in prayer.

What she was saying, I did not know, but she was crying, I could hear it. Yet I knew I had to cross the river to see her for myself.

My hunting had left me strong and silent; I was at my peak. My senses were sharp; I could hear a passing thought miles away in that state, smell a mortal for days in the afterglow of a kill. But her scent maddened me, intoxicated me, and satiated though I was, denied I would not be.

And suddenly, there she was standing before me, like some dark angel fallen from heaven onto the moonlit shores of the river, her feet immersed in the thick brown water. Skirts lifted, strong hands dark against the white crinoline petticoats, hair falling across a bare shoulder like cascading black water, something deep within me stirred like I hadn't been touched in a long time. It wasn't the hunger of blood, the longing; but something else I hadn't felt since I crossed over: the rush of blood filling my loins and hardening me, aching for the softness of a woman's flesh surrounding me.

I stood silent watching her as she emerged further from the water. I was stone, I was silence, I blended seamlessly with magnolias and moss; the breeze lifting off the river and running over me as I fluttered and grazed with the oily leaves. She was singing, and turned back to the shore. The tobacco leaves crushed in her hand, wet by the sweat of her palm, assailed me as she let go of them, and they drifted on the night breeze, into the water. She was liquid heat, simmering molasses and cream and nutmeg; this Creole beauty, this dark Choctaw angel; this sorrowing woman at the shore. In the span of one hundred years I was transported back, back to the edge of the river where I walked alone, to escape the prying eyes and hands of the lecherous few intent upon making a beautiful octoroon boy their own, where I first met my maker in the dappled moonlit shore of the Mississippi River. Now those were hands I would die in, hands I did—if you will—die in, with wisdom of ancient and timeless dark desert skies, smooth, ebony shine and teeth so white that flashed in the moonlight and he was so beautiful, but this part of my story is not about him, it is about her, about how in creating her, she created me.

With a sharp turn of her head, the slightest beckoning glance, she looked across the river, into the leaves and trees there, as if she saw me. Her hair fell in rivulets upon her shoulders, between her heavy breasts, pressed together in the darkness that caused a sheen of perspiration to break out of my forehead and my lip. I could almost swear she could have heard the sound of my sweat pearling in red, shimmering drops in the moonlight, but I was still, so still, like the root of the tree that held me into the ground. Her senses were on fire, alert, and when she was still her scent grew stronger, so strong that I wanted to leap from the trees and bear down on her dark acceptance, her plush tenderness, her liquid heat; to taste her not in the way I had tasted others, but to embed myself within her slick folds, bury my face in those swollen breasts.

"Hutuk awasa," she whispered, the sound of her breathless voice invading my fantasy, "I see you there."

How could she have seen me? I asked myself almost a thousand times, standing there within the trees, yet I knew it was to me she was speaking. She had spoken to me in her language, called me out, and there she was, standing before me, unafraid, there on the river. I stepped away from the trees and moved forward, gliding across the wet earth.

She did not move, did not recoil, just stood there, watching me, still and silent. In one hundred years, since my crossing, I had not felt desire for a woman, or even for a man, until she stood at the river, making a prayer to some long-forgotten deity, in a language that was slowly disappearing from river country and to regions into the west, where the land was red with the blood of her relatives. *"Miti . . ."* she whispered again in that same breathless, succulent voice, "I want you to see me as I see you."

Her prayers were indeed strong, strong as the cords of sinew and muscle that lined her arms and ran across her back. The breeze lifted her scent and there were undertones of musk and gardenia, of jasmine and sweet wine. I so badly wanted to see her skin, to touch the flesh under the cotton and crinoline, that I did my best conjuring of that river wind, lifting with it the thin summer skirts, opening slightly the white blouse she wore—barely covering the shadowed slope of her breasts—grazing a hardened nipple. I felt the heat rise from her in the narrow space between our bodies. My own blood surged through my veins, and every part of me ached with the wanting . . . the wanting of that fiery molasses and cream; the nutmeg and jasmine and gardenia and musk, the feel of my teeth sinking into that sweet flesh, the spurt of first blood upon my lips and teeth and tongue, liquid nectar running down my throat with her life and her heart pounding me with the essence of just who she was.

Oh, I was swollen when I reached her, ready to burst, rock-hard and needing release, and she knew that. When I saw her smile, saw her teeth flash in the moonlight—those perfectly smooth woman's teeth—I knew that she had prayed for me to come, and come I would. She moved to me, her mouth cornered to mine. Her tongue shot out into me, licking the blood off my incisors with its warm insistence. Moving my fingers slowly across her flesh, I raised chicken skin upon her, trailing at the soft pulse-point of her throat. Her skin was on fire, a shock of sweetness and soft, so soft, I could feel the rush of blood between my legs, hammering, wanting, needing release.

She lifted her arms and the cotton blouse slid from her shoulders to the soft earth below. She was standing there, in her shift and petticoats, skirts raised high, moonlight shining upon the darkness of her skin and crackling white hot darkness of night. I moved forward again, reaching for the laces of her shift and with trembling hands, slowly, carefully, unlaced the silken ribbons that held her breasts constricted to her body. They tumbled free as I slowly, so slowly traced a line with my fingertips up the taut flesh of her arms and slid the shift from her. I was careful not to let my nails raise blood welts upon her arms; that would come later.

I stood so close to her that I could feel her breath upon my face. She reached with her hands and slid the waistcoat and vest from me, then the cravat at my throat, then the shirt from my arms. The coolness of the starched silk against my skin made my hairs stand on end, and I growled in my throat her name.

With her left hand, she drew tiny lines and circles upon her left breast, tracing slowly to the dark areola and thick, hardening nipple. I reached behind her, unfastening the skirt around her slim waist, my hands running along the heat of her hips as I pressed the cotton to the ground. My lips grazed her engorged nipple and she gasped, a tiny, breathless gasp of pure pleasure that sent rivulets of blood fire pulsing though me. It had been so long for me that I was unsure where to go next, and her dark eyes darted up to mine. She had heard me.

She took a step back from me, running her fingers across her ample breasts, teasing and pulling on her erect nipples, sliding down the valley between her mounds, across her belly, and moving between the dark thatch of hair between her legs. Her eyes were on me as she moved her fingers slowly, rhythmically across her dampened flesh and I could feel her heart pounding, pumping in my head, as her fingers began to move in time with her beating heart.

The space closed between us as I moved forward in an instant, kneeling before her. God, she was beautiful, skin tawny and deep in the moonlight, a fine sheen of sweat covering her in the river breeze. She trembled in anticipation as I buried my face in her soft thatch of hair, breathing her in, then I nuzzled her hot wetness. Oh, and the strength and delicacy of her scent was enough to send me to heaven then, and I dreamt I was there with her, standing before God in some sort of twisted tribunal, the flowers she offered gave me my salvation, and my penance. I was a hungry sinner and my tongue snaked forward upon the petals of the offering she gave me, licking greedily and laving until my tongue found the hard nub of her flesh within. I took her between my teeth, sucking at her engorged tip, forcing it between my fangs. Her pelvis arched against me, pressing her mound further into my waiting mouth. Her fingers clawed at my hair, twisting it, her soft cries punctuating the molten darkness. I reached around her waist, fingers kneading the soft flesh of her buttocks and holding her firmly against my teeth. I forced her body where her soul would follow; she gave to me willingly and when she did, I drew first blood. Not much, just enough to feel the smooth taste of her running down my throat. She tightened against me again, raw, untamed.

I stood, holding her in my arms, her body stiff and contracting against my body. Her black eyes were clouded with pleasure, with release, with triumph, and once again she was pliant, taut, and I pulled her lips to mine. She groaned against the invasion of my tongue which thrust her blood and her come back inside of her. I would not let her rest. Taking her hand in mine, I guided her fingers to back to her gaping wetness, pushing her fingers inside until they were soaked. I took her hand again and wrapped her fingers around my shaft, wetting me and stroking me, until I thought I would explode all over her. But I would wait.

With her other hand, she took hold of mine, and moved my fingers between her slick folds. God, she was wet, moisture pearling and dripping from her, and I easily slipped two, then three fingers inside her, while she wrapped a long, slim leg around my waist, pressing the flesh of her thigh against my rock-hard cock. Raising her soaked hand, she pressed her fingers to my lips and my tongue darted between my incisors, licking the cream off her fingers. She writhed within my grasp, my fingers pumping against her slick, sucking sex, as I ran my tongue over her fingers and onto my teeth. She was cream and jasmine and musk to me, and she bucked her hips against my hand, arching into me, crying out under the moonlight.

No longer able to contain myself, I pulled out my hand and dove into her, raising her up onto me. Her hands flew around my neck, tangling in my hair, pulling my lips to her swollen nipples, and I thrust harder into her, pressing at her womb with each thrust. Harder and harder I dove, until she was crying out, harder and faster, her voice echoing up the slopes of the riverbank and onto the oiled leaves and magnolia blossoms. My grip upon her hips was relentless, impaling her with each thrust, her cries urging me on. She clung savagely to my neck, pressing her nipples against my face and I dove for each magnificent tip, sucking, running my fangs along the hardest part, and then, only then, did I draw blood.

Ah, molasses and mother's milk, the sweetest, most comforting, most intoxicating blend of hard liquid fire shot through my mouth and down my throat. I fed on her, mercilessly, barely aware of her nails imbedded in my shoulders. Sweet nutmeg and mulled wine filled me and with a great roar of flames I spilled into her, the blood and life of one hundred years erupting from my loins and into hers. I fed on her, giving her the life within me, sustaining her with what I drank from her and what I fed her. The more I sucked, the weaker I became, dizzying and drunken on her flesh and blood, bone and muscle. In a swarm of stars and trees, I felt us fall to the ground, our grips upon and within each other tight and sucking.

Vaguely aware of her slowing heartbeat, I pulled away from her breast, cradling her head in my hands. *Take me into your mouth,* I whispered in my head, and she heard me. As if drunken and weak, she moved her head slowly to my still solid cock, moving her lips across the velvet tip. She took me inside of her, a tangle of teeth, tongue, and soft, wet walls, moving across my hard length. I felt the blood rush inside me again, building fire and flame within me, and I spilled again. She took it all in, sucking, laving, drinking me, and I stroked her forehead, her hair, her cheeks, her throat, her jaw line, and as I watched her in the moonlight, the thin sheen of sweat forming upon her brow turned from a clear shine to a fuzzy red, and she was complete. She pulled away from me, blood pouring from her sex, from mine, from her nipples, from my mouth, and we lay there a long time, licking the sweet blood-sweat from our soaked bodies, our hearts slowing and pounding so deeply, so slowly, that neither could be heard as we drifted in the madness of one another's memories: mine of the soft smells and sights of my mother's kitchen, hers the fires within the women's lodge, sweet herbs and smoke wafting through prayers in a language that was fading slowly from the red earth below us.

Her blood filled me with her life, her triumphs and her tragedies, the loss of three children and a husband at the hand of her enemies; mine filled her with visions of my maker and his maker, of the hushed voices of my mother and father in the moonlight, of my African lover by the light of candled darkness. I looked down upon her, upon her perfectly formed beauty in the darkness, as the life spilled from her into the soft, wet earth, and watched as my blood filled those places where death would never reign. *What I have done,* I thought, *I have done.* I had never made one before. But she was perfectly patterned, and I could feel her power rising within the blood I had given her, blood of my blood, becoming her own. She had once created something, and lost it. Three children buried into the earth, and she would live forever. I had created her, and now she would never suffer the fate her children did, nor suffer the death mask as my mother had, all those years ago. No mother should suffer the death of her children, as mine had, as she did.

They are killing us, I heard her whisper. *I want to live. I do not want lines etched from my blood to make their borders. I want to speak my language, pray my prayers, save my children. How can I if I must die?*

"You will not die," I whispered aloud against her hair. "I have seen to it."

I prayed for you, again her voice, soft in the river breeze, *I came here to the river to ask for your help. My people are dying.*

We are all dying, I answered her. *Our way of life, our people, our language, ourselves.*

What must we do? she asked me in the hallowed shadows.

Forgive them. Hunt them, but never again in revenge for what we cannot ourselves forget. I kissed the top of her smooth black hair. *Do you regret what you asked of me?*

She answered me by holding me close to her, resting my head upon her shoulder.

It was in that moment I loved her, and I knew I could never let her go. I had given her what she had asked for . . . survival. Survival in speaking her language, in singing her songs, in living where her people were dying. But to me, she was my salvation, antidote for my rage, my seed, my lover; and there, upon the river, I began to truly live again.

That night was a lifetime ago. Well, two or three lifetimes now.

I tell this story now, staring not at the shores of the river, but gazing out at the ocean covered with a thick drench of fog. There on that river, deep and dark where we first joined, where our blood became one, the modern world has embedded itself into those old waterways with man-made stone, with cement blocks and mortar and steel; trash dots the landscape where magnolias once did. Oh, my river still is constant; everything and nothing changes in that way in the two hundred years since she came to me on that bank of the mighty Mississippi River. Solitude is not the best revenge for anyone; living is. That river holds memories for me too painful to examine, and it was after that night we first made love on the shores, after she had crossed over, that we left for good. I turn from the window two hundred years later and watch her sleep, a tangle of moonlight and shadow upon red silk, her hair fanned out across the pillow. She is filled, ripe from last night's hunt, drunk upon blood and my never-ending hunger for her. In her reverie, she had sent me a dream of the river early this morning, wrapped in the peaceful confines of my long arms, legs and arms and tongues and fingers a tangle in the shut-out morning light.

In my dream we are not walking the shores of California but on the banks of the Mississippi. The smell of softened tobacco leaves besets my senses. I'm on alert, needing to feed, the hunt starting in the small of my belly, moving through my loins where soon it will become a need so great I will not be able to control it. Standing near the river, in the thick, dark Louisiana mud, I glance over my shoulder. She is wearing a long patchwork coat of many colors, singing a song, emptying the tobacco leaves from her hand into the river. I watch as she moves up the bank and stands behind me, slipping her arms around my waist, leaning her chin upon my shoulder. *Gaston,* her mind whispers, *everything and nothing changes. This is survival.*

"Yes," I answer her aloud, standing before the winter window upon the ocean, breathing in her scent. "We are." Hungrily, I move for her, my fangs erupting. She still tastes of everything I long for, of the home I loved and lost, of the river which hasn't slowed in time, just bore the ravages of progress upon its shores. She is softness and light, darkness and dawn at the same time. My hand slips past her waist, sliding to the familiar places and precipices I have known so well, so long. She sighs in her throat, crying out the sounds I love so well when she is driven mad with the wanting.

She has brought me back, brought me to the land I was born for one last time, where I gave her the gift of life. *Who really gave what to whom,* I ask myself, she waking to find my tongue insistent, hands and fingers splayed across the soft wetness within, and underneath my teeth, and she smiles a girl smile in the darkness. Everything and nothing changes. Blood of my blood, flesh of my flesh, she the darkest dawn, the magnolia in moonlight, and she will live forever.

Hutuk awasa: Choctaw, literally "Little Man." The Little People are Choctaw supernatural beings, benevolent and malevolent at the same time.

Miti: Choctaw, "come here."

Red By Any Other Name

Kathleen Bradean

Scarlet. Crimson. Cerise.

There are so many words for red.

He evokes them as a mantra during the long pauses in our telephone conversations. I wonder if he knows that his thoughts spill into my mind.

I turn away from the muted television and snuggle into my couch. He gives good phone.

"May I meet you tomorrow?" His accent is pure American Midwest. Those stocky Wisconsin vowels make me doubt the rumors about him.

He can't truly be undead, the modern part of my brain argues. He can't be a vampire. He's just a *sub* in search of a *domme*. My rational mind tries to convince me to calm down, but the other side of my brain screams that his voice is too hypnotic.

I've soaked my panties. What is it about vampire voices? Do they resonate on orgasmic frequencies?

"Don't you dare use your voice or eyes to bring me under your thrall." This is like scolding a rabid wolf not to bite.

"Please, may I meet you at the club tomorrow?" my vampire asks. This time his voice lacks persuasion. I can tell it's an effort for him to sound human.

This voice doesn't scare me as much. It's not as sexy either. His words don't vibrate down my spine and between my legs.

I shouldn't meet him.

The phone calls I can handle—just barely. I'm not so sure what will happen in person.

"Please."

Cruel inspiration strikes. "Only if you come to me in daylight hours." There, finally, I've set a condition that he can't meet. This will end his pursuit.

I hear traffic. Wind buffets his cellular phone. It's an eternity before he speaks. "That would be difficult." He measures his words.

I wonder what he hears on his end. The hitch in my breath as I hope he says goodbye? My heartbeat? The movement of blood through my veins?

"But I will find a way." He surrenders.

Of course he will. Damn it.

I click off the muted television. "Let's talk about vampire myth versus reality." Despite my fear I'm curious about him.

I put my heels up on the coffee table. My knees spread when I slouch against the overstuffed pillows. There's no way I can hold a rational conversation while my pussy's so engorged.

If he knows that I finger myself while we negotiate, he doesn't mention it.

I lose the thread of our conversation. My thoughts as I hang up the phone are of summer peaches, the aroma of the ripe flesh, the sweet explosion of nectar on my tongue as my teeth break the sun-warmed skin, the rasp of fuzz in the back of my throat.

When I come on my fingers, I wonder if those visions were mine or if they were his.

My rational brain says there's no such thing as the undead. As I drive towards the club I almost convince myself that the dead don't walk the night. Still, the side of my brain that controls the steering wheel pulls me into the parking lot of St. Thomas Martyr Church. Here, believers in the unknown are offered refuge.

I slip a scarf over my shoulders. I'm not sure if women still have to do that covered-hair thing in church or not. Either way I don't want to attract attention. I'm here for insurance, not redemption.

My sunglasses are lowered so I can pretend to read flyers for a Fire House spaghetti dinner fund raiser and the 5th Grade candy bar sale while I hover in the vestibule of the church. My nose wrinkles at the scent of burning wax wafting from the votive candles.

Finally, one of the biddies in the front pew remembers an old sin. She shuffles into the confessional, dragging the bored priest in with her. Taking quick advantage, I whip vials out of my purse and submerge them in the font of holy water. Bubbles break the surface as the glass tubes fill. I glance right and left, so obviously guilty of something that I'm surprised no one approaches me.

The manager at the club lets me in, then disappears into his office. The place is deserted.

I change from street clothes to my black latex cat suit in the bathroom. The impossible heels on my lace-up boots change my posture. My copper buttocks thrust out.

According to the full length mirror on the back of the door, I look hot. Stalling for time, I lean close to my reflection and examine my teeth.

Water drips from a mineral-crusted faucet into the sink on the wall beside me. Hollow echoes sound as each drop falls into a small pool of water ringing the rusty drain.

Garnet, ruby, carnelian.

I know my vampire is close by. Over the phone his thoughts are faint in my mind. Now his voice reverberates along my spine. I look over my shoulder twice to make sure he isn't standing behind me with his lips pressed to the nape of my neck.

All three bathroom stalls are empty.

Beet, tomato, raspberry.

This is his version of fidgeting, I realize. He rattles off his list of reds while he prepares for our session.

I pass the bar on the way to the dungeon I reserved for us. Empty barstools are set in a meandering line. One has a long gash across the black vinyl cushion. White stuffing puffs out.

Wheezing fans move air conditioning through the exposed ducts overhead.

Dungeon paraphernalia hangs limp in alcoves. I can see that the black walls of the club need a new coat of paint.

I should have met him at night. More people would have been here. Hesitating, I almost turn to the manager's office.

Strawberry, cherry, candy-apple.

There is a tiny warble in his mental tone. The vampire's nervous about meeting me?

When I open the door he crawls towards me. I doubt his subservience. His emotions splash across my mind. He's the one on hands and knees, but his thoughts are condescending.

The vampire scorns mere humans, but he pursues me, not the other way around. He must be desperate.

As he crosses the concrete floor of the dungeon, his wrists and knees tangle in his brown denim duster. He stumbles.

The dungeon is a small, bleak room furnished with little more than a chair and table. I have no time to consider the rings embedded in the ceiling and walls. My focus is on the creature.

He wears gloves and a hat. His face is swathed in a brown and tan wool tartan scarf. Is he the Invisible Man or a vampire?

"So you can come out in daylight, boy."

He knows better than to answer.

I shove at his ribs with my foot. He obligingly falls over. I straddle him and sit on his chest. I slap him through his scarf. "This is not allowed."

He uncovers his face and I feel a twinge of guilt. He suffers. A fine sheen of pink sweat glistens on his upper lip. His sweat has a faint reptilian tang.

My full weight is on his ribs. My pubic hair presses against his coat. His eyes flicker down to the cutout in my cat suit that exposes my crotch. I lean close to his face. He has freckles!

"You came out in daylight," I praise him.

"It is possible," he admits. He breathes calmly. My weight is nothing to him.

Maybe breathing is an affectation for a vampire. Why would the dead need air?

"Will you be okay?"

My concern triggers an alien response in his mind that I can't fathom. Is he insulted or touched?

"I will not be completely comfortable until darkness falls, but I can endure it."

I slap his bared cheek with my gloved hand. "Then take off the damn clothes, boy."

Underneath the coat and scarf and layers of other protections he wears chinos and a golf shirt. No capes or tuxedos for my vampire.

There is the air of autumn to him. Wholesome as hayrides and apple cider, yet tinged by winter cold.

His thick blonde hair is sun-kissed in wide streaks. I wonder if the tan on his chest will fade.

His hands ball into loose fists. He waits for me to make a joke about his white-bread country-club looks.

Instead, I draw a knife lightly across the bend of my elbow. A thick, warm trickle snakes down my forearm.

He stops, pant fly unbuttoned and unzipped, light blue briefs showing. He lifts his nose slightly, moves it barely right and left. His nostrils spread wide as he scents me in the air.

He transforms into a pure predator. There is nothing human in his eyes.

My hand goes to my whip resting on the small table. "Finish undressing now," I growl.

I will not fear, I remind myself. I must not fear. Fear is the little death, the mind killer. Where did I learn that quote? The little death. *La petite mort*. Every orgasm is a little death. Death and sex, that beast with two backs. My mind is free-associating in hysterical bursts. I must not fear. Fear will be the death of me.

Burgundy, wine, claret. This is his mantra to keep control. Red drinks, I notice. It may have been a mistake to tempt him with blood.

He kneels. He knows the proper postures, the right responses. This is not new to him.

I whip his naked flesh. He pretends to flinch but I know that he's bored. Normally my strokes have to be pulled. For him I put my back into it and I grunt with the delivery. He feels no fear, no real pain, no submission.

Even though his eyes are supposed to be on the ground, he tilts his chin so that his peripheral gaze is on my open wound.

He patiently allows me to bind his arms and legs. It amuses him to obey my terse commands.

"Are there no vampire tops?" He's beyond human help.

"Do you know any other vampires besides me?"

"No."

"Neither do I. Not anymore." He turns away from me deliberately. His wrists twist. The leather bonds fall away, torn in two.

I'm defeated. His physical strength and tolerance for pain mock me. There's nothing I can give him.

Sinking into the master's chair, I spread my thighs.

"Come, boy."

He moves in a blur, a gliding motion that I can't quite see. Until now he's acted as human as possible for my sake.

He licks the inside of my thigh. The very tip of his thin tongue is bifurcated, forked. Crouched, he spreads my labial lips and considers my offering.

He uses his thumb on my clit.

I start to correct him, but his tongue explores my groin at the top of my thigh. I relax back into the chair. The sensation is new. I wonder what other tricks he knows.

There's a main artery that passes near the inside of the thigh. I remember that from some class I once took. Then I wonder why that trivia came to my mind.

His crafty tongue dowses my pulse. His fangs press against the skin over it. Not the points, but the flat, smooth surfaces of his elongated canines. He pants.

I'm thinking about something, I remind myself, something I should worry about.

He slaps my clit.

There's something important I need to focus on, something other than the heat that rushes between my legs.

I spread my legs further apart to let him closer. Wicked flashes of forbidden thoughts dart through my brain. I chase those images through dark labyrinths.

My body is warm from my toes to the top of my head. I couldn't rise from this chair if I wanted to.

He suckles my skin. He wants to merge with me.

I shouldn't let him. He has far too much control of this scene.

I'll put him back in his place—in just a moment—I'm almost there—another moment.

Time ebbs.

No, I have to take back control right now. I can't help him if I let him top me.

At some point I closed my eyes. Now I struggle to open them. The exposed florescent lights on the ceiling are harsh. My eyelashes flutter like moths beating their wings against a bulb.

This is wrong. I have to open my eyes and look. It's like swimming through thick water. I'm drowning in lust. It's not my eyes that need focus, it's my brain. I fight to surface into reality.

We share an emotion. It wells inside me, inside him. Need. My pussy thrusts for his mouth. The shared hunger grows, overwhelms me.

I'm wet, slick wet. He penetrates me. I grind into his hard—

He's feeding!

Adrenaline snaps me into full awareness.

I grab his hair and pull him off me.

He snarls. Blood coats his teeth. Thick red smears across his pale face.

I hit him hard, harder than I've ever dared hit anyone before. I catch his chin with force. He barely turns aside, and then smiles. He delicately licks the pool of blood at the corner of his lips.

"You will be punished for that." I shake. I know what bloodlust feels like now. And worse, I know how good it feels to sate it.

He doesn't care. He thinks that he can take anything he wants from me.

"Assume your position."

He smirks but drops down so that his cheek touches the cement floor.

I grab one of my vials of holy water. My gloves make unscrewing the cap a desperately unfunny comedic scene, but it finally pops off. I tip the tube. One tiny drop splashes down on his exposed backside.

He yelps.

Pain, he's feeling real pain for the first time in ages. It repulses yet fascinates him.

I sink back into the master's chair. My legs press tight together. I drag him over my lap.

He tries to wriggle away.

Another drop falls on his backside. He screams. Two welts rise.

"This is what happens to bad boys. Feeding without permission earns you ten drops."

I caress his buttocks. The next drop of holy water lands between his shoulder blades.

This reminds me of a good caning—the catch of the breath as the stroke falls, then the lip bitten to muffle a sob.

The fourth drop makes him suck air in between his clenched teeth. He's beginning to remember fear. He worries that the throbbing pain across his back will never fade.

Parting his ass cheeks, I stroke his anus.

He's engorged. His pale face flushes under the drying blood. Lifting his ass with his strong thighs, he grinds against my leg.

Drops five, six, and seven fall in fast succession.

Vampires can cry. They have pink tears. He sobs. He begs for my forgiveness.

I let him anticipate the eighth splash of holy water. He breathes heavily and postures while he braces.

I force him back down to the floor. He spreads his knees and arches his back.

His back is mottled with welts. They will heal slowly. Every movement he makes now betrays stiffness in his muscles. Yet, as he presses his face into my mound, pleased purrs sound from in his throat.

His long, thin tongue explores inside me.

It tickles, it caresses. I can't decide if I like it or not, but my body has other ideas and soon my hips rise to meet him.

I can feel his laughter. That's good too. Everything inside me rumbles back and ooh—it feels delicious.

He braces my thighs apart and lifts my ass from the chair. He's strong enough to do that.

I grab his head and press him deep into me.

His freckled button of a nose rubs into my clit. I throw myself against it. Every touch brings a twinge of pleasure.

I'm soaked in my juices.

He gulps in my scent.

Heat radiates off me. I sweat underneath my latex. The sharp odor of my perspiration rises in the air. I grasp at the red crushed-velvet arms of the master's chair. My fingers try to slide between my legs, but he is there. He is everywhere inside me.

His straight locks are just long enough to pull. I dig my fingers into that mane. He grunts as I rip some out by the roots.

His thumb slides into my ass and his tongue fills my pussy. I'm not sure who's rewarding who, but my only clear thought is that I'm filled and it's incredible.

I gasp. Pre-orgasmic heat glows from my cheeks and lips. Against my throbbing clit, he flicks the tip of that extraordinary tongue. I can feel myself crest a wave that breaks and rolls into intense primal pleasure.

Rojo, rouge, rosé.

Now he speaks in tongues.

My heart pounds through my chest, my anus clenches his thumb, and my pussy milks his tongue.

I lock my thighs around his head. His lips seal around my clit. He suckles my juices.

Tiny tremors of delight ricochet through me, the ebbing wave of my orgasm.

He dares to raise his eyes to see if I am pleased. I tip the vial again, pouring out a measure equal to four of the previous drops. I swear I can hear it sizzle as it meets his skin.

At first he howls. As he writhes he thinks the safe word. I hesitate. Does that mean I should stop the scene? Does he know I can hear his thoughts?

His focus moves within.

Our minds link. I am drawn inward with him.

The pain follows him. There is no escape.

The tension flees the knotted muscles across his slim back as he surrenders.

Beyond his pain, free from his unnatural nature, he finds peace. He finds relief. He desperately wants this reconnection to his lost humanity. He craves it.

I stand on wobbly legs.

He presses his face to my boot. He rubs his cheeks and forehead across the leather. I lift my toe. He kisses the sole.

Now I'm on familiar ground. I understand him. We have

entered my domain, my area of expertise. I know what I can give him.

His thoughts envelop me. Carmine, cardinal. Pomegranate, vermilion, maroon. Contented thoughts buzz through his brain and into mine like lazy late summer bumblebees. His heavy-lidded eyes close to half slits.

I plan a future of garlic-infused flails and silver-plated cock rings.

He indulges in a connoisseur's litany: sangre, anima, blood.

Bloodletting

Michelle Blaid

It's rare to find a human who really likes to bleed. But when you do, they are priceless to keep around, and alive. I'd never have thought that blood given freely could be that much sweeter, but sometimes it is. You have to be careful with them though, they'll let you drain them dry if you're not, and then where will you be?

My first real regular drain was a few years back. His name was Owen Fields. Sounds sweet, huh? He was. Tasted like raspberries to me. Raspberries with a touch of coppery sanguine mixed in. So kick back, let me tell you about him. If you find one like him, maybe you'll know.

I ran a small club in the green strip called "The Saint's Drop." It was pretty dark, gothic, everything you'd expect with a name like that. The front door had a big cross on it, all in black, under a red and black awning. All of the waitresses were asked to wear industrial goth-type clothing, but since I was the bartender, I pretty much wore whatever I wanted. I remember what I was wearing the night Owen walked in. My favorite shit-kickers with leather pants and a tight cut-off T-shirt that read "BITCH." My hair was curly and wild down my back and my makeup was dark. I liked the look; it gave me attitude. That night was no exception.

I was serving drinks, waiting for closing time, when Owen walked in. He looked so out of place in the Drop, mostly because of his khakis and T-shirt. People turned and stared at him, but he was too intent on getting wasted to notice. He sat down at the bar and said, "Give me whatever is good, and will get me plastered, now."

"You sure you're old enough to drink?" I asked him. He looked maybe twenty, tops, with dark sable-brown hair, wavy and slicked back like a rocker. His skin was light tan, and his eyes a dark brown, the skin around them red from crying. He handed me an ID that was good enough for government work, so I served him. Four shots of tequila later, he was pouring out his heart to me about some girl who dumped him. He caught her in bed with one of his housemates tonight, because he'd come home early from work.

"So then," he said, his words slurring, "she says to me 'stop being a baby and get out, Owen' . . . That slut."

I was polishing the same glass for the thousandth time. It's a bartender thing. "So you left?"

"After I told the fucker I was moving out. I'm not gonna sleep in a place with them and listen to them bang all the time." He knocked back another shot.

I nodded, and pulled the glass away from him. "You've had enough, Owen." He looked up at me with pleading eyes.

"No, I haven't . . . I can still think straight—or at least only a little curved. C'mon lady, let a guy get wasted."

I shook my head. "No alcohol poisoning on my shift, kid, but I'll listen to you if you want me to." *No more for you, Owen,* I thought, *or I'll be drunk off a pint of you.*

He looked mournful for a moment but then relented and talked on and on about his life. Somehow he managed to come across as sad but not pitiful, and still somehow dignified. He was from a family with no father, his mother was a bit of a psych case, and both of his siblings were in jail. Good, no one to miss you. Poor sod.

I looked up at the clock that overlaid a Budweiser ad. It was almost two in the morning, and I was hungry, which meant it was closing time. I clapped my hands and had the waitresses start shuffling people out. Owen stood to go.

"Hey man, don't stress it. Sit until I close up." I smiled at him invitingly, and he smiled back, drunk on the alcohol and now on me as well. He sank back into his seat and slumped against the bar, head on his forearm.

I shut the place down and the waitstaff headed out, leaving

Owen and I alone in the Drop. He looked up when I clicked the lock shut, confused. I smiled, and nodded to the back door. He nodded back, vaguely understanding.

"So what's your name?" He had the confidence in his demeanor that comes to the inebriated.

I slid into the stool next to him, flashing him another smile, encouraging this time. "Maggie. Maggie Stotten."

"Maggie. That's a nice name. I like it." He reached out and touched my hair, as if unaware that he was doing it. I grabbed his hand suddenly and he froze, looking like a frightened animal. Then I kissed his palm and he relaxed, a slow smile spreading over his face. "So Maggie, you got a plan to keep me tonight, or what?"

If only you knew. I didn't answer. I kissed his wrist now, and kissed my way down the inside of his forearm. He closed his eyes for a moment and then opened them, looking at me through eyes heavy with desire.

I stood up and leaned forward, and his eyes roamed to my cleavage as I kissed his forehead lightly. His hand moved to the back of my head and he drew me into a kiss, tentative at first and then harder. My hands ran up his thighs and I threw one leg up onto the stool peg, looping it over his.

He broke the kiss and grinned, looking up at me past the veils of hair that had fallen to either side of my face. I grinned back and almost showed teeth, but decided not to.. I wanted to rile this one up before I drank him, bring him to a height before I struck. They were always best that way.

I slipped my leg down and took his hand, pulling him leisurely behind me toward the back room. My apartment was downstairs in the basement, which was convenient to avoid the sunlight. He followed me past the big metal door and down into the little lair I'd fashioned for myself.

It was more opulent than someone would expect for an urban vampire, but I've always been a slut for velvet and plush. He looked around, a little wide-eyed, and I led him to the bed. It was a king size, with burgundy velvet comforters and lots of pillows. I stopped at the edge of the bed, turned, and pulled his T-shirt up and over his head. He slid his arms up obediently, and then kissed me again, sliding his hands roughly down my chest to my hips.

His hands slid under the edges of my shirt, and he pulled it off, his eyes lighting up as he kissed his way down my neck to my breasts. His manner was still tentative, as though he expected me to object. I ran my nails lightly down his back and he bent down, unhooking the closure to my bra before pushing me back down onto the bed. I lay back, enjoying myself as he ran his tongue over my nipple and closed his lips around it, sucking gently. His knee pushed up and rubbed against my crotch lightly, making the leather of my pants creak quietly.

I liked this one. Most boys I brought down here were just that, boys. They wouldn't know a good lay if it sat on their faces, and I was no exception. No initiative, no spark, nothing interesting. Owen was nervous, but he had something. I wasn't sure what, but he was much more satisfying than many of the others. I was sure he would taste good too. My only slight regret was that I would have to kill him.

His mouth worked its way back up my chest and neck, while my hands unbuttoned his pants and slid them off his hips. Under the khakis he wore boxers, which was cute in a frat boy kind of way. Like college dorm takeout for a vampire. He slid on top of me and ground his erection into my hip, his hands working their way over my breasts again.

I pushed him gently off of me, and unfastened my pants, which he helped me peel off along with my undergarments. Now he paused for a moment and looked down at me, naked on the bed. I smiled and let one leg fall to the side invitingly. He smiled back and knelt in front of me, using his hands to push my legs apart. His breath was hot on my pussy as I squirmed in anticipation, and my breath (despite the lack of necessity for it) was coming in short mewling half gasps.

It wasn't acting—the kid had gotten me really hot, and I was more than intrigued with his abilities so far, and eager to test more. Very slowly, teasingly, he slid his thumb and forefinger up my slit and pushed the lips apart, lightly brushing my clit. Now I was biting my lip, all but begging him to go on. He grinned at me from his position between my legs and then flicked out his tongue, just brushing my clit. I jumped, my hands fluttering over my abdomen as my back arched. His tongue shot out again, and again, just quick little thrusts against me. I squirmed, my whole torso moving except my hips, because I did not want him to stop what he was doing.

Damn boy, I wish I could keep you around. My eyes rolled back into my head and I clenched my hands in the velvet under me, which was probably getting more than a little moist from all the attention I was getting. His tongue worked in tiny motions, chiseling away at my pink flesh. He was patient, this one, very, very patient. I'll admit, I'm not the easiest to get off, but he was doing a damn good job so far. Slowly the tension was building in my spine, starting in my lower back. His hands moved to my hips, where he held me in place and began in earnest, his motions quicker but still so light. I cried out involuntarily, my chest heaving with gasping breaths as my back arched sharply.

He did not relent; instead he gripped me more firmly and began to grind his tongue into me, which sent me over the edge. I screamed sharply and this time the arching of my back had me looking at my mirrored headboard, I was bent so far back. He didn't stop, kept grinding his tongue into me as I thrashed on the bed. The tension in my spine became a fire that roared through me, and I could do nothing to stop it now. I remained on that high for what seemed like forever, as the fire slowly left me gasping in a ragged placebo of breath and hot with sweat. He slowly eased his ministrations, withdrawing and sitting back on his heels.

I blinked like an owl for a moment, my eyes numb from being squeezed so tightly closed. He smiled down at me, a brown curl flopping down next to his eye. I finally looked down, my breathing still crazy, and chuckled throatily. "Owen, you're damn good at that. Don't let anyone tell you differently." Not that anyone will be able to after tonight. It was a shame to kill such talent. He chuckled back and brushed his hair back as I sat up slowly, my own hair tumbling down over my shoulders and breasts. I looked up at him and reached forward to pull his hips closer. I took a deep breath, withdrawing my fangs with only a little exertion. Then I smiled at him and freed his erection through the opening in his boxers. When my hand touched him he moaned softly, letting his knees touch mine as he relaxed.

My hand closed more firmly around the shaft of his swollen member, and I lowered my mouth, slowly swirling my tongue over the head. He groaned softly and tipped his head back, leaning against me with his hips forward. I closed my lips around the head and moved down his length, moving my hand in time with my mouth. His body tensed against me and he put one hand on my shoulder, his fingertips digging into my flesh. I pulled away and grinned, then swallowed him again, although I couldn't fit all of his cock in my mouth.

I kept at it for a moment before he stopped me. His mouth curved in a half-smile and he climbed up on the bed next to me, sliding his hand down between my thighs and playing his middle finger up and down my swollen outer lips. I wrapped my arms around his neck and kissed him again, sliding my tongue slightly into his mouth. He slid his finger slowly inside me and I moaned, biting my lip as I broke the kiss.

He grinned and then kissed my neck while my head tipped back, his finger sliding into me again, a little more firmly. My hand roamed to his thigh and I ran gentle fingers up the length of his erection, my hand jumping a little as his finger slid into me more firmly. His smile widened and his hand slipped away, leaving me hungry. My hands around the back of his head tightened and I dragged him into a kiss roughly.

He thumbed the waistband of his boxers and slid out of them, his manhood slapping lightly against my hip as it was freed. I drew my hand along it and my grip firmed as it slid up the length and back down again. A lock of hair fell in his face as he groaned, his eyes rolling up into his head, and pushed his knee between my legs again, spreading me open.

I pulled him on top of me and kissed him again, flicking my tongue lightly against his. He leaned on his elbows on either side of my head and reached one hand down, putting the head of his member against my opening. He suddenly seemed hesitant, and slightly unsure. His buzz was wearing off and now he was thinking about what he was doing, and whether he should be doing it. I ended that quandary by pushing his hips forward with my heels.

We both cried out as he entered me, the head of his cock sliding in suddenly at my urging. His back tensed and his breath hissed through his teeth as he pushed forward, more of his length sliding into me. I spread my legs wider and his hips met mine as we both gasped.

He broke the silence we had unintentionally made, saying, "Maggie. Oh God." It was not the most articulate statement, but his prayer amused me. *God has no place here boy . . . Just you and me. And this.* I nibbled on his ear delicately between my front teeth, carefully avoiding any premature punctures. He began to move, sliding out and then back into me slowly, and then faster, his thrusts gaining momentum and pushing me against the velvet of the bedspread.

Time became a blur of motion and pleasure. I rolled my hips up to meet his as my bed began to rock with our motions. The lower left post began to squeak in time with our movements, but we both ignored it. Beads of sweat sprung up on his forehead and his breath began to come as a harsh gasp.

I rolled over on top of him. He was quickly reaching a fever pitch and I knew it was almost time to strike. He would struggle, and fight, and it was easier to subdue from on top. I sighed softly, which I know sounded like a moan of pleasure, but was actually one of regret. *Oh well,* I thought, *easy come, easy go.*

I sat up and looked in the mirror on my headboard (that "no reflection" stuff is bullshit, just so you know). His eyes were closed and his head was tipped back, exposing his neck to me, and I couldn't resist any longer. I leaned down and pinned his wrists above his head and then sank my teeth firmly into his neck, bracing myself for his reaction.

My body went stiff and rigid with tension, trying to restrain him. But, to my surprise, he froze for a moment, and then thrust his hips upward at me, groaning loudly. He didn't fight. I stopped and pulled away for a moment, startled, blood dripping down my chin. He looked up, his expression unreadable. I paused, and spoke softly. "I just bit you."

He nodded. "So?"

I blinked, utterly flabbergasted. "I'm draining your blood. I'm a vampire. Why aren't you fighting me?"

He shrugged. "So you're a vampire. At least you're an honest bloodsucker. My last girlfriend wasn't." I had to laugh at that, although I was still very confused. He smiled up at me faintly and said, "So, still hungry?" I blinked again. He was taking this awfully lightly. I started to doubt his sanity.

Some of my confusion must've read in my face. He murmured softly, "Look, I've tried to take my own life now and again, so let's just say I like to play with danger. Call me a thrill seeker. Or just suicidal." He turned his arm over where I had pinned it against the bed. There were thick, white scars along the inside of his wrist. "The first set was when my father beat the shit out of me for being a fag, which he assumed from my hairstyle. The second was when I got thrown out of college."

A slow smile spread over my face. This boy was priceless. He meant it. He really liked being drained. I mean, I know it feels good, but most people still struggle against it, knowing what's happening intellectually despite their body's urges to give in to it. I lowered my mouth to his neck and I drank.

He bucked beneath me, his body beginning to tremble. I was careful, but damn did he taste good. There was no fear in his scent, and all the adrenaline in his blood was from excitement, not terror. His body grew more tense and I released his arms, which closed around my hips firmly, pulling me down. He was thrusting into me faster and harder, and now it was in rhythm with the lifeblood pulsing into my mouth.

I knew he was getting close. I had to make a choice—kill him, bring him to a high that he'd die from, or withdraw. I remembered the look on his face when he'd asked if I was still thirsty. I just couldn't do it.

So I withdrew slowly as he thrashed beneath me, crying out with desperation. He clutched the back of my head and pulled me back to his throat but I turned my face away, my hips still meeting his rhythmically. He moaned once more, almost despairingly, and released inside me, his arms pulling my hips down against his.

I lay against him as he shuddered a few more times inside me, my head pillowed on his shoulder, watching the bite marks close slowly in front of me. His breathing was ragged and harsh, and I could feel it move through my hair and over my shoulder. Once he had calmed more, I slid off him, my body curled against his, our sweat cooling and probably chilling him, since he drew a sheet over us. Without looking at me, he turned away, his back against my chest.

"Why?" The word came out like a choked sob.

I bit my lip, my forehead against his spine. "Because . . . I liked you and I didn't want to kill you."

He shook his head and wiped away tears angrily. "You want to keep me. Admit it."

I winced and my chest felt tight. "No . . . no, I don't. I was just being . . . I mean . . ."

He turned to face me. "Tell me the truth. Tell me the truth and I'll stay with you. Until the end." He put his hand under my chin and made me face him. "Just tell me the truth, and I'll believe you."

I glanced away, my face flushing with his blood. "Yes. I do. You're too precious to me to kill."

He wrapped his arms around me and kissed my head. "Then fine. Keep me. But you won't have me forever."

I kissed his neck softly. "I know."

He moved in to my little basement apartment, away from that bitch he hated and the roommate he wanted to kill. Owen became my housewife, my lover, my drain, and the one I supported. He played with music and school and different ideas of jobs and lifestyles that would fit with mine, but none of them made him happy. I guess I knew even then that we wouldn't be together long, and that he would grow to resent his boredom, and me.

One night I got in the middle of a fistfight between two angry customers fighting over a girl. I would have been fine if not for the chance encounter between my face and a wooden barstool. I went downstairs bleeding and bruised, and Owen offered himself to me that night. He had no idea I would heal from it, but I knew. I remember the look in his eyes that night when he saw my black eye vanish and the cut on my lip heal over. I guess that's where he got the idea. I'll never really know.

A month later I was closing up late and I saw Owen head into the back with a package under his arm. I had given him money to spend so I wasn't concerned, just curious. I finished cleaning up, kicked out the last few drunken idiots, and headed downstairs.

As I passed through the velvet curtain into my room, pain exploded in the back of my head. I hit the floor tasting blood, and rolled on my back, trying to get my bearings and figure out what had happened. Owen was standing over me, a wooden bat in his hands. He raised the bat again and slammed it into the side of my knee and I screamed, feeling the wood crack against the bone.

His face was impassive, almost sad. And for the first time in years, I was crying. "Wha-what are you doing?" I choked on the blood pooling where I had bitten my cheek.

"I'm making you need my blood." He brought the bat around to impact my shoulder and I screamed again. This time it seemed almost like my cry hurt him—the bat dropped from his suddenly nerveless fingers. He dropped to his knees beside me and cried, running his fingers through his unruly curls. He looked threadbare, wearing and old long sleeve T-shirt and pants, barefoot on the floor of my cold basement.

I shuffled back on my ass, pushing with my good leg and cradling my arm against my chest, gasping with pain. "You . . . I didn't know . . ." Tears dripped from my eyes and I wiped them away, smearing my fingers red. He looked up, and I saw him in a different light, worn thin with pain and holding onto a life that he simply wanted to let go of.

I sat with my back against the bed, and let out a sad, dry chuckle. "Well, if that was how you felt, you didn't have to go using wood on me to get your way . . ." I was joking, but I knew it had come to this for a reason. "Do you really want to drive me to that?"

He shook his head, a tear dripping down his cheek. "No. I wanted you to kill me that first night. The way I wanted it . . . while I was inside you."

I nodded, another tear dripping down my cheek and staining the collar of my shirt crimson. "Well, then you'll have to come over here, since I think you broke my leg." My voice was gruff and harsh, and I rubbed my hand over my face to dry it.

Owen looked up, his face still surprised when he realized what I'd said. After a moment I snapped, "Well, do you want it, or not?" And he nodded, swallowing and crawling over to me, pushing the bat away. He pulled back his sleeve, murmuring soft apologies as he saw how injured I was. He pushed his wrist against my mouth and I did not waste any time in taking what I needed to heal.

He gasped, a shock of pleasure jolting up his body. I wasn't gentle this time, but rather drank deeply and took what I needed. He wavered and seemed dizzy for a moment after I released him. My bruises faded, and the pain in my leg, head, and shoulder faded. My leg set with a sickening *pop* and Owen swallowed hard, looking pale.

"You still want this?" I growled softly. My bloodlust was up, and unlike most times, I wasn't even trying to calm it.

He didn't even hesitate. "Yes."

I sighed. I had been hoping he would realize what he was asking. That he would say he didn't want it anymore once he felt the way I had drained him. Another tear slid out of my eye and down my face. I was going to miss him. *Damn it girl, he's only a human,* I thought to myself.

He leaned down and brushed the tear from my cheek, his features softening as he pulled me into his arms. For a moment he was the one in control, stroking my hair, murmuring soft apologies, his arms around me. It was strange; he was so calm, so assured, and so very ready to die.

I leaned against his chest for a short time, until I was rested, until I was ready to leave the comfort of his embrace. When I did, he looked at me with a mixture of sadness and resignation, and then slowly, he smiled. I recognized that smile. It was the same smile I had found so interesting that first night in my bar. Sardonic and yet somehow bright.

Slowly, hesitant for the first time in as long as I could remember, I reached for him, pulled him into a kiss. He responded eagerly, seeming suddenly more alive than he had been in months. I wondered how I could have missed the change in him, if it was this easy to see now. I cried some more at that, realizing more fully the willing ignorance I had been perpetrating for that long. And then I berated myself for being a softie.

He slid his hands under my shirt and pulled it over my head, comfortable and confident where he hadn't been that first time. He scooped me up in his arms, under knee and shoulder, and set me gently on the bed, his mouth exploring mine eagerly as he lay on top of me against the velvet of the bed.

His hand slid under my back, unclasping my bra and pulling it away. I moaned softly as he lowered his head, suckling at my nipple gently, his tongue flickering out from between his lips as they closed around it. The moan turned to a sigh as I relented, letting go to the moment, my back arching to meet the touch of his mouth. My hands roamed down his back, pulling his shirt up. He sat up and yanked it off, looking down at me with hungry, dark eyes.

I reached for him and he leaned back down, kissing my neck and throat, his hands working the fastenings of my jeans, loosening them and pulling them slowly off. They were tight, and he slid them down my hips, peeling them like fruit. He pulled off my boots and then stood there, by the foot of the bed, and slid his pants off, letting them drop to the floor. His cock slid against my leg as he crawled forward, cradling me in his arms.

Owen whispered softly, "This is what I wanted. Please."

I bit my lip, trying not to cry again. I was a damned vampire, and I was crying. I felt like an idiot. "I know. I will. I'll miss you."

He shook his head. "No, you won't. I'll be with you, in you . . . always."

I nodded, but my heart was pounding as he kissed my cheek and then down my neck again, sliding his body against mine. I let go of regrets again, focusing on the feeling of his skin against mine, his breath hot on my neck as he took control. My arms snaked around his shoulders, pulling him down against me. I could feel his chest against mine, the heat at the center of his breast. I tilted my hips upward, lopping my legs around his, as he thrust forward, pushing into me quickly.

It wasn't as panicked or feverish as that first time we had been together. We knew each other now. But there was something between us, a tension, an understanding . . . I'm not sure how to describe it. Maybe it was the fact that for the first time since that night we met, one of us was hunting and the other was prey. I think the strange thing was, I wasn't the hunter. He slid out of me for a moment and lay down beside me, his chest against my back. I pushed my hips back and flung my leg over him, and he slid into me from behind. The sensations were amazing, and I couldn't help collapsing weakly back against him as he gripped one of my hips and thrust into me, he other arm supporting him.

After a moment, he slowed, and rolled me forward until I was face down on the bed, supporting myself on my elbows. His hand slid around my waist and down between my legs where his fingers began to brush my clit lightly. I moaned, falling forward against the bed with my hips pushed up into the air, his cock still sliding into me, faster now. I began to tense as my body got closer to release, and he gasped, feeling me tighten around him.

I felt the fire in my body growing, and suddenly it released, while I tensed in pleasure under him. He groaned and thrust into me a few more times before withdrawing, taking a few deep breaths. After a moment I rolled over weakly, my body shuddering and tired, but still hungry. He looked down at me, blood running from his lip where he'd bitten it to restrain himself.

He sat back on his heels, his hands on his thighs. "It's hard to hold back when you do that, you know . . ."

I smiled and ran my hands over his chest, sucking lightly on one fingertip as my over hand ran over my clit. "That's the point." My voice was husky, seductive. I held back the tears, and the thoughts of this being the last time. If it was, I wanted it to be good.

He bit his lip again and groaned, shaking his head. "I can't . . ." His words trailed off as he lost control and lunged forward, his mouth meeting mine as I spread my legs, opening to him. I could taste his blood on my lips, copper mixed with the sweat from his face. After a moment, he slid inside me, with a groan, his body taking over and driving him on. Then he whispered, "Please." His voice had an edge of gentle persistence to it as his body slid against mine again.

I lowered my head to his neck, and my fangs slid into his skin. His breath came as a harsh gasp as he bucked under me, groaning, barely holding back. I stopped moving for a moment, and drank, savoring the taste of him as I started moving again slowly, taking my time and bringing him closer.

He was trembling now, on the edge of release. I drank with abandon, not being careful, and the pleasure of the kiss was intensifying the experience for both of us. I could feel his heart begin to strain as his lifeblood ran out, and I let up a little, waiting for him to reach his peak.

He moaned softly and murmured, "Yes . . ." His body began to thrust underneath me, his hands holding me steady as he pounded into me. I felt his fingers turn to claws against my skin, tight and hard as he tensed. He tipped his head back and cried out loudly as he began to come, his body shuddering hard. I drank deeply, feeling the pleasure in his blood course into my body as he tensed under me again and again.

After a moment, he stilled, and I pulled away. I wiped the blood from my mouth and felt drips of red hit my hand as my eyes shed tears for him. I rose and looked down on him. His eyes were closed, thank God, and he looked peaceful, his body relaxed. His hands dropped from my hips as I slid off of him, curling up on the bed with my back to him. I shuddered in sobs that wracked by body, trying not to cry out all the blood he'd given me.

After a short time, I turned back to the shell he'd left behind, and I stood, lifting his cooling body as easily as a doll. I disposed of it without a second thought—he was gone. His life was over, and everything he'd left behind, he had left in me. I went back to bed as dawn began to break over the horizon, pale light showing in the cracks of the velvet curtains over my window.

I got over it. I was depressed for a bit. But two guys and an Asian chick later, I was back to my fun. I was back to being a killer, and a hunter. The Saint's Drop folded a few years later. The building was falling apart and starting to fail safety codes, so I moved on.

That's the dangerous thing about drains—about the ones who like bloodletting. They take the hunter out of you and make it their own. They hunt you, to get the oblivion you can offer. It's easier when they scream or run or struggle, because then you can call it the hunter in you and shut down your conscience by knowing you're doing what you have to, to live.

So be careful. It's too easy to love them. And when you love them, you're the hunted.

La Paloma Blanca
A Tale of Don Rafael Perez and Ethan Templeton

Diane Whiteside

Dearest Pearl,

Thank you so much for your letter! It seems like an eternity since we vowed eternal friendship in Concord, outside Miss Amity's Young Ladies Seminary. It has taken every ounce of strength that my sister Cordelia and I can muster just to survive this harsh Texas summer. We hope to return soon to Boston, if only we can obtain Father's permission. But he plans to remain here in Austin, searching for ways to help this Rebel state return to the Union. I suspect he also hopes for ways to line his wallet, but he publicly speaks only of the good to be done here.

You ask if we have met any interesting young men. Most of the young men we meet are army officers. Alas, Father will not permit us to do more than speak to men of the sword. He extended this ban to followers of Mr. Colt so very few men in this martially inclined dust hole are acceptable. Cordelia has been known to say that if we did not meet anyone soon, she would invent someone! However, we encountered two men last Saturday night who were very intriguing. I will tell you everything that I can remember of them.

Father had invited some acquaintances for dinner, which Cordelia and I attended as his hostesses. We were excused when the drinks were passed, a departure we both welcomed. The gentlemen here drink whisky and smoke the most appalling cigars all night long, whether or not there are ladies present! It is very distressing to both of us. In any event, Cordelia went directly upstairs to nurse her headache while I went to say a few words of thanks to the cook. (She had managed to provide a meal without beans, a most remarkable feat.)

When I went upstairs, I could hear voices from within our bedroom. It seemed that Cordelia was moaning, a most intense sound if somewhat low-pitched. I hesitated, then approached softly, reluctant to disturb her in case her headache had increased. Her moans did not sound pained, so I went up to the door, holding my skirts so as to make the least sound. I put my ear to the door and heard words out of Cordelia's mouth. To my surprise, she was begging someone for more!

I could not imagine to whom Cordelia was speaking. This is a most uncouth town, and she complains frequently of the lack of presentable callers. I crouched down and peered through the keyhole.

What should my stunned eyes behold but my sister Cordelia sitting on a man's lap! He was a tall blond man in a threadbare Rebel uniform, seated on the edge of the bed, holding Cordelia arched across his arm. His hair spilled across her generous bosom, so I could not quite make out all the details. He seemed to be kissing her throat and farther down. Her language was rather incoherent but I am certain that she wanted more of whatever he was doing.

I observed them for some time. He was able to unbutton the back of Cordelia's dress so that her underthings were very evident. His mouth was most busy, although I am not certain of all his actions since Cordelia spent much time clutching at his head. I believe his name was "Ethan" since she frequently repeated that word. I blush to say that my hand reached under my skirts, echoing Ethan's movements.

Suddenly, I was picked up in a man's arms! I squeaked with surprise as I beheld a giant holding me as if I were as light as a feather. (Which you know, Pearl, I am not!) He stood some inches over six feet, had black hair and black eyes, olive skin. He was heavily muscled, had an eagle's beak of a nose, and a very nasty scar above one eye. He had quite the look of a conquistador from the days of Cortez.

"*La paloma blanca,*" he murmured. "Little white dove, perched on the gallery to watch the excitement." He smiled at me, then kissed me. It was a very dream of a kiss, one to flutter any lady's pulse.

"Won't you invite me in, *paloma mia?*" he asked. I could only nod yes as I stared at his mouth, hoping for more of his attentions. He lowered me slightly so that I could open the door and in we went.

Ethan lifted his head as we came in but kept his hand busy on Cordelia. He did not seem surprised, but simply lifted an eyebrow. Cordelia twisted her head around and glared at me. (Pearl, you at least must believe me. I was not spying on her so that I could inform Father! Cordelia has always accused me of such reprehensible behavior when, in truth, she is the one who ran to our patriarch with tales of my misdeeds. But she has not done that since this night's adventures, so I have some hope for the future.) In any event, I mouthed an apology for interrupting her frolic and Cordelia soon went back to fondling Ethan's head.

"Continue as you were, Ethan," my gentleman said. "This young lady is desirous of seeing how a gentleman pleasures a woman. So make sure that you provide ample entertainment." Was I mistaken or was there the slightest emphasis on the word "gentleman"?

"As you wish, Don Rafael, but . . ." Here, Ethan hesitated as if seeking words. My gentleman fixed him with a stare that would have made even Andrew Johnson behave reasonably.

"Tonight is the first opportunity to see how well you have learned your lessons, Ethan. You know how to walk into a room and select your best prey from the adults present. You understand how to excite their passion, preferably by seduction but, if necessary, by blanketing their mind with lust. You have thus learned how to walk out of a room with any adult in it, your quarry full of carnal anticipation and more than willing to feed you. Now you must prove that you can dine discreetly, leaving your prey alive. You will not risk my family by killing, thereby making humans hunt us."

Ethan nodded, his eyes fixed on my gentleman, who continued the lecture.

"Remember that feeding is better on emotion than on blood alone. You will answer to me if you forget that and harm either lady."

Ethan flinched as if he had been struck, yet Don Rafael's voice had been low and even. I remembered how the officers had spoken to their men at the close of the late conflict. The slightest word had been attended as well as any minister's thundering sermon. Don Rafael's words held a similar grip on Ethan.

Don Rafael studied him for a moment before speaking again. "*Bien.* Now arrange yourself and the woman to provide the best display. My little white dove has known a man's passion before but now she wishes to watch. Is that not true, little one?"

I agreed, blushing hotly. How had he known of an occurrence that I had only told you about, Pearl? Had he read my thoughts when I wished that drunken oaf had paid half as much attention to my rapture as Ethan paid to Cordelia's?

Ethan bowed his head in acknowledgment, then shifted Cordelia so she came astride him with her back against his breast, draped across his lap and her head arched back against his shoulder. He ran his hands over her and her dress slid away from his touch. He lifted her hips and soon stripped the obscuring cloth from her. My startled gaze beheld my sister's body attired only in a chemise, stockings, and her kid boots, outlined against a fully clothed man. Cordelia smiled at me in the exact manner she uses every Christmas when she gets to open her presents first as the eldest child. Ethan began to touch her in the most intimate fashion imaginable, paying considerable attention to her bosom. Cordelia's arms went up over her head as her eyes closed with a smirk and she stretched, offering herself to him.

Don Rafael carried me over to the armchair and sat down. He settled me on his lap in a similar fashion, facing my sister and her lover. This left his hands free to unbutton my garments. I could not pay much attention to this state of undress as he simultaneously fondled me in a fashion comparable to that wrought upon Cordelia. His attentions were thorough but perhaps a bit absent-minded. He seemed more intent on how well Ethan displayed his education than on myself, although I had no cause for complaint.

Ethan's hands began to center between Cordelia's legs. She twisted and thrashed against him in a most uninhibited manner. I could see every detail of her responses. His hands would move quickly then slowly, sometimes even more cautiously until they were still. Then an abrupt movement would bring such a gasp from her! He drove her up to the very brink of rapture and then kept her there for what seemed an eternity. (I confess that I writhed upon Don Rafael's lap as his hands took liberties with me during this time. My hands gripped his, seeking to guide him between my legs to where I knew release could be obtained. But he retained command of my carnal appetites and did not allow me to become so desperate as to stop watching my sister's burning desires.) I have never seen her lose all discipline as she did under Ethan's touch. She begged him for release, crying that he was cruel, cruel for torturing her in this way. (You would wish to be tortured in such a fashion too, Pearl!)

Ethan licked and sucked at Cordelia's neck, showing some very sharp teeth. She went very still once and Don Rafael growled. Ethan released Cordelia's throat immediately and then licked her. I could see a crimson drop sliding over her white breast as she sobbed again, begging him for still more.

Pearl, I do not know how Ethan could move his hand so rapidly between Cordelia's legs! Suddenly her entire body convulsed and she cried out. She arched against him, anchored only by his hand between her legs and his mouth on her neck. I could see him suckling at her, like a calf on a teat, as she screamed her pleasure. His body shuddered, contractions running through it in concert with the pull of his mouth on her throat.

"Ethan." Don Rafael's voice was scarcely more than a whisper, but it cut like a knife. Ethan's head jerked as if slapped and he stopped pulling at Cordelia.

Finally she lay against him, a few slow ripples passing through her body. His eyes shut and he licked her neck slowly.

I burned to follow Cordelia over the precipice of delight. But Don Rafael had his legs firmly between mine and held my hands tightly, withholding any chance of completion from me. I was forced to sit there and study Cordelia's sated sleep. I cursed and fought him but his strength was too great. I demanded the same ecstasy that my sister had enjoyed! Pearl, he laughed at how little effect my struggles had! Then he kissed my hair, still chuckling, and quickly sought my intimate parts. I jerked in surprise at his acquiescence to my pleas, but quickly fell into delight.

Truly, Pearl, I do not know what I was more distressed by at that moment: whether, his first denial of my satisfaction or, his casual and efficient provision of that pleasure!

I sat astride his legs, panting and tried to recollect myself. I was intensely aware of the contrast between my moistly glowing body and the rough strength of the body supporting me. He did not seem unaffected by the passion that Ethan and Cordelia had displayed. In fact, I suspected that his masculine tool was pressed hard against me in hope of similar pastimes. But his discipline over himself was as great as the control he had exerted over me. He made no further movement but simply held me still as we watched Ethan and Cordelia's exhaustion.

Ethan opened his green-gold eyes finally and studied me. His tongue slid out and cleaned the last drops of blood from his lips.

"May I watch you, Don Rafael?" he asked humbly.

Don Rafael chuckled and stroked the inside of my legs.

"Bien, Ethan, muy bien. Yes, it is time for la paloma blanca to coo . . ."

Dearest Pearl, the most wonderful thing has happened! Reverend Smith has just stopped by. He is returning to Boston and will carry this letter directly to you. I know you will be intrigued by this tale, even half-written, so I must send this with him. I will send you the remainder as soon as I can write it.

Pray convey my love to your family. I miss you desperately and will write more to you soon.

But for now, I remain,

ever your truest friend,

A—

Dearest Pearl,

I have found the ending of my previous letter! I will add but a few words to it so that I can send it off to you immediately.

I believe that the summer heat here is more oppressive than in Beelzebub's domain. Cordelia and I venture out only under protection of the evening's cool, except for Sabbath services, of course! While we have not met any new young men since my last letter (for there are few here worth meeting), at least we encounter them during times of frivolity and friendly congress at the dinners and dances that Father's friends offer. Then we retire to our room and read or dream of gallant men to bring excitement into our lives.

I believe that my last letter ended with me seated on Don Rafael's lap, looking at Ethan. Cordelia slumbered on the bed, so lost to dreams that she would not wake until the sun had almost finished its next day's course.

I am afraid to confess that I broke the silence with a question so unbelievable that even now, I blush to confess it.

"Are you vampires?" I asked, feeling a calm that owed much to my irritation at the gentleman holding me. I felt a slight ripple of surprise go through the big body holding me. Don Rafael tilted his head to look at me.

"We are, *querida*. But I give you my word: you have nothing to fear from us. We offer a simple exchange: rapture in return for a taste of blood. Our friends often find their way eased in matters outside the boudoir, as well. Your sister will awaken tomorrow, suffering only from the aftermath of pleasure and a slight lassitude. Her body will heal itself completely within a few weeks. She will remember nothing of this night."

Cordelia emitted a slight snore as he spoke, her usual sign of deep slumber. (As you well know, Pearl, her other sign is stealing all the covers but that is not likely to happen during a Texas summer!)

Don Rafael continued speaking in the most melodious tones for such a deep voice. "And you, paloma blanca, now have to concern yourself only with your own pleasure. You will sing like a dove tonight, I promise you, low and sweet, your voice quivering with ecstasy."

Somehow I believed him, Pearl! It truly was amazing that I accepted the assurances of this man, a vampire by his own admission! And yet I did trust him, at least for this much.

I must have relaxed in his hold because he slowly lowered his hand, bearing mine with it. My hands finished at my waist, grasped firmly by his strong fingers. I slanted my head back to look up at him for the first time.

"Will I remember this?" I asked. I yearned for memories to set against those of that drunken oaf who'd snatched my virginity away, and then had the discourtesy to fall off a horse and break his neck before Father could bring him to account. (But enough of that old lament, Pearl. I must speak more of the gallant Don Rafael.)

Don Rafael arched one eyebrow in surprise but smiled at me. I was so close that I could see how that dreadful scar cut into him, even denting the bone above his eye.

"*Sí,* you will remember this," he granted me. "But you may only speak of this night's events once. And do not worry about Ethan. He is my servant and will do only what I command. *Comprende, señorita?*"

I nodded eagerly. You have so often yearned for adventure, Pearl, that I knew you would enjoy a tale of dashing men if I could but tell it.

Don Rafael kissed my cheek and then rubbed his against mine. It was a gesture of the most amazing gentleness and, yes, even friendship! I purred under it, enjoying the touch. He smelled like the finest of gentlemen's soap—sandalwood, I think. His teeth were excellent and his breath fresh and sweet. I thought suddenly that his kisses would be more pleasant than those from any of Father's guests downstairs.

"Ethan, convey the young lady to the chaise lounge. Arrange her so that she may comfortably rest for the remainder of the night."

Ethan nodded in obedience and stood up. He carried Cordelia to the chaise and arranged her as directed. All the while, Don Rafael kept me on his lap, murmuring into my ear. I am not entirely sure of what he said, but some of it sounded familiar. Do you remember that Latin book your older brother had? The one that your parents refused to let us see, but we spent an afternoon poring over? Don Rafael's words reminded me of those phrases, sweet nothings that a lover might whisper. My body softened at the liquid syllables and the light caresses of his fingers on my hands.

Ethan returned to stand in front of us, eyes lowered. I watched him idly while preening under my gentleman's touch.

"Curious, my dove?" Don Rafael whispered in my ear. "Would you like to see a man's secrets?"

My indolence fell away in a rush. As you well know, Pearl, curiosity is my besetting sin. I sat up straight and watched eagerly as Ethan slowly began to unbutton his gray jacket.

Ethan took his time removing his garments. I may be mistaken, but it seemed that his every gesture was calculated to tempt a woman. I was almost shaking with excitement when he finally stood revealed in the lamplight. He was a splendid sight as he posed there, white as marble and clean-muscled. His golden hair shone only as demure accents on his torso, not as a heavy pelt concealing his charms. My mouth watered at the sight of him, all ivory and gold. A tracery of thin silver lines covered his backside with one line crossing his breasts just above his nipples. (Perhaps they were scars from a whip or a knife. They did not seem to hinder him in any way.) I studied him, comparing him to what little I knew of men's bodies.

"What do you think now?" Don Rafael's warm breath caressed my ear.

"He is a fine figure of a man," I remarked, striving for *savoir faire.* "But he seems a bit," I hunted for words, "soft perhaps, between the legs. Your body doesn't feel soft there to me."

Don Rafael rocked with laughter. I blushed at my own words but chuckled with him. Ethan blushed, too, but continued to wait.

"Ah, paloma mia, what shall I do with you? So inexperienced and yet so observant! You are a delight! Ethan is very new to the feel of a woman's ardor as it flows through her blood over his tongue. He so far lost command of himself that he followed your sister into passion's release. Please accept our regrets that Ethan cannot yet offer you the full use of his manhood. He will take some time yet to regain himself after tasting your sister. "

Am I mistaken, Pearl, or did Ethan's blush deepen at Don Rafael's words? But I did not dwell on Ethan's experience or lack thereof as Don Rafael continued speaking.

"Would you care to study another man's body? Mine is not so elegant as Ethan's but I can assure you that I am not soft between the legs."

I agreed quickly and soon was deposited on the bed. Ethan dropped to his knees next to the chair, watching Don Rafael, but leaving him space to move about.

Don Rafael divested himself of his garb, the typical attire for a Mexican gentleman here in Texas, without any seductive tricks. His short jacket and tight pants emphasized his intense masculinity. His movements' directness fired my blood so that my breath came faster and faster as his clothes fell away. He was a strongly built man, a veritable warhorse to Ethan's racehorse. Every muscle and sinew spoke of power while his hardness reared up between his legs with a stallion's vigor. (I must confess, Pearl, that I trembled at the size of his staff!) He had more than one brutal scar to emphasize a puissance that had been well tested by life. I was utterly conquered, as eager as any mare in season, before he even touched me.

He lifted my chin up with one finger and his mouth claimed mine. I was an eager pupil and our tongues soon twined and danced . . .

I have few words for what passed next, Pearl. My very senses were so dazzled that memories fail me. We kissed, oh how we kissed! And he caressed me with those magical hands, quickly freeing me of my few remaining items of clothing.

What more can I tell you? The feel of his mouth on my breast as he taught each nipple to beg for him? The slide of his long black hair across my hip as his lips moved below my breasts? Or the feel of his shoulders under my grasp, the muscles rippling as he moved? (His back was deeply scarred, like the former slave we saw at the abolitionists' rally. You would weep, Pearl, to see flesh and blood ruined so! And yet in that instant, I cared more for the raptures that body could bring me than its past torments.)

And his fingers, Pearl, oh such marvels they taught me! I fell more than once off the precipice of delight as his fingers and then his tongue played between my legs. Then his mouth traveled back up to my breasts and I clutched his head in my frenzy, twisting against him like a demented woman as we lay side by side.

Don Rafael said something softly, an order perhaps, but I paid little attention, too lost in passion to listen.

A gentle hand stroked my legs and I instinctively bent my leg to allow it freer access. The hand insinuated itself to where my desire raged hottest. I groaned in an ecstasy beyond all words as Don Rafael's hands and mouth ravished my breasts while Ethan stoked the fires below. Oh, Pearl, it was bliss beyond compare to have two men compelling me onward! I hope that one day you may feel the like of it!

My leg was urged upward until it at last clasped Don Rafael's hip. I rubbed him urgently, the prickle of his leg's hair a pleasant sensation for my sweaty thigh. We moved closer still and I felt his hardness pressing against me. This caused me to grow more excited yet. I gripped him fiercely with hands to his head, leg wrapped around his, and my head thrown back.

I begged him for more and he gave it to me. He entered me easily, sliding home on the liquid welcome my body rolled out for him. I felt utterly enveloped by him and yet marvelously free at the same time. Ethan caressed and licked us both, encouraging us to find our zenith. I sobbed my pleasure, my voice breaking slightly with each breath. My sounds were low and sweet, quavering like a dove's voice.

Don Rafael's lips sought my throat. I yielded instinctively and he rewarded me quickly. A fire blazed in my neck and I flew off my pinnacle into a storm of delight. Tremors racked my body as my blood flowed into his mouth on matching waves.

I must have lost consciousness then. I stirred once when horses went past under the window, perchance the end of Father's dinner party. But slumber returned quickly, held as I was in Don Rafael's strong arms, with Ethan lying on the other side of him . . .

And that is the end of the tale, at least as much of it as I can now speak of. Cordelia and I both slept deeply on the following day, awakening to a few bruises and some lassitude. Cordelia remembers nothing of that evening's events, although I dare not speak of it directly to her. The small red marks on our necks were gone within a few days.

I hope to see Don Rafael again, perhaps in a few months when my body has recreated all of the blood he enjoyed so fiercely. But Father's business dealings have gone uncommonly well since that night. He speaks often now of permitting us to return to Boston soon. Cordelia greets such talk with open delight while I strive to hide my uncertainties.

And so I conclude this letter, my dearest Pearl, in the hope that we will soon be reunited. Boston is my home and my future hopes are centered there. But I trust that you will understand if sometimes my fingers linger on my throat as I watch a full moon.

Your truest friend,

A—

Little Predator

Allison Lonsdale

His dancing makes me think of e.e. cummings's "the boys I mean are not refined." So I dance back at him like the girls in the poem, "who masturbate with dynamite." Already I have my suspicions, because there's another line in that piece:

"they kill like you would take a piss"

And the way he moves fits that so very well. He looks at me with nasty promises in his eyes. I know this part so well I could do it in my sleep: I look back as though I'm half afraid he'll keep them and half afraid he won't.

I go outside for a breath of cold air to "clear my head." He follows, offers me a cigarette. Of course. He lights two and passes me one. I taste his saliva on the filter and it closes the circuit: I can feel his surface thoughts. Don't ask me how it works; I only know it does. And I have to fake a cough to cover up my reaction.

He's no more human than I am. And he thinks I'm food.

I came out hunting rapists tonight. He isn't the right target. I could move on, try to find . . . no. There it is. He *is* what I'm looking for. From his taste on the cigarette I can name the landfill where his last fuck is buried. Poor broken girl with her black PVC corset. She liked it rough.

If he were older, stronger, I wouldn't dare. I'm not as hard to kill as they are. But he's sloppy. A landfill, of all places! Not even any quicklime in the grave! Only a young one would be that careless. This is the club where he picked her up, and he's hunting here again only a week later. Definitely not a full-grown hemophage. They're a lot more careful.

They almost never cross my path.

I blow smoke from my nose, dragon-style, and shoot him a glance. A little afraid, a lot interested. I like it rough. Believe in me. Believe in my fear, in my desire. We talk about music, clubs, nights. Meaningless noises to cover up the moves we're making. We smoke at each other like it's a duel, like we're trying to fuck each other right here in public with the looks on our faces.

By the time the club closes, we've played out the next round. Through smoke and strobes and pounding bass, he has flashed the subtle signs. They are supposed to be subliminal, priming the prey animal to react with terror and fascination. He likes to play with his food. So I am doing a food imitation. I have to go through some extreme emotional contortions to get my sweat to smell like human fear, but it's working, oh yes. I can see the outline of his cock straining against black denim.

Smelling like human desire is no problem at all. I'm horny as hell. He's sexy as hell. And if he had any idea of the drives his bad-boy charisma was waking in my body, he'd just fucking wet himself.

I've never done this before, playing the game with a real predator. It's a shock to me, trying something I've never done before. It's exciting. Makes me feel young. Tastes like risk. Tastes good. I'm getting impulsive after all this time, and I wonder, a little, if it's a death wish. But I think it's a life wish, a longing for something different, something to shake me up, wake me up. Sometimes it feels like I'm just going through the motions. Like I'm a sleepwalker. The taste of danger is hitting my system like Turkish coffee, and—I like it. I can understand the human woman he thinks I am a little more than I like to admit.

He expects me to go home with him when the club closes. He is shocked at my departure. I shoot him a meaningful glance over my shoulder as I go and hope, pray, that he takes the bait. My high heels tick on the rain-slick sidewalk; neon and traffic lights reflect from the inky gutter. Ducking into the alley, I move fast, preparing for his arrival. A rasp of metal teeth is drowned in the nearby sound of traffic. The leather makes no sound as it settles on the concrete.

He turns the corner, comes around the dumpster, and sees me bent over a packing crate, spread open, waiting for him. My dress is on the ground. My legs are spread, and his eyes involuntarily trace the line from my boot heels up to the black stockings and then the pale flesh of my thighs, traversed by the dark garter straps of the corset that binds my waist. Framed in black, the spread cheeks of my ass are a beacon in the dim light, and I know that his impossibly sharp vision can pick out the ruddy glistening of my cunt below them.

I can hear his breathing shift, and the sounds of his subtle motions as he scans for a trap. The prey is not supposed to offer itself, ripe and spread, for his taking. There should be a chase, and then a struggle, to speed the pulse. He tastes the air with his mouth, like a cat, and I sense his confusion. He scents the arousal, yes . . . but something's not right. Damn it, I should have worked more fear-scent into my sweat. How's this: I'm afraid I'm not going to get you tonight, you son of a bitch. That ought to smell interesting.

I deliberately let a tremor show in my legs. Come closer. This is not so alien. Kinky prey, out slumming for a little taste of danger. She has no idea what she's getting into. Come here, little predator. Come on. *Damn your sorry ass, get over here and do it before I grab you by the balls and*—No. I have to stay calm. I can't risk spooking him. He's designed to be stronger and faster than I am; if he bolts, I'll never catch up with him.

I hear his footsteps come closer. My trembling seems to have reassured him. About goddamn time! Another rasp of metal teeth, one only my senses or his could detect over the night pulse of traffic, and then I feel his cold hands on my hips and the swollen head of his cock pressed to the lips of my cunt. There is a sudden sweet ache in my belly, a blisteringly intense longing, but I restrain myself. He is a predator; he is accustomed only to taking.

If he senses that I have bitten my lips to bleeding, he assumes it is terror that stirs me. I feel him grin, see with my mind's eye those sharp white teeth he showed earlier among the lights and music and smoke. With one violent thrust, he buries his cock in me to the hilt. As it strikes home deep in my belly, I groan, and pray that it sounds helpless to him. The need is burning in every cell of my body. I can't believe I've let myself go this long without it. He is eagerly misreading the intensity of my need as fear mixed with arousal; he has me pegged as a hardcore submissive with a taste for freaky kicks. He'll find out soon enough. He has no clue. My kind keep a very low profile. He thinks his people are the only real predators out there.

I am making tiny sobbing noises in the back of my throat now as he thrusts into me, pounding me so hard I can see light behind my closed eyelids. The sensation of his cock sliding into my wet, swollen flesh is so unbearably good that I am losing strength in my legs. He holds my hips with a grip of iron; he will leave marks on my flesh before he is done. A strangled whimper escapes my lips and it seems to speed him to his goal; his sharp nails dig in as he slams his hard flesh into my body faster, more brutally. I taste him getting close; like humans, he leaks a little before he gives. It's dark and bitter and tastes of wet copper and human pain, like nothing else I've ever felt. It's ugly. And it's very, very good.

I can taste his mind along with his fluids, deeper than the surface thoughts now, and it's a shiny little thing, all hunger and vanity. It calls to me like a piece of aluminum foil to a magpie. Pretty trash-trinket, pretty play-toy. If he could taste my thoughts, his cheeks would burn with shame. But he is so self-absorbed that it does not occur to him to wonder what his prey is thinking—in fact, he does not consider prey capable of any thoughts that might interest him.

He is dreaming of feeding, now, and how sweet it will be to tear at my helpless throat when I am crumpled beneath him after he has hammered me into even more helpless submission. Yeah, right. I've got your helpless submission right here, pretty boy.

I am so close, so painfully, sweetly close; I can feel it coiled as a tight knot of unbearable need in my belly. But I have to hold it in check until it is too late for him. It feels like I will go insane with waiting. He is pounding and pounding me, this teasing that I cannot abide, and I am sobbing aloud with hunger. I begin to gasp "please," not specifying please what, and that vocal sign of helplessness inflames him. I feel the tremor in his hands where they grip me, and then the first wave of climax takes him and he snarls aloud with pleasure.

I taste the first wave of it bursting within me and every nerve screams *now.* And I let go, blessed relief, and take him. The ring of hidden teeth just inside my labia slam into the base of his cock with all the built-up tension of weeks of hunger and the last twenty minutes of unbearable teasing torment, anchoring his flesh within mine. Those teeth were already primed with venom; half the wetness that let him drive into me so smoothly was a compound that goes for a viciously high price in Tokyo—if you have to ask, you can't afford it—where even the group that sells it does not know what it is or where it comes from. The venom began welling into his achingly hard flesh the moment the teeth hit; he never felt a second of pain. Trying to pull back for another stroke, he feels himself trapped within me and manages a small puzzled noise even as the second spasm of his climax pours into me. Poor thing; he's used to the puny orgasms of dominance. He has never really lost control.

Linked to his nervous system, I can feel the tsunami of sensation hammer his consciousness as the venom crosses his blood-brain barrier and my cunt spasms violently, a burning whirlpool around his penis. Primed by the link, my feeding mouth, that has been doing such a clever impression of a cervix, opens and locks itself onto the head of his cock, pulling greedily at his fluids, sucking so hard it would make him scream with pain if his system were not flooded with venom. As it is, he is trying to scream through a throat swelled shut with the strain, his nerves redlining with an intensity of sensation that should not be possible—and I am feeding on his pleasure. It's like air to a drowning woman the way I need it and pull it in. What I take from him sends waves of exquisite relief through my tissues. Each amplified spasm that wracks his body, each burst of fluid that I pull from him deep into my belly, has me almost crying with relief. It goes on, getting more intense with each wave both in his flesh and mine, as the venom I'm pumping into his body meets and boosts the reflexes that are pumping semen into mine. My nerves are made to take this load, but his are not. He will not last much longer. This intensity is startling; with the small part of my mind still capable of rational thought, I attribute it to his nature as a predator. Always under control, he has always taken, has never been made to give. This must be blowing open channels in him that were sealed shut long ago, or that never opened.

Then I lose that part of my mind as the sensation roars up to a new level. I can't tell if my eyes are open or shut; I see only a pulsing redness punctuated by brilliant spasms of white light. I am only dimly aware of my nails digging into the packing crate under me, and his nails digging into my hips; there is only our point of joining and the aching heat up inside me where he is feeding me his ecstasy whether he wants to or not. It goes on and on, well past the point of satiation, until it feels like a blast furnace between my thighs and a small supernova in my belly, and I am dizzy and near to losing consciousness from the overload. I can barely manage enough mental focus to wonder what is happening to me, and a shred of recollection floats to the surface of my mind: a warning from one of my sisters, long ago—was it in Prague? Istanbul?—that it could be dangerous to feed on the hemophages. I had forgotten; with so many memories, I misplace things all the time. The storage space is finite.

The recovered knowledge is not doing me any good now; I can vaguely sense that the edge of the crate has splintered in my hands and I have bitten clean through my lower lip. It keeps going, in his flesh past what I could imagine any human enduring, and in mine pushing me into levels of sensation I had never imagined. He may have the last laugh yet; I can feel myself bursting and falling gently into a soft darkness, away from the roaring heat and light he is pouring into my core.

I awaken later; I don't know how much later, save that it is still dark. He is a dead weight draped over my back, pressing me into the crate. My hidden teeth are locked into the base of his cock, squeezing him tight enough that he is still hard inside me, although I can tell by the feel of his flesh against mine that he is out cold. I try to retract them and whimper in sudden agony; every nerve between my legs is amplified and raw. Sinking my teeth into the wood my face is pressed against—and blessing the fast tissue regrowth that has already healed my ravaged lower lip and the spots on my hips where he crushed my flesh in his grip—I force the ring of teeth to retract. They come stiffly, slowly, and I groan as they finally sink back into their hiding place. His penis softens immediately and slides out of me; I can feel a gently aching pop as its seal with my feeding mouth breaks. I grab his limp arms when I rise; draping his body over the crate, I take a good look. The puncture wounds ringing the base of his cock are already vanishing; even if he were human, they'd be almost impossible to detect in a few hours, courtesy of my venom. As it is, they'll be gone in a matter of minutes. The length of his shaft, where it lolls against the denim, is pale; the head is rosy at the tip, the only sign of its recent ordeal. Even a sloppy or a greedy one of us won't do the kind of damage his people inflict without a thought.

When my people kill, we do it deliberately. We taste the brain through the body and we judge. If they need to die, they die without pain. We are merciful.

That girl in the landfill did not die without pain. As sweet as feeding on this one's orgasm was, I cannot forget that. He acted according to his nature, so I can't judge him for that death the way I would if he were human. Not for her, and not for the many others that I know about now, deaths flavoring his climax like the oak char in bourbon. Can I execute him for fulfilling his purpose? I've lived with cats and never thought to stop them catching mice.

I must consider. He'll wake, eventually, and then?

My secret's in no danger. He will remember that it was good, yes, that it was intense. But the venom distorts short-term to long-term memory transfer enough that he will not remember exactly what it felt like, exactly how intense it was. Because then he might piece together just what I have done to him, and that could have unpleasant repercussions. We do not reproduce, my kind; there are a fixed number of us, and always have been. Well, not exactly fixed. Slowly diminishing. There has been attrition over the millennia. Those of us who are still around are careful. With a little luck, by the time technology makes it impossible to hide what we are, it will also make it easy for humans to tailor their flesh as if it were clothing, and when a body-scan at the airport splays my intimate secrets across a screen, the security staff will yawn over another kinky thrill-seeker and mutter something about goddamn West Coast fashion victims and their bio-mods.

Illogical? Yes. I belong to the only species on the planet that makes no fucking sense. Well, the hemophages are a little iffy, but some of their design elements, like the decentralized circulatory pumping system, are far more elegant than what got used as a standard here. But design elegance carried less weight than the status of the researcher on this project when it began, millions of years ago. Publications, grants, connections—having worked in some human universities, I can say with full assurance that academia has literally been this way since the beginning of time (and possibly longer; in my youth I overheard a fair amount of drunken speculation as to whether time and space are themselves projects of someone who is trying to get tenure).

As to what we (and, for that matter, hemophages) are doing here, I will only say that you shouldn't turn your back on bored graduate students for centuries, especially when they're stoned. They tend to do unauthorized experiments and then not sterilize the petri dish properly when they're done.

What to do with him? I could kill him but I won't. I could leave him here (same thing, when the sun comes up)—but I won't.

I have got to try that again. It was just too damn good.

I brush the splinters from my hands and gently tuck his cock back into his jeans—no underwear, I note with approval—and zip him up. Against the black leather jacket, his throat looks paler than it did in the club. I lay a hand against it, feeling the quiet singing of his inhuman metabolism. He has gone without feeding a bit too long himself. I pull back his upper lip, disrupting the perfect Byronic half-sneer on his handsome face. Mad, bad and dangerous to know. Oh, yes.

His fangs are distended from his upper jaw, the signs of need plain on him even unconscious. I close his mouth gently and retrieve my leather dress from the cold concrete. It will be dawn in a few hours. I drape him over my shoulder; the added weight grinds my heels viciously into the concrete as I head for my car. I'll have to feed him, of course, but as full of vitality as I feel right now, I think I can spare a little blood. And if he reacts to feeding on me anything like the way I react to feeding on him, I may have to keep him for a while—because he might refuse to leave.

Back at my condo, I stow him in the walk-in closet and block the crevice under the door with rolled-up towels; all the while he gives no more indications of awareness than a sack of grain. Then I take a long, hot bath, aching muscles almost groaning aloud with relief. I phone out for Thai food—like him, I live mostly on the same things humans do; we each just need our special supplement. Then I fall asleep, trusting in day to keep him dormant and hoping the curtains and my improvised light-seals will keep him intact. I've watched accelerated aging from sunlight shrivel one of his kind down to a husk; it was in Egypt, longer ago than I care to think about. It does the same thing to humans, only on a much slower scale. My species seems to be immune. We are resilient creatures.

By the time dusk gathers, I have slept ten hours, done my kata, watered the plants and logged on to check my e-mail and the stock market. Sunlight is still faintly visible in the sky when I haul his unconscious body to the bed and strip him. The curtains block it, so he does not darken and shrivel, but he is still dead to the world.

When he awakens, nude, his already swollen cock is buried in me to the hilt. Awareness comes to him in a rush and he remembers passing out in an alley. What is he doing here? One thing is clear: he has been compromised, his secret found out. He is startled to find that he is not bound. I know better; tie him to the bed and he'd only break it—and with what I paid for this bed, I am not about to try. No, the only thing in this place strong enough to hold him is my cunt. He snarls at me, his eyes wild with panic and hunger—and cloudy with the remembered ecstasy echoing in his nerves as his cock strains within me.

"Look what I caught," I say with a nasty grin. He wants to fling me across the room, watch me break like a rag doll against the architecture, but he is unable to make any move that would result in his cock leaving the hot tunnel that clasps it. The venom, surprisingly enough, is not physically addictive; this is his hunger coupled to his sex-drive, both kinds of need singing in his blood. We are not so different in that. "What are you?" he hisses.

It is amazing what men will believe, and I know that this one is no rocket scientist. "Never met a master of tantric kung fu before, have you?" I smile . . . and I squeeze. His breathing is quickening, and though he has no pulse I can feel the hundreds of tiny pumps in his circulatory system singing higher and faster. Whatever he uses for adrenaline is pouring into his bloodstream in massive quantities. "Let . . . me . . . go," he snarls, fangs extended. Even as he protests, his hips are pushing up, trying to bury his stiff flesh deeper in me. The head of his cock, exotically cool within my heat, grinds against my enfolded feeding mouth, and an answering ache stirs deep in my belly. "I'm not keeping you by any kind of force," I answer. "You want to be here." I lean forward, trace my tongue over his pale lips as I flex powerful muscles around his hard cock. A low hiss escapes him. Were he not pale with hunger, he would be flushed with hot shame at my teasing.

"Don't you want to taste me?" I whisper, licking beads of sweat from his forehead as I raise my hips, letting him slide out of me with agonizing slowness. He almost makes a little begging noise and I feel his fear that he will slip out completely, and then I slide back down onto him, impaling myself sudden and hard, so that we both feel the impact in our bones. I pick up on the moment of vertigo he feels as my alien heat sucks him in. I know this is a dangerous game; if I push him hard enough, it would be fairly easy for him to kill me. But I feel a certainty, deep in my belly where his cock grinds into my flesh, that he will not try. Much as he fears me and the strange place I sent him to last night, he is even more afraid of never getting to go there again. He wants it as much as I do. And that will keep him from taking too much when he finally takes me.

Why has he not gone for my throat? I know how badly he needs my blood; I can feel that aching hunger in every pulse and flex of his penis inside me, just as I feel my own ache building against that sweet pressure. Perhaps he can only take as a violation; certainly I can tell that what he needs has never been given to him. His shame is paralyzing him; his flesh remembers what I did to him in that alley, and he can no longer see me as prey. Well, his need will overpower his capacity for thought soon enough. I rise up, drawing a groan from him as the angle of my pelvis shifts over his cock, and I run my nails delicately over his nipples, continuing to pulse and clasp my walls around him. He reaches down to grab my thighs as he pushes up, up, trying to get deeper inside me than he can go. If he were not so starved with need, I think he might have tried to kill me some time ago. But his hunger will not let him stop what is happening, even as he aches to drink me but cannot bring himself to cross that line. I reach up to cup my breasts, letting my tight nipples look out between my fingers at him, and begin to rock my pelvis faster, pulsing my muscles inside in a tight fluttering rhythm. His eyes roll back in his head as my hips pick up speed, and his mouth is open, a building roar in his throat as I move harder over him. So soon after last night, his nerves are raw, still somewhat amplified, and the sensations are almost too much to bear.

As I continue driving my hips forward and back over him, it suddenly crosses the line into pain, and he cries out and seizes my hips in hands as cold and hard as metal, forcing me to stop moving. It does no good. My insides are still working him, writhing, clamping down hard, milking his cock mercilessly. I know it is hurting him. So many he has hurt to feed; he feels it now, what it is to be helpless. Not, I reflect, that it will work any great change in his personality. But I get a kick out of it.

Very carefully, working the muscles by an act of will so as not to waken my full feeding reflex, I unfold my un-cervix and let it delicately suck at the tip of his cock while my muscles squeeze his shaft. A terrible lucidity comes over his face as pain crosses the line into something else; his eyes are perfectly focused but not on anything in this room. The slippery inside of my feeding mouth pulls at him and I feel with exquisite clarity his conviction that he is drowning. He has stopped breathing—I know enough not to worry at this—and is staring intently up into nothing, face twisted in torment and ecstasy. Bernini's St. Teresa looked somewhat like this. I hold him on the edge for long minutes, feeling his nerves sing of ache and promised release, need and exquisite relief. Then I put my wrist to his lips and his reflexes take over. The fangs drive into my flesh and a sweet hot rush of my blood fills his mouth; for a second I am only aware of the taste of it through him. His orgasm begins wracking him just as I feel the fire of his bloody kiss tearing through me. This? He has been giving *this* as pain and violation? He has been mixing single-malt with sewage. It starts like a climax unfolding in the veins of my wrist, and then runs wild through my whole body, electricity in the marrow of my bones, a divine edge of inexorable glory. My control, everything, is gone; with dim panic I feel my own feeding reflex take over, driven by the pull and the need in his flesh and mine.

He swallows convulsively, body trembling as my unleashed fangs drive in and start flooding his system with chemical ecstasy. The blood pouring into his mouth tastes like light made liquid, an alien tang to it so sweetly different from the thick salty rush of feeding on humans. So rich, so dense, such a bright burning. He won't be able to take much of it; it's beginning to overload him already. A low groan vibrates through my wrist as his clenched teeth grind into the bones; he is feeling the venom-orgasm overlaid with the ecstasy of feeding on me, and it is so sweet he cannot stand it. Deep in my belly, he gives; pulling at my wrist, he takes, and the circle of fire is moving faster through us, pushing us to heights where the air is very thin. I am not draining him as hard as

I did last night; I am satiated, and it is only the unexpected ecstasy of his drinking from me that drew my fangs from their hiding place and drove my feeding mouth from delicate sucking to the fierce hot pull that is draining him now. I can feel that he has fed while coming before, and he thought it an impressive sensation. But my blood is as far beyond human blood for him as his orgasm was beyond human climaxes for me, and this is mingled with my nerve-amplifying venom and the exquisitely unbearable things my insides are doing to his penis.

When it finally ends, when both sets of fangs retract and we feel our efficient flesh repair the damage, I am a little light-headed with blood loss, and I know he is drunk on me. I collapse on top of him and he puts his arms around me, then flinches at his own unaccustomed gesture. Still, he does not let go. I turn my head and lick the sweat from his neck, and he trembles for a moment as though he were human.

I know what I will do with him now, this puppy, this tasty mouthful.

Humans are so short-lived; they flicker by like landscapes from the window of a bullet train. No sooner do I become fond of one than I have to watch it eaten alive by time, and that is depressing. The hemophages are long-lived, certainly—technically immortal, they inevitably die by violence—but the adults have a personality like flint shards and do not qualify as pleasant company by any stretch of the imagination.

But this one, still young enough to be cute, is also still young enough to be malleable. I can break him to the leash, curb his bad habits (he has *got* to learn some table manners; there's no reason to kill every time he feeds) and enjoy him long enough to make the effort of keeping him worth it.

I run my fingers through his hair and he looks at me with wonder. He is already eager to please me, though he would never admit that to himself. The echo of my venom singing in his bloodstream has made him forget, for a little while, that he is supposed to be cold and hard and edgy. Yes, I think he will be trainable. Good boy. Heel. Play dead (easy enough if the sun's coming up). Fuck me. Stay.

Come *here,* little predator.

I've always wanted a pet.

TAKEN

GENEVIEVE ISEULT ELDREDGE

And so it was that on the eve of her birthday, one hour before she turned eighteen, Anastazia Tzigane stood before the grand ballroom in Castle Walpurgis. She had come here to slay the fiend who had murdered her family and brought misery and death to the lands.

She hesitated before the great doors, unable to catch her breath. Her bodice heaved, the hilt of the Dagger nestled safely between her breasts. Its weight was both a comfort and a dread. For the magick of the Dagger had failed her two sisters. On their eighteenth birthdays, they had both met their end in this castle, drained of blood by the monster that lived within.

Anna began to tremble; and she prayed that her purity would be enough to inspire the blade's power.

The dark red of her gown reflected like blood in the torchlight, the wrappings round her waist disguising the small bulge of the Dagger. She put her hand to it, to steady her resolve. Now that she was past the guards, she felt unsure—a little girl lost in a fortress of doubt.

She laid her forehead against the door. The strains of music seeped through cracks in the wood; and off in the distance, she could hear the bells from the tower toning the hour of eleven. The far-off echo galvanized her, and she took in a deep breath and held it.

The stroke of eleven resounded, and before it had faded, Anna burst into the ballroom. The sound of the doors striking the wall stopped both the guests and the music.

Anna swept into the chamber like a troubled storm, one hand on her bodice, her eyes scanning the crowd. Desperation creased her fair features. So many of them! If they came at her, she would be overwhelmed in seconds.

With a politeness that bordered on sinister, the guests made way for her, and she walked among them, the only red in a sea of black. Anna turned herself in circles, her eyes searching the decadence of the throng, the opulence of the ballroom. The nervous clatter of her footsteps on the slate floors echoed in the tense silence.

"Anastazia, I am so glad you could attend."

The voice came from behind, sudden and masculine, sending a spatter of dreadful shivers down her spine. Anna forced a deep breath, and turned to face the man she had come to murder.

Like all of his guests, Baron Kondrati was dressed in regal black, his collar and cuffs velveted. The darkness of the attire made his stark white skin stand out in the candlelight. His black hair was cropped short. His face was austere, yet youthful and comely.

But his eyes!

They blazed an icy blue, burning with a chill no mortal man could endure.

Anna met his gaze with all the strength she could gather. "Baron Kondrati, prepare yourself, for this night, Anastazia Tzigane will see an end to your evil."

The Baron smiled and started toward her.

Anna stepped back, and the crowd of dancers made way for her. Her green eyes flashed, and her breath began to quicken. One hand strayed unconsciously to her bodice, where the Dagger lay hidden. "I will not fail like my sisters. I will see your wickedness turn to ashes."

"Ah yes, the Gypsy prophecy." The Baron's piercing blue eyes locked on hers for a moment, then fell to her bodice. For a completely different reason, his gaze lingered there.

Anna found herself blushing, found her heart beating faster.

"On their eighteenth birthday, the women of the Tzigane clan will gain the power to slay the vampire." And he laughed, showing the brilliance of his fangs.

The obvious display made Anna falter, but only for a moment.

Her heart hammering, she tore the Dagger from her bodice and rushed him. The crowd surged forward, and she found herself caught, the blade an inch from his black heart.

She cried out and struggled, but their iron grip held her fast.

The Baron approached with slow and dreadful deliberation. Anna found she could not move, could not breathe. His striking blue eyes pinned her to the floor.

Fear blossomed in her belly, and on the heels of it, came excitement, hot and unbidden. Her knees became weak, and she was suddenly glad of the arms holding her up.

His shadow fell across her. "The Prophecy also speaks of surrender." He was so close, she could feel the chill of his undead flesh. "Surrender yourself to me this night, and you will awaken to a new life—free of the chains of mortality." One long finger stroked the high angle of her cheekbone. "Yield to me and rule beside me as my bride."

His glacial caress was abhorrent, yet compelling; and Anna lingered under it for a moment before tearing herself away. "You repulse me!"

"If I repulse you so, why do you remain?" The Baron stepped closer, and held out his hand. "You need not resist. Surrender yourself to me."

"Never." She strained toward him with the Dagger. "This blade will send you to the Abyss!"

His gaze intensified, and he grabbed her, crushing her fingers against the hilt. Anna cried out, tears of pain springing to her eyes.

He bared his fangs. "The Prophecy speaks of purity, Anna—a trait that does not run in your family." He paused, his face an inch from hers. "Are you pure, Anna?"

She looked up, tears streaking her cheeks. Every word was an effort. "I . . . am . . . pure enough to vanquish you."

He gripped harder for a moment, and she whimpered; then he released her with an abruptness that sent her falling back into her captors' arms.

"We'll see . . ." he spoke almost gently. "We'll see if you still want to use it after I have done with you."

Anna looked at him balefully, cradling her throbbing fingers. But the Baron turned away to look upon the wall clock. "The time has not yet come. Your eighteenth birthday is still an hour away."

The offer of his hand remained. "Come, let us have a dance on this, the eve of your awakening."

"No." But even as her lips spoke, she watched her hand reach out and take his. The cold of his touch splintered up her arm, and took the breath from her lungs. The Dagger dangled in her brittle grip.

The violins began to play and the Baron swept her away into the crush of dancers. Her feet went willingly enough, her body like a marionette doomed by the bidding of its master. The Baron's hand was light on hers, but he controlled her every movement as the dance wound on and the music reeled out of control.

Black velvet swirled around them, as the other dancers spun and twirled about the unlikely pair.

Anna felt dizzy, and she shivered under the Baron's hands. The chill of his touch raced along her spine; and with each passing moment, she became more and more lost in his embrace. The weight of the Dagger in her hand was little comfort. She did not have the strength to lift it. Her limbs were lead and ice. And yet, a need began to burn hot in her belly. She felt it welling up inside her, but she knew not what she craved.

As they danced, his arms enfolded her from behind. His face was close by her ear, but she could feel no breath from his lips. His hands moved down her body. The iciness of his flesh seeped through her dress, making her entire frame quiver. Her breath came short and hard, pluming frost into the air; and her heart raced in her bosom.

For eighteen years, she had been without the caress of a lover. Her body ached from neglect. She yearned to be touched, to be explored, to be taken.

The Baron's hands found her bodice and he filled his palms with her full breasts.

Anna's face grew red, and her hand went to his. But as she moved to pull them away, gooseflesh rippled over her fair skin; and a shudder of unexpected, unwanted pleasure wracked her. Instead of pulling away, her hand merely held his.

He caressed her breasts, cupping and squeezing them gently. Her nipples grew hard against the velvet, and her breath froze in her throat. Anticipation raced up her spine, mingled with fear—fear that he would persist, fear that he would stop.

The Baron laid his wintry cheek against hers, and a shiver—part revulsion, part allure—slipped down her spine. His strong body pressed up against her, and she felt somehow safe and yet completely endangered all at once.

"Anna, you have finally come to me. After eighteen long years . . ."

Anna struggled in his enthralling grip. The shine of the Dagger's hilt caught her eye. "You . . . I have come to kill you . . ." The words came out before she could stop them. Terror shot her through, liquid-quick, but the Baron only chuckled kindly.

"My dearest Anna . . ."

His hands fondled her breasts through the crimson velvet. Anna let her head roll back onto his shoulder as he pinched her nipples, rolling his fingertips across them. He leaned in, his hips insistent against her buttocks. A hard bluntness stabbed at her tight ass, and the Baron let out a throaty moan.

Shame made her face red as the bittersweet relief of his touch shuddered through her, bringing tears to her eyes. Caught in his embrace, she was assailed by sudden desire, scattering fire through her body, and sending her thoughts to the winds. She no longer cared about anything, only the solace she found in his arms.

Her eyes passed over the other guests and their partners, and propriety made her whisper: "But the others . . ."

"They will not watch . . . unless you would like them to." His lips brushed her ear, and his hand slid up her leg, gathering the velvet there. The chill of the night was nothing compared to the chill of his flesh. She shivered, her thighs quivering as he slipped his hand around to caress her bottom. She felt the stiffness of his manhood through his breeches as he ground himself against her. Cold fingers barely brushed the warmth of her inner thigh. "Would you like that, Anna?"

"I . . ." She could not form a rational thought, only the most base, sacrilegious desire: that the burning of her flesh could only be quenched by the ice of his touch.

He smiled around his fangs, and knowing she was captive, let her go, spinning her into the mob.

They received her greedily. Their hands rained softly over her body, running through her brown locks, touching the brocade on her bodice, pulling at her skirts with an exigency that began to seep into her bones. She held the Dagger overhead with both hands, trying to summon the strength to use it, fearful that she would use it, and put an end to the desires she could not control.

Her eyes fell upon the Baron, fell upon his heart. She imagined plunging the Dagger deep into him, penetrating him with her cold steel.

The crowd of dancers swarmed her. Two of them took her by the arms and held her fast. Another lifted her dress above the knee. Anna fought against them, but their grip was relentless. Cold hands groped at her thighs, her bosom, chill fingers tousled her hair. The more she fought, the harder they held her, the quicker her heartbeat pulsed, the more labored her breath. A light sweat sheened her skin.

She saw the Baron watching her. Lascivious intentions flashed in the ice-blue of his eyes as they explored every inch of her thrashing body.

He gave a small gesture.

Hands, abrupt and rude, came round her ribcage and grasped her breasts, lifting them up, displaying them for the Master.

The Baron's eyes drank in the sight of her, held by his minions, skirts lifted, long legs exposed, manhandled from behind, her cleavage heaving in the grasp of a stranger.

He leaned in and his lips brushed the tops of her exposed breasts. She trembled, though she tried to keep still. He inhaled the scent of her fear, and smelled something else . . .

"Ahh, is that excitement I smell upon you, Anna?"

"No!" She struggled in vain against their grip and against the ecstasy rising within her.

His minions pulled her hair away from her neck. The Baron gently laid his lips to her throat. Anna grew very still, her green eyes wide in fright.

Although she stopped breathing, he could feel the blood pulsing hot through the vein, fiery and defiant. It throbbed with her fury and anger.

"I look forward to tasting you."

A small cry escaped Anna and her legs almost buckled. Her hand tightened around the Dagger—the salvation she could not find the strength to use.

Before her, the Baron sank to his knees. His minions lifted her dress, exposing the warmth of her thighs. She strained in their grasp, a terrible thrill blossoming in the pit of her belly. The Baron brushed aside the red velvet and laid his cheek on her inner thigh. She recoiled from the bitter chill of his skin, and then his hands came across her legs, caressing them, his fingers teasing past her virtue.

Anna gasped; and she could feel a sudden, throbbing heat between her thighs—a wet, sticky ache that brought a shameful blush to her cheeks.

The Baron looked up, and seeing her captured in the grasp of his servants, he smiled. Anna writhed in frustration. She bit her lip, and a small bead of blood welled. "Please . . ." she whispered, not knowing what to beg for.

The Baron's tongue flicked up her leg, licking the droplets of sweat and chrism from her inner thigh. The cold of his touch was lost in the flushed heat of her flesh. His hands slipped between her legs to spread her gently.

A low moan escaped Anna, and she struggled in fearful expectation.

The Baron licked lightly, once to tease; and then he parted her forcefully, and pressed his face against the hot wetness between her thighs.

Anna bucked, straining to get away. She drove down with the Dagger, but his minions held her tight. Gasping, crying out, she struggled to knife him; but as his lips and tongue bore down with cruel insistence upon her flesh, she went faint with a pleasure she had never known.

Held captive, she could not be responsible for her actions. Her struggles began to drive toward him, to press herself harder onto his face. Her hips writhed. Using her captors as support, she spread her legs.

The Baron licked and sucked at her pussy. His tongue lashed her, licking, probing deep, and his fingers came in to spread her wider. The heat of her warmed him and he pressed deeper into her, exploring her virginal cunt. She quivered under his touch, the soft petals of her sex responding with an eagerness blossoming into lust.

Anna could not control herself. Her head rolled back onto a stranger's shoulder and she closed her eyes. Her face was red, her need exposed, her modesty shattered. The Dagger was all but forgotten in her hand.

His lips brushed against her clit, and the rush of blood swelled up under his ministrations. Her heartbeat pulsed against his lips even as his tongue prodded deeper into her.

Anna cried out. Her thighs tightened and he knew she was nearing her crisis.

"Not yet, Anna. We must save you for midnight." He took the clitoris gently in his teeth, and then bit down. A single fang penetrated virginal flesh.

Anna screamed, spasming. Her body, close to climax, froze, both pleasure and pain spiking her. The tugging pull of his teeth, the pressure of his lips, sucking her harder, drawing her clit further into him. She could barely move, barely breathe. She could feel her own pulse beating hard between her legs. The cold, the pain of the wound made her lose her breath, and she collapsed back, letting him take her.

The Baron suckled at her sex. Her untainted blood pumped hot and sweet. Mingled with the flow of her lust, it was heady, intoxicating. The Baron lapped at the liquid fusion with beastly greed. Anna pushed against him, urging him to take more, and for a moment, he indulged her.

Her voice rose high and winding, urging him on, uncaring of her fate, so long as she could spend herself against his suckling mouth.

And then he retracted his teeth, and pulled out of her, leaving her gasping and unfulfilled. He caressed her thighs gently, calming their heat with the chill of his caress. His tongue lapped gently at her clitoris, closing the wound; but not before a thin rivulet ran down her pale thigh. He chased it, his tongue catching the sweet droplets of her chaste blood.

He stood to face her. Anna was disheveled, breathing hard, her cleavage heaving, yearning to be free of the confines of her dress. His eyes fell to her lush body, and he imagined taking her, sinking his flesh deep into hers.

The Dagger was limp in her hand, impotent, no longer a threat.

He embraced her, and the stiffness of his own craving nudged against her thigh. "Anna, you are mine."

"N-no!" But even as she raised her hands to push him away, she fell into his embrace. She buried her face in his chest. "Not here. I . . . I want to be alone with you."

Her words were an admission of guilt, a surrender.

The Baron smiled, and he gently took her from the arms of her captors. Anna's head spun, dizzy from blood loss and the feel of his teeth in her. She ached inside, with a burning that would never be filled. The touch of his hand was not enough. She wanted him to take her, to ravage her, to tear her body apart with his caress.

His hand was cold in hers, leading her past a dark blur of opulent hallways and chambers. And then he was laying her down on velvet cushions.

He stood over her, and his eyes grew a deep red. He smiled and she saw her own blood on his cruel fangs. "I must have you, Anna." I am no beast, but neither am I a gentleman. If you say no, I will take you."

The thought of him ravishing her flashed in her mind, hot and carnal. Her face blushed a dark red.

"There are other ways I can please you, my Lord, my Master."

Anna got down on her knees before him. Her hand went tentatively to his breeches. The Baron stood still as she unlaced his pants, and slipped her fingers inside.

The skin was cold and soft, yet hardened quickly under her touch. She stroked the rigid shaft with two fingers, and gently brought it out into the light. It was pale white like marble, with thick veins running its surface. Slowly, Anna began to stroke it.

The Baron leaned back as she fondled him. Her hand worked the length of his shaft, twisting gently and arousing him beyond reason. The warmth of her, the pulse of her heartbeat through her fingertips. He felt the wave of his pleasure rising, threatening to burst forth; but he stilled himself.

"Anna . . ."

The young girl leaned in and took the tip of him gently in her mouth. The Baron gritted his teeth with the effort of holding back.

She looked up at him, green eyes dilated. He took her face in his hands, the softness of her brown locks falling around his fingers.

Anna struggled at first, as he penetrated her. She pulled away, but he held on, pumping at her gently. His shaft slipped in and out of her wet mouth. He pushed gently at first, and then harder, thrusting between her pursed lips.

Anna surrendered, taking him deep in her throat. She sucked him, her tongue teasing the soft stiffness. He began to moan deep in his gullet, and she dominated him, ruling over his pleasure with tongue and mouth and hand. She reached between his legs and ran her fingernails along his inner thigh. She raked him.

The Baron's eyes rolled back in his head, but Anna pulled away, letting his hard cock fall from her full lips. His eyes flew open in icy fury, but she smiled up at him, and reached for her bodice. With one hand, she exposed herself, her breasts heavy and ripe. He groped blindly, desperate, and thrust himself, plunging into the cleft.

He fucked her, massaging his straining cock against the softness of her cleavage. He clamped down hard on her breasts. She whimpered, but her head was thrown back, her hand clenched to her heart, breath coming in short gasps. Looking upon her, kneeling before him in her shamelessness, his cock riding between her full breasts, took him over the edge. His eyes rolled back into his head and he spurted hot come all over her pale, perfect orbs.

He pulled away, and lust shone from his eyes. He drank in the sight of her body, half-naked and stained with his jism.

"I am not satisfied Anna. I will not be satisfied until I can come deep within you."

The thought both terrified and excited her. She stood, the seed of his hunger trickling down between her breasts.

She moved to meet him, pressing the heat of her living flesh against the cold of his undead frame. The wintry chill stole the warmth from her body, and she began at once to shiver. Frost plumed from her mouth.

The Baron's hands came up, tangling into her hair. He brought her head down to his chest. Obediently, she laid her deadened lips to his skin.

She stayed still, listening, praying to hear the tower bells toll midnight. And yet, she knew with awful certainty that there was no escape this night—that her only release would be found in his carnal embrace.

He arched his back, and she bit him as if to tease.

He smiled. "Soon, enough, my love. You will taste my blood. And you will become one with me."

"Yes . . . my love . . . my Master . . ." Anna straightened and pressed the length of her body against him. The cold shot her through, breasts and belly, thighs and hands. But even as it froze across her bones, the visceral burn of desire rose within her.

The Baron's mouth opened, his tongue meeting hers. She explored the taste of him, daring to feel at the edged teeth with the tip of her tongue. She pressed a bit too hard, and felt the sharpness bite into her. She winced back, but he captured her, and sucked gently at the tiny droplet of blood.

The taste of her drove him to madness. "I can wait no longer."

He threw her down on the bed and began tearing her dress with his claws. Velvet ripped and tore under the force of his need.

Anna struggled and screamed, but it was pretense, a charade. Her own desire rose in her, hot and wild, and uncaring of his nature. She was already spreading her legs wide, and pulling him down on top of her. Their clothing was like a shield between them; and he pumped against her impotently, while she writhed and cried out her frustration.

"Surrender yourself . . . give yourself to me for this one night and you can rule over me forever."

"Yes!" She breathed. "Yes, I want you. I want you to take me."

Her dress tore wide. The Dagger fell between them, forgotten.

She began pulling at his clothes, ripping them in her frustration. His pale body gleamed like bleached bone in the moonlight. She paused to look at him, and the thought registered in her mind—her sacrilege, her sin. But she could not care, she could not stop herself.

His clawed hands bore down on her breasts, pulling the torn velvet aside from them, to take their firmness in his hands. Under his chill touch, the nipples sprang up hard and taut.

Anna lost her breath and squirmed under him. His tongue licked down over one rosy bud, teasing. And then his mouth closed down and he sucked gently. The sharpness of his teeth grazed her nipple and she shuddered.

Her mind whirled as she imagined those teeth penetrating her, drinking deep of her virgin's blood.

Anna spread her legs wide, and he lowered himself on top of her. The soft tip of his cock prodded against her, and she felt herself, hot and wet and wanting. She looked down and saw the shaft—pure and smooth as marble. His hands came down over her hips and he thrust.

Anna cried out as he split his way into her, his icy cock defiling her pussy. His shaft was cold and hard, but the fire of her lust warmed it. He thrust deeper and deeper into her tight, virginal flesh, burning himself on her wanton heat.

Anna cried out again, tears welling in her eyes as he filled a need she had never known existed.

His voice rose in the chamber, guttural—a beast's voice—and hers joined it, screaming in pleasure as he took her. His cock speared her without mercy, ravaging her soft, chaste pussy. She clung to him and sobbed, crying out for her own ruination.

The echo of the bells began to toll midnight. Panic sped Anna through—she feared she could not hold back. "Yes, my Master, yes. Take me. Fuck me. Make me yours."

His fangs pierced her skin, penetrating her deep. He sucked her hard, drawing her blood to him. A chill trembled over her body, numbing her fingertips and toes. She cried out softly as he took her, but she did not struggle.

The bells thrummed a race against time.

The Baron took her blood as he took her virginity—penetrating her with cock and fang.

Anna fell into his dark embrace, her limbs going limp as the warmth bled out, stolen by his sensual kiss. Blood ran from the corner of his lip, and trickled down her neck. She could taste her own blood at the back of her throat. She felt his unyielding cock thrusting inside her, slick and wet with her juices; felt his fangs within her, like twin slivers of ice.

Her lust smoldered against it, fighting the chill of his embrace. But even as she burned to a fiery inferno, her body grew colder and colder—dying as she satisfied her darkest urges.

The bells toned on, monotonous and eternal.

Anna struggled not to come against the hardness of his cock. Sobbing, crying out, she clung to him as he fucked her without mercy. He thrust up into her hips, splaying her legs aside.

And oh, she wanted it, she wanted forever with him.

The Baron drove harder, the smell of virgin's blood spilled and the scent of her sex driving him mad. He lifted his head, her blood trickling down his white throat. A scream of ecstasy escaped his sanguine lips.

The bells tolled on, closer and closer to midnight. Anna's breath went out of her and her body bucked under him. Death throes wracked her.

Her cold hand fumbled in the bedsheets. Her fingertips brushed the hilt of the Dagger and then it fell into her hands. She gripped it tight.

The stroke of midnight.

She was eighteen.

Her blade penetrated him to the core. A scream tore itself from her throat, and sunlight shot over the Dagger.

Locked into his bestial rutting, the Baron cried out in a crisis of agony and ecstasy. Sunlight shot over him, riddling his flesh. Even as he took her virginity, the sun began to swallow him.

He bared his fangs in defiance. "You . . . are . . . still mine . . . Anna." And he thrust into her one final time. He shuddered, his cock straining as it spurted hot come deep within her.

Anna screamed her throat raw as he spilled his immortal seed into her virginal cunt. And as his corpse began to writhe and turn to cinders before her, she felt her own body start to spasm and wrack, and she came against the dying of his ashes.

THE PERMANENT

CATHERINE LUNDOFF

Run, my mind sings. *Run.* And I do. I am almost flying now, my heart thudding against my ribs like a rabbit pursued by hounds. My bare feet pound against the dirt as I do my best to outstrip whatever it is that hunts me. *Bare?* I glance down at a frothy lace confection of a nightgown, at my pale naked feet twinkling below me in the darkness. *Why am I wearing this . . . thing?* The thought jars me awake just ahead of the phantom grasp of my pursuer.

Just ahead of the alarm as well. I sit up, heart still pounding as I turn off the clock radio. When I look down, my nipples are gradually relaxing and I can smell the dampness like rust between my legs. I scramble for a tampon, coffee and clothes, then drag my carcass out to catch the bus. It stops in front of a big red brick building with high-arched windows. Two large stone pots filled with scraggly brown leaves and twisted stems stand on either side of the doorway. I wonder what it was before it died.

I'd also wonder why they don't shell out for landscaping, but I've been inside. I know the answer to that already. Genteel decay doesn't begin to cover it. Once through the doors, I have to stop and blink for a while to adjust to the dimness and the dust. There are ancient red velvet curtains and musty old Persian carpets and dark, dark wood everywhere. I don't see Terese until I almost bump into her. Not that I mind that part. She and her brother

Gerard are the best part about working here, besides the pay, of course.

"Hello, Magda," Terese purrs down at me, not bothering to step back. She's about five inches taller than me and round and curvy in all the right places. Her big black eyes come into focus as my eyes adjust and she flashes a bright white grin at me.

I love hearing her say my name. In her deep voice with its undefinable accent, "Magda" becomes an exotic Eastern European beauty with cheekbones to die for and yards of black hair. Of course, I do look just like that, except for the cheekbones. And the hair. Well, all right, and I'm not particularly exotic; can we drop it already?

Terese moves slowly away from me as Gerard comes into the hallway. "Hello, Magda. We've got some fun stuff for you tonight." He smiles reassuringly, teeth dazzling in the gloom. He is long and lean in contrast to Terese's abundant curves. They both have the same melting eyes though, and black hair that looks more like ravens' wings than ravens' wings if you know what I mean. Their hands are pretty similar too, all long fingers and slightly tapered nails. Just the right size to fit into all kinds of inappropriate-for-the-workplace things.

On the other hand, Samuels, the other employee, is more than a little creepy. He has eyes that kind of slide away before they really catch yours. I follow Gerard into the next room where Samuels wanders up to us. When I glance up it looks like he's trying to smell my hair or something.

I back up until Gerard speaks. "Didn't you say that you wanted to get started on the billing, Dick? I'll be in to talk to you about it in a few minutes," Gerard's voice has just the right authoritative ring to it and Samuels dutifully trots off without a backward glance. I hope the office lights are too dim for Gerard to notice my small sigh of relief. I wouldn't want him thinking that I don't play well with others.

He keeps the lights low and they work mostly at night because he and Terese are both light-sensitive. I'm finally getting used to it; soon, like their general gorgeousness, I'll just take it in stride. I tell myself that when he leads me over to his computer. His hand rests lightly on my shoulder. All of a sudden, I want that frothy lace horror I was wearing in my dream. I wonder if he'd like taking it off. Then he breaks the mood by taking his hand away and standing tantalizingly out of reach as he tells me what he wants me to do.

But I'm having trouble concentrating. The room is getting warmer. Maybe it's just the dark red velvet of the curtains drowning out the setting sun's watery light. Maybe it's the rise and fall of Gerard's voice as he speaks to me. I reach up and unbutton the top two buttons on my blouse but he doesn't seem to notice and it doesn't cool me off at all. The room spins slowly around me and instead of listening to the wonder of invoices, I find myself imagining the touch of his lips, the feel of those long fingers on my skin.

"You're confusing her, brother dear." Terese slinks in to sit on the edge of the desk, as close to me as she can get. I turn my chair a little so my leg touches hers ever so slightly, just enough to send shivers up my spine. I am getting wet listening to them banter back and forth above me, soaking my tampon until I wonder if my blood will pool beneath me in a small sea. I contemplate throwing myself at both of them. But what if they say no? How humiliating would that be? *Coward* says the little voice inside my head.

Terese leans forward to point out something on the screen and I can see down the front of her dress. Round breasts glow like alabaster against the soft dark blue of the cloth and I long to bury myself in them. She reaches out and I feel her white fingers caress my face. I turn to kiss them. *Wait, that's not it at all. She's reaching out to get a paper from Gerard. Damn, Magda, get a grip.* I drown in her eyes anyway and come up gasping.

My fingers play with the next button on my blouse. "Are you too warm?" Gerard purrs solicitously, and from somewhere a cold breeze startles my flesh from its daydreams. Goosebumps run down my arms and my nipples leap erect and I gasp aloud at the sudden chill.

"Too much, I think." Terese stands up, her fingers now gently stroking the goosebumps from my bare arm. I chew my lip in a frenzied effort at self-control. I should go get a glass of water, take a break, do something, anything so I don't make a fool of myself. Not here, not in front of them.

With a huge effort, I make myself say, "I'm fine, really. Well, I should get started on this stuff." They both smile down at me and for an instant, I remember my dream and my body braces for flight. Then the moment's past, leaving nothing but my pounding heart behind as they glide like panthers from the room. Terese gives me what I interpret as a smoldering gaze over one shoulder and my lips part in a soft pant.

The door shuts behind them and I am left alone in Gerard's office with its ancient wood furniture and red velvet curtains and a giant stack of invoices. When I look down I can see the rivulets of sweat run down between my breasts. *Are you showing enough cleavage there, Magda?* the voice of my common sense demands shrilly, but I ignore it in favor of wishing that I had worn my good lace bra today instead of my sad nylon one.

I don't rebutton the shirt, but I do make myself work for a while, make myself pretend that the growing wetness between my legs isn't there. I try to squelch my new fantasy of being chased through the woods by both of them. And better yet, being caught. It works for a while. Then I give up and begin typing with one hand as I unzip my boring khaki skirt with the other. I stick that hand inside the waistbands of both skirt and underpants.

My fingers swim upstream to my clit and I imagine they're Terese's tongue, circling, stroking, then darting inside me. Heat washes up my thighs and I quiver against their touch. I abandon the keyboard to stroke my nipples through my shirt and bra, first one then the other, pinched into points with my—no her—free hand. My clit hardens beneath my fingers, her tongue, skin slick with my own juices, with her imagined softness. Her phantom fingers slip inside me and I ride the wave, cresting it with a soft moan, legs shaking against Gerard's chair.

I hear the click of the door before I open my eyes. In an instant, I am looking doggedly at the screen, both hands resting on the keyboard. Casually, I reach back and zip up my skirt. But when I look up there's no one there.

Dinner time rolls around eventually and I go and eat my sandwich in the backyard. It's about the size of a postage stamp and overgrown with old rose bushes and morning glories. I can pretend that I'm Sleeping Beauty while I sit on the old iron bench and remember what summer looks like. Samuels glances out the door at me, faded eyes sliding all around me, but he doesn't come outside.

I'm overjoyed when he disappears back inside. There's something creepy about that wrinkled face with its weird eyes shifting and wandering but never quite coming to rest. If it weren't for the pay and the chance to lust after hotties like Terese and Gerard, I'd ask to be pulled from this job. Not that I think that way once I'm back inside.

I close the door behind me and notice Terese through the open door of her office. She's meeting with someone, perhaps an actual client. They don't seem to have all that many of those, possibly because of the evening hours. Or maybe it's that silly slogan: Forever Insurance Insures You Forever. I mean, who needs insurance *forever?* Lifetime total is usually enough for most people.

Terese leans forward, talking with her hands all the while and looking earnest. Definitely a client. I wander back to Gerard's office in time to find him sitting at his desk. He gives me a sleepy grin and ushers me back to his chair. The way he hangs over me when I sit down almost makes me wonder if he can smell my wet warmth, and I squirm against the upholstery at the thought.

I wonder what would happen if I turned around and unzipped his fly to take his dick in my mouth. In my mind, it's just the right size and he groans at the touch of my tongue. I rock my head back and forth, then pull away to lick my way slowly down to his balls. His breath quickens into short gasps as I embrace him with my mouth once more. He clutches my shoulders in an effort not to ram himself down my throat. I can feel him shake with desire and I smile a little. I just love polite boys.

He reaches down to grab one of my hands and pulls it up to his mouth. I can feel his mouth on my fingers, then his tongue on my wrist: distracting, but not unpleasantly so. I work harder until I can taste his salty tang and as he comes in my mouth, I feel his teeth sinking into my wrist. I groan in surprise and desire, panting as I watch him drink from me. His tongue pulls at my wrist like a tongue on my clit and I spread my legs, straining against the chair. My fingers stroke my clit until I forget where I am and come in waves.

When I'm ready to start paying attention again, he's gone and I've got nothing better to look at than the computer screen. I remind myself sternly that there was no way Gerard was going to be doing the temp at work, not with the door open, anyway. The voice of my common sense takes over despite the imagined slight ache of jaw and wrist.

I type listlessly until it's time to go home. Terese's client is gone and she and Gerard are talking softly to each other when I say goodnight. They stop talking to smile at me as Samuels holds the door open for me. I wonder if he lives upstairs. He's always there when I get there and still there when I leave. I look up at the curtained windows of the second floor where I have yet to venture. They look deserted but my flesh crawls a little as my eyes meet their glassy, blank stares.

The dreams are more intense tonight. This time, I worry that something serious will happen if I get caught and I run faster than ever. Still, something grabs me and I fall, tumbling not to the ground but into the afternoon and safety. The last thing I remember seeing in my dream is the curtained windows of the second floor of Forever Insurance as I run past them, pursued by whatever it is. Terrific. I hate it when my subconscious works overtime.

I decide to take the proverbial bull by the horns or any other available body part and check out the second floor. Once I knew there were no dead bodies or whatever up there, I'd get over this whole thing. Or so I tell myself.

The groovy ghoul is the only one at the office when I show up. "Terese and Gerard are meeting with clients downtown," Samuels informs me in a voice like a damp fog. His bulbous, colorless eyes gaze just past me until I get impatient and slightly queasy. I flee to Gerard's office and my very safe invoices. Joy.

But at least I'm not working with him. He has his own office down the hall. As long as he's busy, this is probably my best chance for checking out the dreaded upstairs. I just need to know that I'm overreacting, then I can make it all go away. Tomorrow I'll go have lunch with some friends, maybe catch a matinee. Get back to normal, whatever that is.

I do remember being normal. That was the time when I wasn't having weird dreams about things chasing me and could enter invoices for hours at a time without even once thinking of fucking my bosses. Back then, I wasn't looking at little cuts on my wrist and wondering where they came from. It's not like anything actually happened yesterday so I really don't have a clue. I rub them a little and they fade under the pressure, disappearing into my skin like they were never there. Bizarre.

I wait a reasonable amount of time before I head out into the hall. I poke my nose around the door of Samuels's office and wave the universal signal for "see you later." He bares his teeth at me—whoops, no that was a smile. Sort of. He goes on talking on the phone, so I move as quietly as I can to the big staircase, just out of sight of the door. It has dark wood banisters that curl at the ends and it's very dark up at the top. *All right, just go up, look around, then back down,* I tell myself.

I'm shivering a little on the first step and more on the third. By the time I get to the seventh I know this wasn't a good idea. But on step ten I know I might as well go all the way up. Five steps more and I'm on the landing. There's a little light coming in from somewhere, but not much. The air is really still up here, like it's anticipating something, and it's a lot cooler than downstairs. There's a short hallway to my right and I walk down it, swearing to myself that I'll just peek into that open door on my left. Then I'll go back downstairs. Just one little look . . . the room is almost empty, except for the two long boxes on the floor and the hurricane lamp on the table above them.

I make myself open the boxes. I just have to know. They aren't sealed or anything but the dirt inside doesn't tell me much. Maybe they're into gardening. Or maybe, they're . . . *What?* My little inner voice demands. *Bloodsucking fiends from Transylvania?* Outside in daylight, I would have laughed. Up here in the dark, crouched over two big boxes of dirt, I start shivering.

I close the boxes as quietly as I can and stand up very slowly. Just a few steps and I'll be down the stairs and out the front door. Then all I have to do is call the agency tomorrow and tell them things haven't worked out. I don't see Terese in the doorway until I bump into her. "Hello, Magda. I see that I don't need to chase you this time." Her eyes are black pools and I fall in, drowning until I would crawl over broken glass to get to her. Or let her chase me through my dreams until she catches me.

Then she kisses me, with lips so cold they burn mine and a tongue that freezes the inside of my mouth. I kiss her back, trying to warm her with my breath, my desire. We move slowly down the hallway to another room, her hands busily unbuttoning my shirt. Tonight, I wore my good bra, the red lace one with the snap in front. She has both shirt and bra off in moments. Her cold lips pull away from mine and drop to my breast. She takes my nipple in her mouth and it hardens until it's almost numb.

I don't feel her teeth sink in, just the sense that she is drinking, draining me of something I didn't know I had. Something I hope I don't want. She unbuttons my skirt and it falls to the floor. My underpants follow after an expert tug. I am pushed backward onto a bed, an antique four-poster with curtains. *Black velvet, natch,* the analytical portion of my brain notes, as my eyes adjust slightly to the glow of the single candle.

Terese releases my breast and looks up to meet my eyes at the thought. I whimper as I watch her lick my blood from her lips and she smiles knowingly and slides down between my legs. Her icy caress finds my clit and strokes it, first with fingers, then tongue and I shiver and shake with longing and desire. She tugs the tampon from me and I close my eyes as she slides her tongue over it. Then I come, bucking wildly against the glacier of her mouth, and she drinks from me like a goblet.

One moment, it's just us on the bed, with me writhing against the persistent pressure of Terese's fingers and teeth, then Gerard's there. His pale skin glows against the velvet of the curtains as he climbs in next to us. Terese lifts her face and bares her fangs at him, my blood staining the pale glow of her chin. "Share and share alike, sister dear," he responds as he kisses me and I know they've done this before. For an instant, I wonder what happened to the others: are they dead or what?

Then I find myself on all fours, my face buried between Terese's suddenly very naked thighs. I lick fiercely because I want to be the one they keep, the one they share between them and tell all their secrets to. I want them to want me like I want them: desperately, all barriers gone. Terese is very dry against my tongue, but I hear her breath hiss against her fangs, feel her body stiffen slightly.

Gerard slides up behind me, his fingers guiding himself inside me until he fills me with his biting cold. Terese pulls my hand up to her mouth and sucks fiercely on my wrist as he rides me, my groans muffled in her flesh. I try not to get too distracted, my tongue still coaxing her clit, begging her to lose herself in me. Gerard sinks his teeth into my shoulder and I whimper at the momentary pain. I want to surrender but my instinct for survival is too strong and I struggle, fighting against losing myself utterly.

Terese releases my wrist and slides down between my arms to

kiss me. "Gently, little one. We will not hurt you. Much." Her voice purrs on the word and I relax into her arms as Gerard shifts position so his fingers can stoke their way up between my thighs. He is still inside me when I come again, howling against Terese's neck. As one, they drop their mouths onto both sides of my neck and begin to feed. My body shivers in arousal, in terror, until I pass out.

When I come back around, I'm at Gerard's computer, fully dressed and very tired. It's the end of my shift. I notice that the stack of invoices is gone from the basket and I feel as empty as it is at the sight. Are they out of work for me? What if they don't want me back? The place is very quiet as I log out and get my jacket and there's no one around to ask if they have work for me to do next week. I crawl home, depressed at the loss.

I don't remember why I'm so tired or sore, at least not at first. But I don't have any dreams that night. Then Bob from the agency calls in the morning and says that Forever Insurance loves my work, but they don't have anything for me just now. He tells me about some other gig and I answer like a robot until I can get off the phone. Then I curl up and cry around the big empty space inside me. I wonder what used to fill it. My fingers find my wrist and I massage a sore spot, dully surprised that it hurts at all.

I get up to look at myself in the mirror and I look like I haven't slept for days. Bats could nest in the dark caves of my eye sockets. I wonder what Terese and Gerard would have seen in me, if they could see anything in me at all. The imagined touch of their hands thrills me for a moment, and I close my eyes, then open them and make myself head for the fridge. It wasn't real, none of it. I just have to get over them.

I'm insanely hungry this morning, for whatever reason. It's only after I rummage around for a while and the cold freezes my fingers that I realize that I'm supposed to remember last night as an elaborate fantasy. But what if it wasn't? Then I got used: a little blood, a little sex and then put away like yesterday's news. The words hang there in my mind until I get good and pissed. *Who the hell do they think they are?* I wanted them to keep me, maybe even make me one of them, but what do they do instead? They try to glamour it all right out of my head.

That night I will myself to sleep, thinking of nothing but my dream until I am back on the road. Nothing pursues me yet because no one knows I'm here. I lean against a tree in the dark, waiting, my own blood running freely down my legs. They will come, called to me by its rusty scent. My fingers toy with a small crucifix, then stroke the rough wood of the stake that I dream into being. They need a new employee at Forever Insurance. I just hope they can see that before I have to hurt them. Much.

The Twelve Nights of Callicantzaros

Renée M. Charles

Oral vampires, the ones who plant their gobs right on a victim's neck, then pierce and suck, they don't know what they're missing. Up close like that, there's no way you can properly see the person's eyes go wide with that delicious segue from fear to . . . fancying. All you see is a blurry bit of cheek, and feel their hair (if they've any) slide across your own cheek as you sink your fangs in. Oh, true, you can get a whiff off blood, all coppery-pure and steaming hot being that close, but of all the sense memories, personally, I consider sight the best of the lot. The brain simply can't process memories of smell, or touch, as well as images. Granted, sounds make for excellent memories, too, but just how many noises do vampires really make? There's that wet rending of flesh, but that's so terribly brief, and afterwards, you might as well suck your own arm, for all the sonic good that action will do you, afterwards. The victim screaming? Some don't, some do, while other merely . . . grunt, which is far too porcine a noise to be truly-madly-deeply sexy.

But to blood-let at a distance, arm's length for the best view, now that's a bang-on delight. Watching my nails go in, once I've raked the flesh into mottled pink and white striations while in the teasing stage, seeing the shiny, hard, painted talons dig in and rend . . . now that's something for the old brainpan to feast upon. And the follow-up, twisting runnels of rich coppery-red, glinting with white-hot sparkles of coruscation where the overheads hit it, dripping, dripping downward, or around and over, if I've mined the flesh closest to the round bits . . . and the best part, the way the victim starts breathing hard and noisily, when he or she sees their very ruby essence spurting out over their soft matte-textured flesh. A sound wholly unlike the slurping sucking other vampires have to put up with . . . a unique rhythm, air, music, from the deepest center of the victim's being.

Just remembering it can get me off.

And once I've watched the person's body go all latticework with cinnabar cross-hatching, the flesh below all the whiter (or sometimes all the brewed-coffee translucent) for the combined effort of my nails and their thudding, hard-pumping heart, it's up to me . . . to simply sit and watch, or lean down, kiss it better with long slow lingering tongue-laps and open-mouthed suction-cup osculations.

Lately, what with all this public fascination with scarification, branding and tattooing and piercing of a non-vampiric sort, I've found myself going with the latter option come that time of year . . .

Two

Vampire or not, being born on that last day of the year sucks. At the very least, you have to literally wait all year long for your special day, not being able to say you're X-number of years old no matter what the simple arithmetic of This Year minus Birth Year should equal. Nope, it's sit around and wait all year clinging to your old age, then *bang,* it's the day, and *bang-bang,* tomorrow it's another year to wait until the endgame to score that proper age.

But where I originally came from, that other set of small islands called Greece, being born on the last day of the year—or anytime during the week between Christmas and New Year's—went beyond annoying, straight past Go (do not collect two hundred pounds) and into a nether-region far worse than Go to Jail, Hell on Earth, or where ever quasi-celebrities go after their fifteen minutes of fame have long ticked off the clock. Not that my family ever heard of Monopoly or "I'm a Celebrity, Get Me Out of Here" analogies . . . just let me say that when I was born, the only board game around was that white stones/black stones Go brainteaser, and as far as the telly went . . . well, even if someone had had one of those contraptions, there was no electricity to power it up.

Let's just say my family, my people, called me "feast-blasted" and let it go at that. Oh yes, and there was this other small detail, having to do with us being destined to become vampires, after death.

Not that all of us actually made it, mind you. But when you're considered doomed to a certain lack of luck from one day, coupled with the name they saddled me with—Desmona, which means "unlucky" (something my transplanted kinsman Shakespeare latched onto when giving a similar name to his doomed heroine in *Othello*)—well, I for one am not surprised that after I died one wintry afternoon I've no idea how many years ago, after ailing for nearly a fortnight with some lingering malaise the medicine-practitioners of the day couldn't recognize, and certainly couldn't cure, I didn't *really* die-die, not in any recognized sense.

An occurrence which brought little surprise to my family, who promptly cast me out, in the most ancient Biblical sense . . . not that I blame them in the least. My early years of vampiric "life" as what my people called a *callicantzaros* (go on, try to say that three times fast) have become a blur—almost an entire year's worth of aimless, vaguely-recalled rambling about, going from one nameless village to equally anonymous hamlet after another, existing the best I could, and then . . . come Christmas day, to come violently, brutally, into my own. A twelve-day time of personal celebration of the flesh, of feasting and tearing, leaving my earliest victim in bits and bloody pieces across the countryside. Not my finest work, but I *was* rather new to my destined life's labor, and wholly without any sense of aesthetics, and never mind any possibility of fulfillment of the sexual sort.

After all, being born when I was, I was hardly the most sought-after woman in my village. It didn't matter how round my bits were, no one was willing to give them a squeeze. That whole innate hostility thing, the cultural bias against me, all because my mother and my father went at it one fine March day without bothering to do the baby-math, let alone considering the possibility that I just might be born in that feast-blasted one-week window of lack-of-opportunity.

Which, I suppose, shows you the consequences of shagging when the mood strikes, and not minding the date you go at it.

Three

It's ironic. Try as I might, I can't put a face to the majority of my victims over the years (all that comes to mind are snaking runnels of blood, and the sight of my nails digging, rending, and revealing still more blood), yet, once I began to refine my technique, actually starting to view the process as something to *experience,* not merely *do,* mindlessly, like the addled, drifting, undead being that I merely happened to be, it became easier to put a face with the bloody body. And when I started to let them live, afterwards names, as well as faces, became a part of my catalogue of remembered pleasure, a little something to keep me going during the foggy remainder of the year.

And that's when the whole sexual gratification part kicked in. I think it was the '60s, when skirts rose up to skim the ladies' naughty bit on the bottom, while necklines scooped low enough to almost reveal the nipples, and the men's clothing merely became a tight enough to see the outlines of every round and long and most definitely naughty bit to be had for the touching—that was when I realized that there might be more to this whole Callicantzaros Christmas holiday phase of mine than merely raking and running off. By then, I'd jumped the pond, after leaving a trail of Father Christmas-red across lower Europe, and found my sorry self in England.

Not that I looked the part of the wandering, doomed flesh-tearer—the biggest advantage of this whole undead state of being is that physically, you don't change. And I died while in my twenties, so my hair remained glossy black, my eyes sparkling blue-grey, and my own flesh stayed creamy milk-tea warmly tan, with a most life-like bloom of red about the cheeks. Just as my nails remained long, gelatin-chugging, hard and resistant to breakage and once people started putting colored polishes on their own nails, I was suddenly desirable. Women wanted to know how I kept them so long, so perfect, and men couldn't wait to feel them raking across their backs while I was wriggling under them, or parting the hair on their chests or crotches. There were even a few ladies who wanted to see my nails finger-combing their hair too.

And so I became part of the shagging '60s, one of the Mods who experimented with revealing clothes—revealing what was under those clothes whenever an opportunity arose. I worshipped at the alter of Mary Quant, and wore skirts short enough to show off my own naughty bits whenever I sat and crossed my legs—and once, I uncrossed them long enough to let one bloke trim my abundant pubic hair into a heart shape, just like Quant's husband had done to hers.

When my time of year rolled around, I found that my victims were far more willing to be participants—I was exotic, and my raking, tearing nails were a turn-on, while their blood became paint upon fleshy canvas, to be artfully smeared with each sharp caress of my clawed hands. Then, later, when my needs were sated even as my victim still breathed, still actively bled, I learned to kiss them all the better, before bidding an actual farewell to them come the next morning, rather than a final good-bye.

One of these nights, past Boxing Day, but before my former birthday, is deeply embedded in my mind: His name was Jarvis, and we met in the underground, after he'd drifted away from his mates who were still celebrating Boxing Day, ale on their breaths, unpopped crackers in hand, leaning on each other while waiting for the train. His hair was long, with the requisite bangs brushing his sandy eyebrows, and his suit was artfully tight about the thighs and waistline, and what little skin I could see was ruddy with suffused blood, just waiting to spurt out in hot double-helix twists all over my raking hands.

He'd deliberately bumped up against me as I stood there, waiting, and before you could say Father Christmas, he had his hand on my bum, and was giving my left cheek a squeeze.

"You've got a bloody cheek," I hissed through frosted-pink lips, even as I stayed in place beside him, not jerking my ass away from his fingertips, all the while imagining how his cheeks would look, bloodied and parallel-scratched, before my hands went down, down on that lean, waiting torso.

"Blast it . . . overstepped the mark, and I don't even have your name—"

He was rat-assed, like his friends, but still aware enough to try to salvage the situation by putting me on a first-name basis.

He was expecting me to be cross, but I simply smiled at him, and said, "It hasn't done much for me so far, so you can have my name and the best of luck to you with it—Desmona's a funny name for a bloke, but you're welcome to it."

"It's not much worse than mine . . . Jarvis. Got me beat up more than once in the lower forms. Yours is . . . different. I like that. Too many Janes and Marys and whatnots, all four letters of boredom. Now you . . . you do *not* look boring."

"And apparently I don't feel boring, either . . . your hand hasn't left my bum since you walked over here. I'm afraid it isn't a cracker, so no matter how much you yank on it, it won't pop open—"

"But might there be a prize inside? Something worth my effort?"

"Cheeky bugger," I smiled, as the rest of his mates lurched into the waiting train, then said, "Your friends are getting on—shouldn't you, too?"

"Oh, sod it . . . they know the way home. Besides, they all have their crackers from the party . . . but I left mine there. So I guess I'll have to find another to pop open—"

Jarvis was the first potential victim of mine to have go at me before I lured him to a private place, and when I replied, "I think this place might be a bit too noisy and open for you to find your prize," I could tell he thought he'd gotten his Christmas gift a day late. But he had no idea who'd be doing the real opening that night.

FOUR

His flat was typical of the time—deep shag carpeting over the worn wood floors, albums lying about on the tabletops, pop-art posters attached to the cracked, painted walls. And the bed was simply a covered mattress on the floor, with fake-fur pillows strewn on top.

But the jumble-sale tilting mirrors were a plus—this was the first time I'd get to watch myself at work, and something about that prospect awakened something in my ages-old, undead flesh that went beyond mere bloodlust, and the anticipation of sating my innate need to rend flesh, to see the blood spurt and seep and drench the surrounding bedding. As we undressed, quickly, awkwardly, with coats and belts and hose and knickers flying in every direction while our bodies briefly goose-pimpled thanks to Jarvis being cheap with the heat, I saw myself as he saw me—creamy-tan skin, long tumble of curls across my shoulders and the tops of my tits, the growing-out fine hairs surrounding my heart-shaped mat of pubic curls, my long lean legs, and—standing out in bright contrast to my pale hands—those bright-painted hot-pink nails, each coming to a knife-tip sharp point. And I knew he was waiting to feel those nails raking his back, but first . . . first, I needed to see those nails in action.

Naked, he was fairly impressive—not the handsomest bloke, but lots of thick, curly hair on his chest, which tapered down in a thick darkening rope to his crotch, where the hair fanned out to a full matting around his right-swinging prick and groin-hugging, slightly jerking balls (after all, the room was rather cold, and I wasn't expecting them to dangle). And in one of the mirrors which surrounded the mattress, I could see his bum—two tightly muscled, smooth-skinned orbs above rather hairy legs. Just as I liked a man (or woman, for that matter)—with a firm, fleshy bum, just waiting for my cross-hatched raking caress . . .

He was about to reach for my tits when I put one long-nailed forefinger to my lips, and shook my head, before whispering, "Not so fast . . . first, I get to play with *yours.* A little scratch, before the tickle," I found myself adding, something new in my approach before the attack. Maybe it was his forward manner that made me so bold, so willing to risk the entire encounter before I struck the first stinging, raking blow.

Jarvis nodded, and flopped down on the mattress, arms crosses behind his head, legs bent at the knee, so his lower legs and feet were off the mattress and on the floor, with his round bits resting near the edge of the bed. His prick was already at attention, aiming for my heart-embellished cunt. But as I knelt down over him, breasts hanging close down close to his own chest, I whispered, "Don't scream too loud," before placing my clawed hands just below his collarbone, and letting the nails seek out the hidden blood below the waiting skin.

He didn't scream out like a girlie, but he bit his own lip so hard an independent trickle of blood slid down the side of his face, to pool at his earlobe. His chest was soon pin-striped with his own vermilion essence, and as I worked my way down his flat belly, down close to his straining, clear dew-tipped prick, I noticed that he was actually arching his body up to me, eager for each new tearing pass of my pressing fingertips. For a reward, I lowered my crotch onto his, and felt his rigid, blood-filled prick sink deep into my ridged, wet vagina, and with each upward thrust, I felt a bloom of white-hot come fill my quim. With every gouge and rip of my nails, he spurted more come into me, until his prick finally quivered inside me, grew flaccid, and slid out, creamy-white and glistening against the bloody bedspread.

And just as he was sated, so was I . . . blood had spilled, yet he was still whole, albeit torn, below me. And smiling, through the reflexive tears which made his eyes glitter even as he smiled at me with blood-ringed teeth, before whispering, "I'm still waiting for the tickle . . ."

Five

Jarvis hadn't been the first of my holiday-time victims to live, but something of him continued to live in me, during the long year which followed my time of blood-feasting—and no, he did not get me preggers. Vampires have their own natural birth control, namely, being dead in the first place.

What Jarvis gave to me, that fleshy gift of spirit and blood fire, was the need to seek my *own* pleasure, even as I filled that more basic blood-need which was my doom, and curiously, my salvation, in that in kept me in a state of quasi-life for all these centuries. I may have spent some of that hazy pre-Christmastime limbo which I suppose you could call half-life shagging as many people as would have me, but until Jarvis happened, it had simply been that—mindless shagging, for lack of anything else to do with myself. I certainly didn't need to eat, or actually work—there were plenty of places to squat, and plenty of folks who'd pay me for their pleasure, so I could afford to keep up with the changing fads in clothing, just to keep looking like my live fellows. Plus I had to move, periodically—not aging has as many drawbacks as benefits.

But even after Jarvis and I were quits, just before New Year's Day, he'd infected me with his lust for living, for experience . . . and eventually, I ended up doing something I hadn't even considered during all my previous centuries roaming the unsuspecting, bloody earth—I learned a trade. A real salary-earning job.

Six

For a while, until the '90s, my job as a body piercer was rather limited to doing ears and the occasional navel, so I had to branch out, learning how to do tattoos, even though my long nails made handling the tattoo needle gun a bit dicey. But people do bleed when you give them a tattoo, just as they bleed when you stick a needle into their flesh, and make a permanent hole. Then came the boom in body modification—the piercings in nostrils, genitals, even eyebrows. All those body parts, close to my hands, my face, waiting for me to open the skin, let the blood hit the air . . . sadly, I had to stopper them up right off with rings and orbs of gold, but still, there was blood, every day I worked.

And there were some customers for whom mere piercing wasn't enough.

Seven

She called herself Caeneus, which, being Greek, and especially being a Greek person who was around when some of these names were fairly *new,* I knew immediately what her new name actually meant—a woman who asked to become a man. Her name came from mythology, which used to be religion where I came from, before the whole Christianity thing mucked up people's minds and made them fearful of things like babies born during a certain week in December.

She was old enough to be a student of mythology, but not old enough to have settled down physically as a true woman, a mature woman.

Her tits, under a tight wife-beater T-shirt, were still small, close to the chest, with only the nipples sticking out more than a finger's width from her ribcage. And her hips, under those too-baggy, low-slung jeans, were almost bloke narrow, with a lean, flat belly and one of those bums that juts out only minimally over the back of the thighs, with little of that sweet swelling men tend to look for when giving women the eyes on a street corner. She'd had her hair sheared close to her head, with only a flat buzzed fringe above her forehead, and the rest sidewalled to a stubbled haze of reddish-gold.

I knew her age, but she tried, nonetheless. The eyebrow ring did give her a rakish look, but I'd seen the sort of dyke the femmes seemed to go for—older, heavier women, more muscle than fat, with that self-assurance which comes from real age, not the addition of hardware about the face and round bits.

Even though it was Christmastime, I volunteered to work the shop during holiday time, just in case someone decided to redeem one of the gift certificates we sold just for the holidays. And as luck would have it, there was no one else about when Caeneus stepped into the shop that chilly, wet afternoon, when everyone else was at home, opening boxes, shagging their thank-yous, getting stuffed on pudding. As soon as she cleared the door, she'd shucked off her leather jacket, and shook the melting flakes of snow off her roan-buzzed scalp, then said, without preamble, as usual, "I need something new."

In the past, "something new" had included a clit ring, a tattoo of a dragon with a pearl in its claw on her lower abdomen (which used an existing appendectomy scar as its backbone), and even some branding on her right upper arm—the latter done by one of those other workers in the shop, since I'd yet to learn that skill.

But today, there was a deeper yearning in her voice, something which went beyond her usual physical-whim-of-the-day need for more bodily decoration.

"So, what'll be? Tattoo? Piercing? I think I've pierced everything that can be pierced on you already—"

"Sod off—" she started, but I could see in her eyes that she didn't mean it. I knew she was attracted to me, with my long hair, and ample tits, but we'd yet to go at it—she was too steady a customer, and even though I handled all her round bits, and already had gotten to know to unique smell of her blood, and felt it on my gloved hands, the heat boring through the latex, she was more like . . . family than a potential sex partner, or blood-victim.

"No, wait, I think I forgot to do your tongue—"

Sticking out her gold-knobbed tongue at me, she said around the protruding pink mass, "Got that done before I met you . . ." then, pulling it back in, she went on, "I'm not in the mood for a piercing, today . . . but I want to *bleed.*"

"What, you've stopped having monthlies?" I teased, but she muttered "Sod it" while sticking both hands deep into her pockets. Her pants weren't baggy enough to hide what those hands were doing, moving in toward her shorn crotch and massaging herself.

I watched her play with herself for a few moments, then she

said, "I like that best of all when I'm having something done . . . feeling the blood *on* my skin, instead of under it. It's sensual, like sweating when you're boinking . . . only it's richer. It . . . slides on your skin, instead of just dripping off and leaving you all wet and smelly."

"And blood doesn't smell?"

"Is this a slanging match, or am I going to bleed?"

I could tell, she was serious, even if a trifle unfocused about what was going to happen next. But I didn't smell any liquor on her so I weighed my next words carefully:

"Well, there's many ways I can make you bleed, but I need to do something specific to you before the blood flows. There's no set price established for me just cutting into you—"

"I wasn't thinking of a cut . . . tell me, have you ever scratched yourself, after taking a piss? Those claws . . . leave nasty marks on peoples' backs, do they?"

So. She and I were on the same sexual path, after all . . . .

Eight

Since it wasn't likely that anyone else might actually walk in that afternoon for a nose piercing or an "I Love Mum" tattoo (and if anyone did pop by, the place would simply be closed for the holiday), I locked up, before fetching Caeneus home to her flat. It was only a short walk away, three flights up, but clean once you got past the noisy hallway. Dun-colored walls covered with R.C. Horsch posters, including the lovely one of the bare-pubed woman standing in front of a brass footboard, holding a cow skull aloft, and the one of the two short-haired women wearing sunglasses, lying spooned on their mattress, a futon covered with an Indian-woven spread, and lots of carved wood and brass animal sculptures, mostly Indian in origin.

Noticing my appraising stare, she said, "My last lover left these. She was half Paki . . . loved those Bollywood pictures. I used to take her to the pictures every weekend . . . when they were playing. Sometimes we'd go at it with henna on each other . . . which is what got me to wondering about what you might be able to do to me. With these," she reached for my hands, and placed them nails-down on her barely budding breasts. I could feel the nipples go raisin-hard under my palms, as she reached down to undo her pants snap, and unzipped. The oversized blue jeans billowed down around her blackwork-adorned legs in a sighing chuff of fabric. She'd left off her knickers, so her close-shorn quim was exposed, the outer lips already moist and musky-smelling. I pulled off her T-shirt, exposing her wrinkled pink nipples and unshorn armpits, holding her hands aloft before wrapping her tee around her wrists. Leading her backwards by the bound hands, she had to step out of her jeans to keep from tripping, so all she was wearing were a pair of black lace-up boots by the time I'd backed her against the nearest wall, where a clothes hook jutted out from the door frame.

Securing her fabric-swathed hands on the brass hook, I felt that familiar maniac euphoria which always comes before I take my latest conquest (the concept of a victim had gone the way of micro minis and knee-high plastic boots, back in the days of Jarvis), as I began to lightly tease my sharp-tipped nails over her flat tits, down along her taut belly, and along the contours of her plump outer labia, whispering as I drew the first small dribbles of blood along the way, "What sort of designs did your lover paint on your body? And just how long would the henna last?"

Grinding her silky-wet round bits onto my raked fingers, she groaned, "Not nearly long enough . . . not nearly—" before I balled one hand into a tight fist, and rubbed the knobs of my knuckles against her quivering inner lips, feeling them cling to my flesh in a slippery-wet kiss.

Part of me wanted to simply start the bloodletting there and then, but since the night with Jarvis, I'd learned the rewards of restraint.

Pausing to bend my head level with her breasts, I tongued and lightly nipped each in turn, before lifting her off the brass hook, and walking her into her bedroom, then into the loo beyond, where the bathtub had one of those old-fashioned center-mounted shower heads, which suited my intended purpose perfectly. Securing her hands to the shower head, so that I could turn her around within the tub, I shucked off my own clothes, and left them in a heap on the cistern, before stepping naked into the tub, and approaching Caeneus, fingers in that ages-old familiar clawing position, ruby-red lacquered nails poised centimeters above her waiting sweat-sheened flesh.

"So . . . just what sort of patterns did you have in mind?"

Thrusting out her chest toward me, she whispered, "Surprise me . . . make me look dangerous. . . ."

NINE

The bottom of the tub was dotted with small splashes and drops of blood by the time I'd finished with her front. Holding back, I'd made sure I'd scratched only deep enough to scar upon healing, not so deeply as to truly please myself. Her body was fiercely arabesqued with sets of parallel lines, wavering circles, and swirls encircling her breasts, swelling scratched that dribbled sweet blood that I longed to lap and suck from her flesh, but there was still her back to attend to. . . .

Her bum took patterns as well, as did her broad-shouldered back, and by the time my own body ached for release, for the hot spurt of deep-tapped blood splashing against my own flesh, she was done . . . my most delicate, restrained handiwork yet, but also my most lasting. I longed to mark her face, but kept my hands below her neckline, out of deference to the fact that no matter what her sexual needs, she also needed to be able to work, to pose for a driving license snap, or for a passport.

But once I was done, and I released her hands, she ran them slowly over her tender, freshly sacrificed body, then raised her bloody hands, palms out, to roughly caress my body, starting from the shoulders and working her way downward, until I was covered with her coppery-sweet essence. When we both stood deliciously red, her hot skin touching my not-warm-for-eons flesh, in that tub, she smiled at me before saying, "*Your* turn holding the shower head . . ."

TEN

Obediently, I grasped the cold metal projection, then let Caeneus tie my hands loosely with her blood-flecked white tee. Once I was held in place, unable to freely move about, I waited, my body now covered in drying, flaking blood, as she studied me, taking in every rounded curve, every back curl on my body, even as she held off touching me. This had never happened to me before . . . always, I'd be on top, riding my willing shag toy, always in control, always, *always* the dominant partner.

To be . . . helpless was something I hadn't experienced in

centuries, not since I was really alive-alive. But even as it brought an unknown icy coldness to my already cool insides, there was something else . . . something exciting.

Something I couldn't control, but definitely looked forward to.

Eleven

It was only when she stepped out of the shower, out of the loo itself, with only a sly backward glance in my direction before quitting the room, that I realized that no matter her age, no matter her outward sex, I was in the presence of someone powerful, someone able to outwit even the likes of me . . .

And when she returned, wearing an elaborate strap-on double-ended dildo, one which looked achingly familiar to me, I realized that my latest conquest was truly a student of the Greek, in all ways. I hadn't seen a double dildo like that since my own youth, and even then, only on some pottery. True to the Greeks, this thing was made of leather, well-oiled with what had to be extra virgin olive oil—I knew that odor from childhood, ages ago.

With her close-shorn hair, and nearly flat tits, Caeneus looked to be well on her way to having her desire to become a man—or to at least be perceived as one, of a sort—especially with that generous jutting leather phallus hovering above the top of her thighs.

Stepping into the tub, her body covered with the raised, already scarring designs I'd so recently incised in her flesh, she looked up at me, and asked, "How long have you been a *callicantzaros*? I'm assuming you have a birthday coming up soon, too—"

"Don't tell me . . . you studied Greek history, mythology? Or you're a vampire freak?"

"Vampire freaks are stupid prats. All that sighing and neck biting . . . by-passing all the round bits. Really useless . . . but I saw those nails, and noticed they never break . . . those aren't glue-ons, either. And your boss, he said you're Greek . . . never underestimate the benefits of a public school education. O levels and beyond. You know I'm old enough to have gone to university . . . and now you know I what I studied. Before I got fed up and quit. But back to you," she ran one fingertip along my nipples, then moved downward, to my bloody-damp thatch of curls, "I wager you haven't been properly impaled in donkey's years, right? Oh, don't worry, this isn't wood . . . I don't know what's under the leather, but it isn't any sort of stake. You just made me feel so bloody good, I had to return the favor . . . but I must admit, I do fancy older women. If you care to tell me just how old you are?"

"I would if I could . . . can't remember. But it was before virtually every convenience in this flat, if that's a help—"

My answer must have pleased her, for she came close enough to brush my thigh with the tip of the dildo, before saying, "Fair enough . . . but you *must* know your birthdate—"

"December thirty-one," I panted, as that pliant, oily dildo slid along the outside of my thigh, then began nosing around against my hair-covered mound, poking lightly along my labia before honing in on my own oily depths—and when she slid it all the way inside me, while wrapping her arms around my body, and grabbing my ass tightly with both surprisingly firm small hands, I moaned, "You . . . you wouldn't happen to have known a bloke named Jarvis, would you? He'd be . . . oh, fifty, maybe sixty-some now . . . sandy hair, in the day—"

"Not sandy anymore," Caeneus grunted, as she nuzzled my nipples, licked them lightly, then added, "More like shiny on the top, and stubbled grey on the sides. He's my dad."

She stopped thrusting for a second, as I took it in, and while she stood still before me, I could see it, as if for the first time—the eyes were similar, as was the shape of the mouth. The reddish hair could've come from her mum, of course.

"And he told me all about this woman he shagged one Boxing Day night . . . used to drive Mom up a tree, before she up and left. I don't think she could stand the competition, even though she came along years after the two of you were together. He still has the scars you know . . . I remember them from when we went swimming. They're what got me interested in tattoos, all that—"

"Did they make you a dyke, too?"

"Don't flatter yourself all that much . . . me being this way was something I was born to do. Dad wasn't too keen on no grandbabies, but that's the way things happen . . . just like you didn't ask to be born when you were born. But once I read up on Greek history, and saw that passage in Leo Allatius' *De Graecorum hodie quorundam opinationbus* about *callicantzaros,* I knew what Dad had shagged . . . and I just had this feeling about you.

Remembering that night with Jarvis, so many years, decades

ago, just as clearly as I remembered meeting that Allatius fellow, back in the late 1600s, knowing full well that no one would wholly believe what he'd written about me and my kind in that treatise of his, I found myself shaking in place in that cold, blood-splashed tub, finally saying in a small voice, "Does he know you've met me? He was the first who . . . made me feel something other than that maniac blood-lust—"

"No . . . why would I want to make him feel older than he is?"

I felt a wave of relief pass though me; seeing Jarvis as he was, now, would surely negate what we'd had, ever so briefly, on that night thirty-some years back. But Caeneus, now she was another matter altogether—knowing, and knowledgeable, and willing to be with me despite what she knew of my kind.

Twelve

The nice thing about a dildo is, even if you've both tired yourselves out shagging and boinking and just plain fucking, the darned thing stays beautifully, deliciously erect inside you. And this double one joined me with Caeneus, especially once she untied me, so we could gingerly walk as one out of the tub, and into her bedroom, where we sat down, legs draped over each other's legs, on the corner of her futon. It sat a bit higher off the floor than her dad's old mattress, but we were still low to the ground, and the cool floor below.

Face to face, my thickly-curls-covered head touching her close-clipped scalp, I rubbed the back of her neck, and asked, "Before you changed your name, what was it, really?"

"You're not going to believe this, but . . . Desdemona. Almost like yours, he was going to name me directly after you, but Mum was a Shakespeare nut—"

"Did she realize what the name meant? That it stands for—"

"'Unlucky'? Yes, she did, actually . . . it's really funny, but you're what you are because of when you were born . . . and Mum named me what she did, aside from Dad's urging, because I was born on a Friday the Thirteenth . . ."

Funny, isn't it, how superstition can make people do the strangest things?

Broken

B.K. Bilicki

It had all been so simple.

It had been his life, changing as he had changed, ebbing and flowing as did the man harbored within his ageless frame. An ancient process, he had honed it, shaped it, turned it from an act of supreme violation to a subtle performance of tender beauty.

It had kept him alive.

Now it was over.

His mind's eye flew back to his most distant memories, the shards of hate and pain that had followed his transformation. He had spent his days taking others as he had been taken, consuming his victims in a frenzy of malice and self-loathing. Bathed in blood, he became that which he feared most, the same manner of dark beast that had sunk its evil fangs into his neck, robbing him of his humanity. Unaware of his growing powers, he lived only for the hunt, seeking to kill all around him, leaving him alone to wallow in his unending misery.

His savagery had come to an abrupt end in a long-forgotten back alley of Victorian England where he suddenly reclaimed a single shred of his discarded self. Just as he was about to pounce upon some tender morsel of a woman, a hunter of a different kind struck first, roughly grabbing her and throwing her to the ground. He took no notice of the new one's brutality, only paused to smile at this addition to the upcoming feast, but a sudden shift in the air made him hesitate. The new attacker recoiled in disgust as his assault revealed the woman was in the course of her menses. Gathering his drunken ire, the man resumed his plundering, plowing into her tender flesh despite her screams.

The combination of the rich scent of her blood and her pitiful cries for help stirred something he thought long dead inside his undying being. He launched forward from the darkness, swiftly ripping out the would-be rapist's throat with little more than a bloody gurgle greeting his efforts. Tossing the body aside as if it were a dry leaf in the wind, he looked down upon the sobbing woman. Her world was still awash in endless suffering, so she had not even noticed he had dispatched her attacker. Her wailing cries and his ever-present hunger gnawed at him until he could stand it no longer and he roared, "Enough!"

The woman's eyes opened wide and stared directly back into his. His command burrowed deep into her brain and she immediately fell silent as his will became hers. He felt the hold he had on her mind and it surprised him, as he had never known of his other abilities. "Close," he said, his rough voice quieter now. Her eyes quickly closed but his mind still enveloped hers. Though amazed by this newfound ability, his hunger would not wait and he pounced upon the man's body, draining it of every last drop of blood he could. When he had finished, he stood over her once again. She remained there on the cold ground, her dress torn, her legs still splayed and smeared with her blood where they met.

This last detail was not lost upon him. Although he had fed well, the aroma wafting up from her was too good to resist. Falling to his knees, he leaned down between her legs. Again, something inside him held him back so that instead of sinking his fangs deep into her thigh, he only licked at her tentatively. The simple touch sent a bolt of pure pleasure rocketing throughout her body which resounded in their shared mind. The force of the feeling made him bolt upright before sending him staggering back on his heels. He looked back at her in confusion as he fought to steady himself and the events of the night ignited a sudden rush of panic within him. Standing back up, he stared down at her and said, "Forget." The memories of the night's attack were wiped from her mind in the blink of an eye and he helped her to her feet. Pointing her up the alley, he whispered "Go" and released her mind. Her eyes opened and without a word or a glance back she followed the implanted suggestion and hurried home.

He stood there, frozen by the rush of sensations coursing through him. The secrets of his powers were now all laid bare before him, but they were overshadowed by his rediscovery of pleasure. True, it had been akin to the feeling he got after a feed, but that was more a sense of relief than true happiness. In addition, the pleasure was twofold. Part had been due to the woman's passion streaming in through his mind's link to her, but the other had been simply that which he felt just from doing good. He had saved her, both from the brutal attack and from his own hunger, and in the process he had saved himself. The human heart hidden in his inhuman breast had awoken.

His life changed that night. Pain and hate were replaced with a growing caring. He still needed to feed, but he no longer attacked indiscriminately. His victims were now chosen carefully from those he felt were worthy of his particular brand of final justice. He watched them from the shadows, looked for the evil he had seen on that first night of his new life. His newfound other forms—the bat, the wolf, the nightgloom—all served him well in his new quest, but it was his growing knowledge of human nature that proved the most useful. He listened to their conversations. He observed their strengths and weaknesses. With growing frequency, he even ventured out of his beloved shadows to walk among them, posing as one of them to gain further insight into this forgotten family from which he had been cast out. His travels took him to many countries until he found himself in the so-called New Land. Here he found new opportunities and yet another change in his eternal life.

One night near the turn of the previous century, he saw his new beginning replayed in startling similarity. A young couple stumbled arm-in-arm out of a tavern he had come to frequent, each sharing hushed giggles and saucy banter with the other. His sharp hearing had caught most of their conversation from his unseen vantage point in the back booth and their exchange troubled him. His mind had touched upon each of theirs and he knew that the man's inevitable advances would likely be rebuffed. Further, he knew that the rejection would not sit well and was concerned for the woman's safety in that event. Without a word or sound, he rose from his seat and hurried outside in pursuit.

Looking around through the gaslit fog, he sniffed the air deeply and caught their scent. Just as he determined it was coming from a nearby alley, he caught a muffled shriek from that direction. He moved with unnatural swiftness, his feet moving so quickly they appeared to float over the pavement. Coming around the corner, he was greeted by a scene from his past. The woman lay on the ground, pinned beneath her boyfriend. Her skirts had been bunched up around her midsection and her undergarments torn in a fit of lust. The man's trousers were down around his ankles and his pelvis was thrusting forward between her outstretched legs as he kept his hand clamped tightly over her mouth.

The entire scene was so similar that he wondered for a moment if it was only an illusion, a flashback to that night of long ago. In his confusion, he called out, "Stop!" The command carried a rush of power with it that had two distinct effects. The woman instantly fell under his spell, but the man felt a wave of fear crash over himself. In a flash, the man shot to his feet, hitched up his pants and ran away down the alley. He considered pursuing the man for a moment, but the unmoving heap that was the woman worried him, as did a peculiar but somehow familiar scent. Hurrying to her side, he dropped to one knee and looked down at her.

The thought of this all being some kind of strange memory play crossed his mind again. The woman's legs were still spread wide and her undergarments were stained a dark red. Instantly he knew the source of her objections to her beau's advances. Sadness filled him and he released her mind and placed a hand upon her thigh. Both the contact and the absence of her boyfriend startled her and she swatted at her voluminous skirts to see who was now touching her. She started to scream when she saw his dark eyes staring at her with an unnatural intensity, but his mind leapt at hers again and commanded her to remain silent. Her mouth closed and she stared at him with the same glazed expression that every person he had mentally dominated did, but a curious glint in her eye hinted at something else lurking inside her.

His mind idly searched hers as he struggled to ignore both the sweet scent of her blood and the hunger it inspired which bloomed inside him. Suddenly his mind touched upon something in hers and he blinked at her in surprise. She was not being attacked as he had thought. She was crying out in joy as her boyfriend made love to her despite her condition. Now her beau had raced off in fear and unfulfilled desire coursed through her body with every beat of her heart, a sound that grew louder to him with every passing moment. Regret and confusion warred within him when he realized what he had done. Glancing down at her smeared sex, his remorse faded as he recalled the sweetness of a similar woman long ago. He moved between her legs, fighting the bloodlust within, and licked once up through her delicate folds.

The woman gasped as his tongue delved into her body. He likewise felt his breath catch in his throat as the intensity of her reaction churned through his mind. The rich nectar trickling down his throat drew a ripple of visceral pleasure from him and he swiped at her sex again. Again, the trio of sensations bombarded him and he cast restraint aside, licking and nibbling at her glistening vagina, feasting upon her as he had no other. The woman thrashed wildly below him, lost in a world of intense passion as he consumed her. Fastening his mouth over her entire sex, he sucked strongly and she burst into a furious orgasm which bathed both of their minds in a shower of white-hot sparks.

Catching his breath at last, he opened his eyes to find her looking down her body at him. A bubble of panic started to rise within him when he realized she was no longer under his control, but it dissipated when he saw her wide smile of gratitude. "Thank you!" she whispered breathlessly.

Her words astounded him. Quickly binding her mind to his own, he stood and commanded her to do the same. She obeyed without question, of course, but now her complete submission felt wrong to him. She would do what I ask willingly, he thought, because I have pleased her. He thought of his hunger and was perplexed as he found himself devoid of all desire to feed. Though he could quiet his incessant hunger in the past, he had never been completely free of it before and the sudden silence warmed his heart further. Releasing her mind, he drew her close and murmured in what he hoped would be a charming voice, "You are most welcome."

The woman lunged forward and kissed his lips firmly, both surprising and delighting him even more. He returned her kiss passionately, but knew that questions would soon follow, so he reluctantly bound her mind once more and erased himself from her memory before commanding her to return home. She went without question, his dark eyes following her every step of the way.

For the second time, his unending life had found a new purpose. This time, however, he had found a way to feed that not only appeased his hunger, but brought happiness in its wake. Moreover, the rich lifeblood quelled his appetite more thoroughly and for a much longer time, enabling him to go longer between feedings. This newfound freedom allowed him to expand his life outside the realm of shadow and he found himself suddenly leading an almost normal existence among humans.

Tonight he had come out, as he had so many times before, to find another to assuage his hunger for both blood and passion. He had grown to enjoy his newest role of the mysterious bringer of pleasure to women who often thought their condition would preclude such delights. His sharp senses had scented her as soon as she walked into the club and he knew she wanted release badly. It was a simple matter to engage her in conversation, having had the last several decades to hone his approach to a razor edge. Her current lack of a lover did startle him, but it also cheered him somewhat. She was so young and vibrant, the thought of sharing her, if only for one night, somehow seemed wrong to him.

Later, it came as no surprise to him that she led him to her apartment willingly. They had talked about many things throughout the night and their newfound closeness was like nothing he had ever experienced. True, every woman he had fed upon in this manner held a place in his heart, but he always knew that they were destined to be single nights of passion, sparkling jewels that glittered against the solitary backdrop of night that was his life. They came together and their minds made contact as he disrobed her. Laying her back upon her bed, he slowly kissed his way down her body, savoring every gasp of delight, every bead of sweat, every silken expanse of skin.

Arriving at last between her thighs, he nuzzled the fine hairs of her mound and sighed in elation as he felt her passion rising to nearly unbearable heights. Keeping only the slightest touch on her mind with his own, he proceeded to make love to her with his mouth. He licked and nibbled at her flesh endlessly, slowly building her up and easing her back down until she writhed in supreme need under his ministrations. Finally he brought both her body and mind to their ultimate pinnacle and, with a final thrust of his tongue inside her, he sent her tumbling over into the abyss of lust waiting for her on the other side.

As she came, his eyes closed and his mind suddenly ignited in a combined burst of pain and rapture that knew no bounds. All his love, all his hate, everything he had ever been during his life as a creature of the night thundered through him as the peculiar sweetness of her essence washed down his throat. Fear ripped through him for an instant, only to be replaced by a heavenly tingling that seemed to light him up from the inside. All hint of darkness fled from his being, as did the powers his status had brought him. This was both an end and a beginning, his mind told him, right before it revealed what had happened. The tingling and light receded, retreating to become a faint glow which pulsed with every rapid beat of his heart.

His eyes opened to find her looking down at him with the overjoyed expression of the well-loved. "That was incredible!" she whispered with a bright smile before noticing his look of absolute shock. Reaching down to him in concern, she caressed his cheek and asked, "What's wrong?"

"You—you're a virgin!" he gasped.

Her eyes widened but she nodded in reply. "Yes," she answered hesitantly. "Is that a problem?" she asked as she started to draw away from him.

In a flash, his hand came up to grasp hers and he held its softness to his cheek. Kissing her palm gently, he shook his head and smiled at her. "I—I didn't think there were any left," he stammered, sheer wonder overrunning the hint of sarcasm in his voice as, for the first time in twelve centuries, he looked upon the world with fully human eyes.

The curse had been broken.

Veil of Skin

Maria Alexander

"He then created a woman for Adam, from the earth, as He had created Adam himself, and called her Lilith . . . She said, 'I will not lie below,' and he said, 'I will not lie beneath you, but only on top. For you are fit only to be in the bottom position, while I am to be in the superior one.' Lilith responded, 'We are equal to each other inasmuch as we were both created from the earth.' But they would not listen to one another. When Lilith saw this, she pronounced the Ineffable Name and flew away into the air."

—The Alphabet of Ben Sira, *medieval text*

"They found (Lilith) beside the Red Sea, a region abounding in lascivious demons . . . 'Return to Adam without delay,' the angels said, 'or we will drown you!' Lilith asked: 'How can I return to Adam and live like an honest housewife after my stay beside the Red Sea?'"

—Hebrew Myths *by Robert Graves and Raphael Patai*

She tucked the riding crop under her arm, the tack-tack of her high heels punctuating her authority, green eyes razing any resistance. Auburn hair brushed the seat of her leather lambskin pants as she circled him, garnet lips parting wetly over the Venus gap of her front teeth. Black leather bindings securely fastened his hands to the head of an 8-foot post by thick metal loops embedded in the wood. When she slowly unbuttoned his black Levi's, he responded with a sweltering erection in his cotton briefs. The swell of her ample breasts brushed his bare back as she stood behind him, a leather bustier laced over her cleavage. Sweat trickled from the line of his wavy brown hair down his neck as her fingers worked under his belt line here and there: then, a swift pull downwards exposed his smooth posterior—among other things—to the voyeurs. Wishing desperately he had worked out more, tanned more, not agreed to this, and realizing it was far too late to even wish, he instead relinquished his concerns to more pressing matters:

Snap! Snap! Snap! Snap! Snap!

She reached down and gently rubbed the glowing patch on his buttock where she had riveted him with the flap of her jet-black crop. If he didn't already associate pleasure with pain, he did now, although he was pretty sure journalists were somewhat masochistic to begin with. Her finger traced his jaw and those green eyes burned, smiling into his as she reached to her looped belt.

"I told you this story would cost you," she said and slipped a black leather blindfold over his pleading hazel eyes . . .

Of course her beauty had attracted him initially, as well as her vampiric reputation. But later in that back room of the dungeon, he realized she was also highly literate, a constant thinker and weaver of detail. She hid her age, as well as her true identity, but he guessed she was somewhere between 25 and 35. After the scene she improvised for him when he requested an interview, she wore a blue satin shirt that covered her like a smudge of watercolor light. As she spoke, her eyes were languid under lids lined with a thick sweep of kohl. Her gaze never traveled away from his brow.

"Aren't you going to sit?" she asked playfully, gesturing to the stuffed vinyl chair.

"No, thank you," he replied, "I think I'll stand—" His posterior still stung from the exhibition. He bent a bit stiffly, his worn Levi's and T-shirt chafing his tender skin, and turned on the tape recorder.

"—Mistress."

She began.

I

It was fall and the tree leaves in Pasadena had turned from green to coppery green before dropping, chased by rippling winds over celluloid streets. She stretched on the wooden floor under the bed in the dust, fishing out a soiled pair of black lace panties as she cleaned the bedroom. She had worn the panties three weeks ago when she and her husband last made love, after she swung around the bedpost in glossy black pumps like Jamie Lee Curtis in the movie *True Lies*. She had to imitate cut-and-dubbed intimacy to arouse her husband: it had to have gloss, a script, a man yelling "Speed!"—or something. Whatever it was, all she knew was that it was happening less and less frequently.

The phone rang as she emerged from under the bed. It was her husband's friend Kannic. Good old Kannic, publisher of horror novels and now a fledgling director/producer. So fledgling he hadn't beat his way out of the eggshell—and couldn't—but that didn't stop him. "Well, well," he said when she answered, "I wanted to talk to you."

Her relationship with forty-year-old Kannic was one insubstantial conversation after another intermingled with lingering hugs and insinuating touches. Although Kannic's Freudian stare unnerved her, she tolerated his advances, hoping her husband would notice and become jealous. He didn't. But he did notice the cable channels had changed . . . again.

"Can you come to the shoot tonight and be an extra for the club scene?" Kannic asked. "And, um, bring a friend?" he said, in that I'm-not-hitting-on-you voice. He was always hitting on her.

"Sounds fun," she replied. It did, actually. "What do I have to wear?"

"Anything extreme," he replied. "You know . . . industrial. Leather. Vampiric."

She knew what he meant. At least, she had some idea from her eclectic friends and reading. Kannic had hired her husband's special effects company to create the werewolves. She agreed to go and he enthusiastically thanked her, a happy stutter in his voice.

She hung up the phone, examining the wrinkled white T-shirt and ragged jeans she wore. She didn't really own anything extreme. Her husband didn't even like it when she dressed sexy, except during her poorly coordinated romp with the bedpost. For many years she had been a good Christian wife, yet the first weakening of her beliefs came when they chose a compromise church—something more liberal to accommodate his Methodist background. Neither thus spiritually impassioned, they went to church less frequently over the years and now stopped altogether. Further, her beliefs were slipping into the gap between faith and experience. Yet, like the cat sweeping its paw under the stove for a toy, as long as she still saw her beliefs, they were still hers. She'd be damned—literally—if she gave up on them entirely.

Fortunately, she had friends like Kari who were not only damned but had the proper clothing for it. For her lesbian friend, dressing extreme would only be borrowing a little reality for make-believe. She called Kari—who had shown a nervous, curious Becky her bondage equipment on a few occasions—and left a message on her voice mail. A massage therapist who usually had clients all afternoon, Kari was too busy to return calls during the day.

Meanwhile, she strolled out to her husband's work studio in the guesthouse. It contained both his expensive CGI equipment for creating computer special effects, prosthetic material, and a collection of props. She dug around in the dusty wooden prop closet and found a whip hanging from the coat rack. It looked real enough: the leather wound around a wooden, 10-inch handle, studded with brass tacks. From the handle hung six braided ropes of 5-foot-long blackened cord twisted inward on itself. A leather thong feathered from the end of each rope. Over all, it was weighty and impressive, though unwieldy.

As she closed the prop closet door, the computer made a faint grinding noise. She examined the tower, its accessories, and the monitor. A light flickered over the "HDD" label on the tower, indicating the power was on. Before she switched it off, she realized the darkened monitor blotted out a running program; it was probably turned off in haste to save energy. Hesitantly she pressed the monitor's power button.

Her husband's malaise became clear when the screen's image

flickered brightly and her long fingers found wads of tissue in the waste paper bin: his come, another woman's nude picture.

II

What was sin? Was it intent? Was it the act itself?

> *The journalist stopped her at this point. "You never told me your name." "You're not going to call me 'O' or 'Lisa' or something like that?" she teased. "No, I'd like your name." Her gaze carefully explored the terrain of his face for motive and found only his natural intensity. She grinned slyly. "You can call me Becky."*

When they were teenagers, they did everything but have sex. They were Christians: Protestant, conservative, sin-conscious. Yet in the back seat of his car, her hands felt his stiffening anatomy through denim, his wet mouth mauling her thin tank tops and gauzy, see-through bras with tongue and spittle. She would get so aroused from him sucking on her this way that she'd orgasm before he lay between her legs . . .

Was that sex? Was that sin?

Becky burned with anger at her discovery in the studio. (The bastard had refused couples counseling.) When Kari enthusiastically called back that evening, Becky went eagerly to her friend's apartment in West Hollywood. They originally met when a coworker at the bookstore she managed referred her for a massage two years ago. Kari was a good friend: supportive, understanding, and loving. Warm heart, cold hands . . .

One evening, when Becky was lying nude under the thin flannel sheet on Kari's massage table, Becky announced that she had to urinate. Kari stepped into another room so that Becky could slip off the table in privacy. As Becky made her way back from the sparse bathroom, she spied Kari warming her hands over a steaming pan of water simmering with drops of grapefruit oil. Becky worried that the steam would surely burn Kari's skin . . .

She liked the smell of Kari's skin—ylang-ylang it seemed today.

Kari found her a black leather bustier that laced up the front and a pair of tight leather shorts that caressed the crease of her posterior. She sat on the mattress and pulled on a pair of thigh-high black leather boots as Kari admired her. Becky herself had only once noticed a woman, when she worked at a lab in Sacramento during college. The woman was in her late thirties and everyone complained she was promiscuous. She wore short girlish dresses, her lab coat hanging open to reveal just enough of her freckled chest. The woman's long bare legs and warm blond hair drove Becky to distraction, unsettling her profoundly with her own heat and obsessions.

No lab coats for Kari. She wore black fishnets stretched provocatively over her white legs and a special black polyvinyl bra that cradled her dove-white cleavage. A barely cheek-length polyvinyl skirt held her heart-shaped ass in a slick embrace. Handcuffs clipped to her belt and nipple clamps fastened to her bra strap, she looked like Dark Fantasy Barbie (batteries included).

Kari wiped a lock of dyed black hair from her eyes and winked, her cool lips glossed bubble-gum pink. "Are you sure you don't play with girls?" she ribbed. Her soft, sloped shoulders rippled muscularly from all her massage work. Kari narrowed her gray eyes and looked as if she could plunder and rape villages.

Slightly unnerved, Becky stood and examined herself in the floor-length mirror propped against Kari's art table. She stood fully four inches taller in the steel heels of the thick pirate-style boots flaring at her thighs. A single sweep of black liner on the upper lids of her green eyes widened her look as she assessed the mixture of embarrassment and delight swirling somewhere around her navel. Kari was a Pygmalion with the esthetics of Emma Peel. Brimstone and treacle, indeed . . .

"Wait!" Kari said, handing her the large whip from the prop closet. Becky had dropped it sadly by the bed with her other things but now she felt the weight of it in her hand and gripped it with a vengeance. "There now," Kari continued. "So where's The Lone Gunman tonight?"

"Disneyland."

"You are *not* serious."

"He is!" Becky insisted, wrapping the whip ropes around her hand. They chafed her fingers, she noted, reddening her fair skin. "His uncle took him for his birthday." Becky despised Disneyland.

Even in her holier days, all that random cheerfulness was revolting. She preferred her purity stern and disciplined.

Kari shook her head, grinning slyly. "Come on, hot stuff. Let's go."

III

"Submit to one another in love."

—Ephesians 5:21

No one ever remembered this Bible verse in Ephesians, Becky thought as she and Kari drove. The verse varies according to translation, but it always appears just before, "Wives, submit to your husbands." Until this afternoon, she would have gladly submitted to her husband's desires over and over if he'd had any. There was little chance of him submitting to hers.

The two women approached the small club located in Hollywood, south of Sunset. The entrance was slotted inconspicuously between a single-story concrete building and five-dollar lunch deli. Its address spray-painted on the metal door, Kari pried it open with ease.

They entered and the club yawned beneath their feet as they descended concrete steps into a smoky vat of home-brewed Kannic chaos. The crowd of extras swirled on the dance floor in a nightmarish stew of vampiric capes, inky velvet frock coats, spiraling tattoos, piercings, leather corsets, starlit headdresses, and thick blue-violet makeup. The beat of heavy electronic music hit Becky square in the chest with a dull, heavy echo under the hand of a glass-encased deejay.

Beyond the busy extras, the set lights bent in all different directions over the activity of her husband's effects crew.

"Becky!"

Henry, her husband's makeup supervisor, called to her, his form and voice fading in the club haze. Tall and bony, with an indigo goatee and thinning raspberry-dyed hair shaved close to his scalp, he walked with a stiff leg. His hands were coated in powder, his flannel sleeves pushed up above his freckled elbows. The fishy smell from the foam latex mingled with the strawberry oil of the fake fog. He motioned to her with his head to follow him. He carried one of the werewolf paws. Apparently the skin had torn and he was taking it to the makeup area to repair it.

Kari kissed Becky on the cheek and, with a little wave, swept out to the dance floor.

Becky followed Henry to the men's room, which the crew had shanghaied to apply the actor's elaborate, mechanical werewolf masks. An intern sat on a stool at one end of the restroom and carefully brushed cornstarch on the eye area of a seated actor wearing one of the hairy masks.

Henry gently rested the torn arm on the Formica counter and dug into his supplies, talking all the while. "So Dave skipped out on us tonight."

"Yup. Heeee's in the happiest place in the world—"

"—and we're in the scariest. This job's a fuckin' nightmare," he intimated. "Even Kannic's out back smoking a joint."

She pointed to the arm. "Is that what we're waiting for?"

"Yeah," he replied, dabbing an extra foul-smelling glue to the tear, "that and someone named Edgar." The actor's wolf lips pulled back into a toothy grin. It never ceased to amaze Becky how real it all looked.

"Edgar?" she asked.

Henry shrugged in his flannel shirt. Becky noticed for the first time the numerous muscles working like large piano strings in his arms under his pasty skin as he painted the glue. She imagined wrapping the leather cords of the whip around them just to see if the chafing would produce deliciously plump welts . . .

"You look really hot by the way," Henry informed her with an appreciative look. "Dave will be sorry he missed this."

"Thank you," she replied, a little embarrassed. Then more dryly, "I'm sure he will be."

She left them to their work and entered the dance floor. She loved dancing, but her husband did not and he rarely took her out. Unsure what to do with her newfound freedom, she stood by the cement stairwell and surveyed the dance floor chaos. She spotted Kari with a predatory gleam in her eye coolly circling a buxom girl in a black velvet dress, her long black hair piled high on her head in ringlets. The girl watched Kari like a child wondering if the kitchen knives were really as sharp as Momma warned.

The skin on her back prickled and every pore opened. Becky turned to see what had just descended the steps behind her when she caught the line of his fair face, traced with shadow and gilded with femininity. He stood perhaps five feet, ten inches tall, medium build, with shoulder-length ash blond hair curling around his ivory temples and chin. Crystal blue eyes sank beneath bowed brows and a widow's peak. A blond, well-trimmed goatee and mustache circled pink lips resting gracefully beneath his roman nose. As for the rest, there he stood, act for act, Byron's Manfred: a white shirt with billowing sleeves and jewel-pinned, white cravat, his torso draped elegantly in a burgundy velvet vest . . .

Becky's eyes moved down his body and the bones of her legs dissolved into pure marrow. From a thick, black leather utility belt hung several feathers, fur gloves, small whips, gynecological instruments, a black mask, and leather handcuffs. He wore black cotton riding pants with black leather riding boots.

"So, what's going on?"

He approached Becky as casually as if he'd always known her and now looked around the club. Then, when his eyes turned toward hers, Becky felt something deadly slide into her stomach. "I think they're having makeup problems," she said, a blaze rising from her solar plexus, "and they're waiting for someone named Edgar."

"That would be me," he said, smiling as he seemed to assess the cast and shape of her face. That's when she noticed the long, perfectly white canines peaking pointedly from beneath his upper lip. Her legs weakened further.

Something fell into place for Becky—on a cellular level, not a conscious one. Something about power and passion, an inexplicable ordinance. A vampire's physiology embodied this law; her body obeyed it. The leather of her bustier stuck to her bare skin from sheer nervousness. "I'm Becky." She offered him her hot hand and he took it, kissing it carefully with cool, girlish lips. Becky noticed him assessing everything of hers from waist to shoulders as he lingered.

Kannic ran by that moment wearing an oversized sweatshirt and crumpled jeans. His silver hair was matted to his head with perspiration. He didn't look the slightest bit stoned, but rather frenzied and desperately rational. He was heading off to the "makeup room" with his assistant when he spotted them.

"Edgar!" he called loudly, running to place a hand on Edgar's shoulder. Kannic stood a full half foot taller than Edgar. "I'm so pleased you . . . could . . . come . . ." he trailed off, his mouth slackening as he noticed Becky.

His first A.D. pulled at his sweatshirt and insisted they had to hurry. Only then did Kannic relinquish his lewd, helpless stare and allow himself to be lead off to the makeup room.

Becky and Edgar shared a moment of amusement at Kannic's reaction before Becky's heart began to pound. Edgar was suddenly everything: audience, director, sound, light. If he left her side, her theater would be empty. "So, what do you do?" she asked. Such a grossly cliché conversation starter, she thought, her stomach twisting with embarrassment. She couldn't let him go, however. Any ploy would do.

But he seemed to enjoy the question and explained he was an artist. For a living he made vampire teeth, using dentistry molds and bridges. He even colored the teeth to match those of the wearer. As he explained the process, he dismantled her fantasy of him. Of course his teeth looked real. Like her husband, it was his job to create realistic fantasies. For other people. Not her.

Then a curious thing happened as she told him about her job managing a book store in Santa Monica. He listened, those crystal blue eyes probing into her, and her mind easily lifted the fallen facade, working it back in place. When she tried to discover a little more about him, his face shone alabaster, a wall against her prying. She only wanted to know his secrets so she could please him. She very much wanted to please him . . .

"My friend Kari is into bondage. May I introduce you to her?"

They found Kari. She had seduced the buxom girl and had her standing perfectly still against a shadowy pillar, dress unbuttoned, hands cuffed behind her back. Kari was teasing the girl's breasts out of her bra with her teeth, slowly, now kissing and licking them tenderly, working them rock hard with her bubble gum lips. Just as they peaked pink and sweet above the girl's plunging neckline, Kari placed the nipple clamps on them, whispering something in her ear. The girl moaned and her lips trembled, her face flushed under the pale makeup. Kari kissed them lightly.

Clearly, Kannic had lost control of this shoot.

Becky stood in a burning waterfall. She wanted Edgar to cover her with his darkness, his ghostly whiteness. She wanted five different foods in her mouth at once, soaking in her saliva. She wanted all these sensations and more, yet all she could do was stand there dumbly, the whip in her hand dangling uselessly to the floor.

Edgar appeared cool yet interested in what was happening, a practiced voyeur. His poise reminded Becky of someone admiring artwork.

Kari noticed them watching and told her submissive to wait, blindfolded her, and left her exposed against the pillar. Becky introduced her to Edgar, then immediately regretted it as they talked. She wanted his attention urgently, but now didn't know how to retrieve it. To make matters worse, he asked Kari if he might participate in the scene she was creating. To Becky's astonishment—as Kari only played with women—she said yes.

Kari turned and gently kissed the girl's face, one hand in the ringlets and the other caressing her clamped breast. Then, as her mouth worked along the jaw of the girl, Edgar moved behind Kari and, drawing on a fur glove, reached under her skirt, brushing all her curves. Kari arched her back like a cat in heat. He then whispered something in her ear. Kari nodded and whispered back, her brow furrowed with either consternation or concentration; Becky could not tell which. His long, thin tongue then flickered over the sway of her neck. He closed his eyes and opened his mouth, dipping those molded incisors, those prosthetic prongs, into her flesh . . .

Or, at least it looked as if he had. Becky's imagination pressed its face so close to the veil between fantasy and reality she peered straight through the weave.

Kannic entered, and his first A.D. shouted for everyone to take their places. The actors then entered, monstrous in their werewolf makeup, skins repaired. "All right, everyone," Kannic told the actors, with more authority than Becky expected from him, "it's going like this . . ." He swept his hands this way and that, giving directions.

But Becky didn't move. Couldn't move. As he backed away from Kari, Edgar's crystal blue eyes turned toward her, collaring her reaction. He seemed pleased by it, and before Becky blinked he was at Kannic's side. The would-be director flushed like a young girl caught dressing when Edgar put his arm around him and whispered in his ear. Edgar motioned toward Becky, those eyes unmistakably touching her body. Kannic nodded, distress lining his forehead with sweat.

Meanwhile, she casually examined Kari's neck, which didn't look the least bit worse for wear—perhaps a bit rosier—and Kari wrinkled her nose happily. "He's a great biter," she exclaimed. "For a boy, that is," she added, kissing the cheek of the poor girl trembling ecstatically against the wall.

Edgar kissed Kannic on the temple tenderly. Kannic's sight momentarily wandered into the hot lights as Edgar approached her and Kari. "I'm leaving now," he said, more to Becky than Kari. "I have a scene scheduled at the Play Pen. Would you like to watch?"

The two women agreed to meet him there.

Becky walked him up the concrete stairs to the club entrance, glad for these last few moments alone with him as Kari attended the girl. She glanced back at the set below and noticed Henry standing against the far wall, watching her. She suddenly worried what he would think, what he would say to her husband, his friend and colleague. The guilt welled in her, then quickly dispersed like candle smoke. She couldn't possibly do anything wrong. It wasn't like her, no matter how badly she wanted it.

They emerged in November air and stood on the sidewalk outside the club, he pulling on his black leather gloves as he gave her directions to the Play Pen. A fresh kiss on her hand, she watched him leave, dissolving into the filthy haze of midnight Hollywood.

IV

He leaned against the wall, arms crossed. "You liked vampires?" he asked. "When did that start?" "All young women 'like vampires,'" she explained. "They are the most erotic figures in our culture. To Christians, vampires are the antithesis of everything Holy. They possess you and make you a creature of their bidding." She grinned devilishly. "What else could tempt a Christian girl and rob her of responsibility for fulfilling her fleshly desires? Yet ironically Dracula was an indictment of the sexual repression of Victorian England. The sexually open Lucy becomes an infant-devouring Lilith and that the patriarchal Von Helsing stakes the vampire brides." "Who's Lilith?"

he asked. He watched her carefully, the sexual tension between them pulled taut. "The first wife of Adam, who would rather fuck demons than lie beneath her husband," she replied.)

They were six inches from hell.

Tall, thin men with long wild hair danced, bare-chested and latex-painted, on smoking platforms. The masses danced below, not entirely unlike the extras at Kannic's shoot. Amidst the darkness and darting, multi-colored lights floated the reek of liquor, cigarettes, and sweat. Becky and Kari passed through draped and torn black netting suspended from the ceiling. They then slid between clumps of people past the bar to a table where a large, bald man in a leather harness hawked slave collars with sturdy steel hoops for attaching leashes.

"Up the red velvet stairs," the bald man half shouted. "The pen's up there."

The staircase, once elegant but now threadbare, was soiled with spilled drinks. Faded on the upholstered walls was a one-hundred-year-old floral design, scarlet upon deeper scarlet, the balcony stairs of an old opera house or theater. Her steel heels dug into the soft carpet.

Just before they reached the second story, the upholstered walls gave way to great glass windows overlooking the dance floor. Overhead, lurid lights glowed steadily. Becky followed them over the crest and onto the next floor.

Drunken college boys crowded against a velvet rope that marked off a roughly 15- by 20-foot rectangular area, using the far glass wall as the back boundary. Over the voyeurs' heads stood a tall wooden post topped by thick metal eye-hole rings; from the ceiling chains hung a horizontal steel bar with a fist-sized eye-hole dangling from each end. Muscles, shoulders, frothing plastic cups, and T-shirts obscured everything else. Behind them milled the darker, quieter types from Kannic's shoot, the ones who huddled under floor-length black cloaks with stark white faces, indolent eyes, and sooty hair.

They all parted for Edgar. He unlatched the velvet rope and moved through the crowd of voyeurs. "Good to see you," he said, hugging Becky, then Kari. "Apparently the girl I was supposed to do the scene with isn't coming." He glanced around the crowd, weighing his options. "I'll start as soon as I find a replacement."

Becky's throat hardly held down her heart, nor her body any objection. Her morality stood alone against her maelstrom of desires, a straw man argument in a tornado of resentment—against her husband, herself, and every rule she'd let become a strut or beam in her moral framework. Sometimes we don't know what we want until we see it. Becky saw exactly what she wanted and her flesh—her soul—cried havoc.

She reached out and touched him lightly on the shoulder as his eyes cast about for a bottom. "I'll play," she said, her voice barely escaping the grip of her throat. Her weak stomach stung with fear.

He turned to her, as if he didn't fully hear what she said, and bent his ear to her. "I'll play," she repeated into his ear, her lips brushing his lobe.

Kari stroked Becky's hair and leaned close to her. "Honey, are you sure you want to do this?"

She nodded to Kari. "It's not sex, is it?"

Kari gave her that who-are-you-kidding look. Or, maybe that's just how Becky's guilty eyes interpreted it. "Do you think he's not safe?"

Kari's brow furrowed again. She shot Edgar a look of bottomless familiarity. Did they know each other? Becky trembled in the threads that stretched between the three. Kari smiled reassuringly at Becky, drawing her close to whisper in her ear. "I'll be watching. If anything happens, I'll knock 'em sideways."

Edgar took Becky's hand and kissed it, soft pink lips upturned. She had definitely pleased him. He led her like royalty toward the crowd of voyeurs and unlatched the velvet rope. She saw the dance floor through the glass behind the pen and felt the music pulsing seductively. A ripple of appreciative whistles and yelps ran over the crowd when they saw her. As they crossed over, Becky felt she was approaching a stage. The eyes on her gave her a rush she hadn't felt since her wedding. Here was a most sublime submission, something darker and holier than Saint Paul ever scribed.

Once he closed the velvet rope, the crowd vanished from her awareness. Audience, director, sound, light. He filled her every sense and was everything she cared to feel.

He embraced her gently. "Do you mind removing your boots?" he asked.

She shook her head and accommodated him, dropping the boots by the wall. "Will this hurt much?"

Edgar removed the handcuffs from his belt and clipped one to each eye-hole on the metal bar hanging above them from the ceiling. "I don't so much believe in the application of pain," he replied, "as the withholding of pleasure."

Kari pushed her way to the front, her hand on the velvet rope. She carefully watched every movement.

Edgar then led Becky to stand directly under the metal bar and carefully placed her wrists in each fleece-lined leather handcuff. He finished buckling them closed and his face met hers, milky, ghostly, pure beauty. "Are you comfortable?"

She nodded.

He then brought his fingers to the laces of her bustier and stopped, those eyes asking her permission. She did not object. He pulled on the laces, loosening them, and the leather slackened slightly to give way to the soft inner curves of her full breasts. She heard a low, satisfied hiss under his breath. He gathered all her hair in his hands and expertly piled it on top of her head in a Victorian twist, tying it in place with her own locks. With the toe of his boot he gently prompted her feet to move apart, making her privates more accessible. Becky's legs trembled as they slid open and her skin burned. She felt herself completely safe yet in extreme danger all at once.

> *"Every strong woman wants to be possessed," she added. "It's the struggle, you see. There's more passion in an even match of power." He moved from the wall to the tape recorder, adjusting the volume, then tested the stuffed vinyl chair. It received him more kindly than he thought it would, and his wincing amused her. "You mean women do want to be controlled?" "I said possessed," she corrected, "not controlled. There's a difference." He sensed the subtlety of her words as those lovely green eyes painted a whole new scenario over his body.*

Edgar stood back to admire her as she hung Christ-wide before him. Then, he reached to his belt and withdrew a large, wispy red ostrich feather. The fingers of one hand played in the loose strands of her auburn hair, his palm brushing her lips, and with the other he stroked her cheek with the plume, blue eyes sinking deeply into hers. The tiny tendrils worked over her forehead, lids, cheeks, lips, tracing her jaw. Fairy fingers, wisp-thin, brushed her long neck and crept to the swell of her chest, delicately slipping into the bustier to stroke her most sensitive, hidden curves. As her head lolled backward, he withdrew the wisps and stroked her arms, her waist, stomach, and finally her legs with broad, slow, patient sweeps. Curling and trailing, the wisps reached between her legs; even where she couldn't feel it, she felt it.

He donned a silky, rabbit fur glove and repeated this, his hand carefully moving over her entire body so lightly that everywhere he touched left her skin weeping for something more definite. But he would not give it. He swept his hand over her breasts, circling deliberately until she wanted him to take a knife and slice through the remaining strings. And when he reached between her legs, he swept all around her most sensitive area and not on it. At this point, the cuffs were unnecessary: they were an elaboration on her already delicate state of possession.

Edgar next removed from his belt a spiky, metallic revolving disc no bigger and no thicker than a quarter attached to a palm-sized handle: a neurowheel. What physicians used to test for numbness he drew down her legs, the small wheel rolling as its teeth nibbled into her calves. His teeth, she easily imagined them to be. The sensation traveled straight to her swelling sex.

> *"These two are different, possession and control. Possession implies that they have you because you will it; you want to belong to them for whatever reason. You fantasize about being his captive, an exquisite creature sleeping in his gilded cage, waiting for his fingers to open the door, reach in, and find all your softest, dampest places. You yearn for him to release you from your dreaming, however temporary. Vampires naturally arouse this desire, this want. Control implies someone directs your actions whether you will it or not, which is rarely erotic."*

Cold metal tips of a suede cat-o'-nine-tails dangled into her cleavage. He unsnapped the leather shorts, unzipping them just enough to let the tips dance over downy, tortured flesh. She wanted him to rake his nails—and more—into her, to tear away every last bit of her. Instead, he took a thinner whip strung with soft amber horsehairs and stood behind her, pummeling her posterior, thighs, and shoulders with rapid figure-eight movements. The scourges lit the delicate folds of her flesh on fire as the tongues leapt up between her legs, the rhythm matching her spasms.

He stood behind her, toys tucked neatly away, and then began the true torment. With the tip of his velvety nose and tongue he nuzzled her elbows, arms, and shoulders. She gasped as he moved to the nape of her neck, sending shocks of sensation to the base of her spine. He painted between her shoulder blades, the lost erogenous zone, and repeated this artistry on the canvas of her thighs, tongue flickering its wet brush into the hinges of her knees. Working his way up the front, he stopped, his face dangerously close to the furnace. Blue eyes reached deep into hers from below, his mouth close to the opening of her shorts under her navel. The moist heat of his breath on her skin . . .

"Possession is nine tenths of passion," she continued. "The other tenth is love, but anyone can do that . . ."

Becky strained to her tiptoes, the sensations a pyre beneath her. As the flames caught her breath, a snake of smoke uncurling from her womb, she realized in her passion how close to death she was. "To die the little death," the Elizabethans called orgasm. But this was not just a little death. It was a fiery wave of darkness washing over her, an ecstatic torrent flooding every chamber of her flesh.

Edgar stood, his breath slow and heated as his mouth printed obituaries over her cheekbones, down the slope of her neck, and across the supple velum of her chest. He circled behind her—his body covering her back. The fingers of one hand gently reached under the bustier flap and caressed her nipple, heightening her spasms. The other hand traced maddening designs across her waist and over her hip.

Then, fiery waves rippled through her in deep shudders as those fangs grazed her jugular. His cruel pink lips dabbed at her ear as he whispered into it: "Do you want to see the sun again?"

Her breath carried more intent than sound. "No."

"No . . . what?"

"No . . . Master."

Piercing the last veil between fantasy and reality, his fangs pricked her skin and merged with the cataract of her climax. The orgasm folded over and over upon itself, spilling and turning, wrapping her within and without like a turban of black shot silk. She slumped against him as his mouth continued to work against her neck. Becky did not doubt in this old theater, this place of suspended truth, that her enraptured suffering was the result of losing her life's substance.

When finished, he tenderly kissed the place he'd bitten and loosened her auburn hair, letting it fall over her shoulders and chest. He emerged before her, his cheeks glowing as he released her from all bonds. His soft warm fingers found her temples, lips, and neck, as the other hand crept to the small of her back and pulled her to him. He kissed her, and her world stopped. If he was aroused, Becky couldn't detect it. He hugged her and she inhaled his ash blond hair, heavy with club smoke but faintly perfumed. Musk, ambergris, civet and rose water. "The favorite perfume of Henry VIII," Kari later explained. The velvet of his vest wrinkled under her fingers as they wandered up to his shoulder blades. When he relinquished her, his blue eyes lit up as they gazed into hers, but they smoldered with some regret that was not lost on Becky.

After she restored her bustier and boots, Edgar opened the velvet rope to a swooning crowd and a wide-eyed Kari. Edgar hugged Kari good-bye and, as before, he kissed Becky's hand. "We'll play again soon."

Kari held her tightly as they left. "Oh my," was all her friend said as they wound back down the staircase. "Oh my."

"I need to make a pit stop," Becky announced a little unsteadily once they reached the bottom floor. She felt wet, which was not surprising, but she also needed to relieve herself.

The two women found the small restroom towards the back of the club. Becky entered one of the narrow stalls and peeled down the leather shorts. She checked the lining of her g-string: Her period had started. A woman's menstrual flow is like her personal new moon, a time of new beginnings, her womb eagerly shedding everything infertile. And here she was, a week early, the infertility of her life shedding quickly, brought by the power of newfound desire. Becky wanted to shed everything: her marriage, her vague religious inclinations. Everything she once held sacred.

When she finished cleaning herself, she tried to pull up those tight leather shorts, but her legs were too sticky with sweat. She took handfuls of toilet paper and dried herself carefully until she could reclaim her second skin. Her legs were florid, heated. She needed out of these shorts, not in, but in she went after Kari helped her purchase a tampon from the restroom machine.

On their way out, the large bald man stopped them. He'd closed down his table to watch the scene. "Never seen him like that," he said loudly, shaking his head. He wouldn't explain.

V

They changed at Kari's house. Becky was back in her jeans and T-shirt, and Kari pulled on her nightshirt, her eyes widening with realization.

"Becky," she said, "I played with a man!" She waved her hands in the air in mock distress.

"Well, I played with a man, too!" Becky exclaimed, waving her hands. They both looked at each other, then burst out laughing.

"Oh my," Kari sighed yet again. "How do you feel?"

"Like I need to get laid," Becky replied. Then, she looked down at her tennis shoes.

"And . . . ?"

Caught, Becky's heart thudded, but she said nothing.

"I saw the looks between you two," Kari explained. She sighed and kissed Becky on the forehead with frosty lips. "Try to get some sleep before you make any decisions. We'll talk tomorrow, if you want." Kari helped Becky to the door. As she opened it, Becky turned to her.

"Did you know him?"

Kari's eyes glistened as she shook her head. "I know his kind."

VI

He knelt on the floor between her open legs as she caressed his ear with her hands, running her long fingers through his wavy brown hair. She allowed his lips to work down her body, drowning in the water color light. "I taught my first slave to go down on me, to move his kisses into the hinges of my thighs as I spread my legs. I taught him to hesitate, to linger, then make rapid, unceasing movements with his tongue . . . there . . . escalating pressure and intensity. I used Vivaldi's 'Winter' movement to illustrate the darkness, rhythm and vigor. Start slow—dolce, largo—with gentle kisses, then build ferocity. Don't bite. Don't flicker your tongue—at least, not for long. Just swallow me as you want me to swallow you. He could make me come twice: once orally and once inside me if he entered me soon enough afterwards, and only if I let him. Of course, when I'm alone, completely sensitive to my own body, I can make myself come seven, eight, nine times. But that's now, not then. I'm amazed at how little I allowed myself to feel . . ."

As she drove home, Becky raged inside. She had been assured that in marriage she would have sexual freedom, a safe place to express herself, to fulfill her desires. It was a lie. A horrible, miserable, ugly lie. Those fucking bastards. They ought not to lie to little Christian girls, she thought. In those pre-marital classes at church, they told her she would be free.

Pricks.

She wasn't free: She was controlled. And now, for the first time in her life, she'd done strictly what she wanted to do, not what she'd been told. As a result, she found some new truth—a new piece of herself that she could never deny again.

Yet . . . she felt ill-prepared to face the consequence of her new hunger, for fantasy, for submission, for the vampire master, Edgar. What it meant precisely for her marriage and her life she was not certain, although she suspected it would end everything she knew.

When Becky entered the back entrance to the house, like Anaïs says, she felt innocent. She walked through the dark hallway, past the peeling storm windows and into the moonlit kitchen swirling with dust motes, as lightly and quietly as a phantom. Once she composed herself, she entered the warm bedroom. Guiltless. He'd not see, not know. For now, she wore her true desires under her skin.

As she undressed, she wondered how long she could keep it up, him not knowing. He would suspect a change in her, a shift. She decided then that she would just tell him the experience of watching affected her, even if it was a lie. When she pulled the sheet away from the pillow and crept under the cover, Dave roused.

"Mmmm . . . got your note. How'd it go?"

"It went okay."

"Went late."

"We went to a club afterwards. A bondage thing."

"Oh." It was more of an "Nnh," a disapproving grunt.

"A friend of Kannic's took us." She paused. "Honey . . . I really liked it. A lot."

Quiet. She sighed, turned her back to him, and snuggled deeper under the cover.

"That's nice. Let's sleep now."

"Okay. Good night."

To Becky's surprise, the mattress creaked behind her as he rolled forward. The sheets hissed as he reached under and his hot hands sleepily groped her bare ass. She wanted him to reach around between her legs and plunge his fingers deep into her, not giving a fuck about her period. He could fuck her in the ass, for all she cared. As long as he had some reaction. She wriggled backwards against him but found him flaccid against her ass cheeks. Tired from Disneyland, he cradled her like a child, not a lover. She decided to not let it upset her tonight. She would try to sleep, although she knew she couldn't. She crackled like a lit fuse of dynamite.

"Good night, honey," he said at last with that I'm-going-to-sleep-now sigh.

He leaned forward, brushed her long hair from her shoulder, and kissed her neck . . .

A hoarse yell blasted Becky's ear. Before she knew it, he'd leapt out of bed and the lights were on. He was looking at her, horrified. Then she knew.

Her still-fresh blood smeared his lips.

The journalist knelt as he did before, but now his hands and feet were bound—hogtied—with reams of glistening cassette tape. Becky wound the soft yet strong bonds behind his head and into his open mouth, his saliva soaking the interview. The floor bit into his knees and sweat ran from his temples as cold as fear. The marks on her neck. Because of her hypnotic, possessive power, he couldn't dismiss them as scars from some mere mortal blood sport.

"I'm not positive about the metaphysics," she said once he was secure, biting the last ream free and tying off the gag. "But it seems to take more than one bite to become a vampire."

So she was mortal after all. His anger at losing the interview now yielded to his unexpected arousal from the binding.

"I looked for Edgar, but the club people said he'd left suddenly for New York. They thought he had family there. I went to New York, but I never found him. When I came back, I discovered my husband had abandoned me in terror of what I had become—or what he thought I had become. He'd spoken to Kannic, who convinced him of what Edgar was. He never let me explain. So I did the only practical thing: I went to spend a few delightful nights with Kari. But she raged with disappointment when she saw the master's wounds.

"'He *had* you!' she screamed as she hurled a large earthenware jar at the wall, shattering it into hundreds of terra cotta shards. A lampshade swayed on the stand nearby as the whole apartment quivered. The predatory edge of her gray eyes flashed unsheathed, canines budding from under her glossy lips. 'He asked me if I wanted you,' she cried tearlessly. 'But I said I could not take you. You would not want it. It would be by force. And I loved you.' She sobbed and wailed like a woman in birth pangs; her skin gleamed, as if weeping pearly scales in the shifting light. I could scarcely believe what I was hearing and seeing. But I was not afraid. I refused to discuss the master's wounds any further until he returned."

The journalist swallowed bile at the thought of Edgar the vampire reclaiming the exquisite creature that stood over him. Then he realized it was not an even match of power. Between her and the vampires, he knew who was stronger.

"He never returned." She paused, smiling. "Thank goodness."

She shut the tape recorder with one long, beautiful finger. Then, because it pleased her to see him so aroused, she caressed him to an extraordinary climax and left him there, wetter and wiser, bound by more than her epistle.

When We Rise

Jason Rubis

She was the one who wanted to do it, it had been her idea from the beginning. Later on some of their friends thought he had pressed her, like the whole thing was some little kinky fantasy of his. No. Sara was the one who started talking about it in bed, she was the one who found the support groups and started going to the meetings. Jack wouldn't go with her, but pamphlets started turning up in his apartment, with titles like *Loving an Undead Person* and *Towards A Relationship of Perfect Interdependency.*

Jack wanted them to talk before she committed to anything, maybe go somewhere for the weekend. Then one day it was three months later and he came home to her message on his answering machine. She had left it in the early hours of the previous morning. Three sentences. The thing was done, and she had done it without him. Jack had read up enough to know the preparation and recovery time required were minimal. It was as easy, in its way, as getting a flu shot.

There was no answer when he phoned her apartment. He went over there, swearing all the way through the cab ride. When she finally opened the door he took her by the shoulders and raked her up and down with his eyes. There was no change in her that he could detect. Her skin was warm and he thought he saw a pulse flutter in her throat. He let himself believe for a moment that she hadn't really done it, that she had backed out at the last minute, but then she smiled at him.

"You promised you'd wait," he said, knowing she had promised no such thing.

"I couldn't wait forever." She wasn't used to the fangs yet. They gave her a very slight lisp. "It was something I wanted, Jack. Can't you—"

"Why? Why'd you want it? What did you want? To sleep in a fucking coffin? Suck blood off strangers? Fly around like a bat, be dead?"

Her eyes flared. "Those are all lies! You'd know that if you came to the meetings! We don't do any of that, we . . ."

So it was "we" now. She cried after him as he strode down the hall, but she didn't follow. He went out to a bar he'd never been to before, but by now it was dark. There were three girls and one guy in the place, and they were all like Sara was now. One of the girls tried to talk to him, and the hunger he imagined he saw in her eyes drove him out, his drink left half-finished on the bar. He ended up on his building's roof with a six-pack, watching the city lights blink like—as he thought—red eyes. As he finished each can he flung it at the eyes and swore loudly.

Eventually they got back together. It took several weeks. She made him start going to meetings and couples-counseling sessions with her.

The counselor they had been assigned was named Vernon. Jack knew he was needlessly torturing himself, but he couldn't help wondering if this was the one who'd done it to Sara. Vernon was a tall heavy-set black guy, beautifully dressed, with a thick mustache that Jack was sure had been grown to divert attention from his fangs, which were formidable. His office at the Center was cramped but pleasant. Soft blue walls, a little table of pamphlets, and a coffeepot and tower of styrofoam cups on another table in back.

"I'm just . . . I'm having trouble with a lot of this." Jack felt like he was a kid in church again, making confession.

"With what, Jack?" Vernon's voice was a deep liquid rumble, earnest as hell. He really wanted to help. "What specifically?"

"Like, when we were—apart. These last couple of weeks. I know she went to other guys."

"She had to, Jack. She needed someone to use, it's a condition of her survival now. Would you deny her that? I'm sure it hurt her very much to have to seek out other patrons."

Patrons. Jack snorted; he didn't like any kind of jargon, and this bunch was full of it. Sara squeezed his hand hard, smiled—carefully, without parting her lips.

"The point," Vernon said, steepling his heavy brown fingers, "is that she came back to you when you were ready. She didn't hesitate. Isn't that the most important thing?"

Sex took some getting used to. Sara's skin was cool to the touch, it had no smells anymore. Jack missed the salty tang he used to get while eating her. Her perfume seemed strangely flat now.

She didn't get wet anymore, but that, she told him, was what lube was for. She still loved fucking, but now that hunger was mixed—inextricably, it seemed—with her new appetites. They fucked hard, since he didn't have to worry anymore about hurting her. She gasped and swore and clawed at his back like always but she didn't seem to ever come. Instead, she waited until he came, when he was lying wet and breathing on the damp sheets. Then she did the other thing. Jack had come to refer to this—with bitter humor—as "Sara finishing herself off."

It was perhaps the hardest new thing for him. When he had come, after the fury with which they had gone at each other, he would be exhausted, could barely move. He felt helpless then, and there was something about how she did it. She would begin by creeping up him, licking gently at his chest and throat with tiny movements of her tongue. Like a cat licking. Like he really couldn't move and she knew it and was taking advantage. But pushing her off, or telling her to stop never occurred to him; it was delicious, too, like biting a lemon-slice. He still told himself that he didn't look forward to it.

When it came time for the real deal, she did it with a razor-blade, so deftly he barely felt it—they had trained her at the Center, and had shown her where cuts could be made safely without endangering the major arteries. Just a swipe of the blade and then her lips tickling on the wound.

A few weeks later, on a night when he seemed calm, Sara used her fangs. She didn't ask or wait for him to come that night—she might have been too hungry. She turned the whole thing into a bite-and-grapple fest while he was still in her. The moment when the points of her fangs broke skin, when he could feel the fuckers slide in . . . that was so good, the good was such a burn in him he couldn't make himself pull out of her. His balls boiled. Every motion of his cock against her walls engendered more motion. His only option was to get into it, thrust hard. His skin took on an outlandish sensitivity; Sara slid a hand over his chest and he felt each separate hair crushing back on its root.

"Love you," she gasped, and to his ears it was an electronic shriek. This was it, he knew, this was what they talked about in the pamphlets, the "indescribable mutual joy of the using, which so many describe as reminiscent of a psychedelic experience . . ." This was why so many people wanted to be used. Something in the saliva? Or was it some kind of telepathic echo-effect, the pleasure bouncing back and forth between the two of them until it reached a kind of critical mass? Afterwards he ended up lying still again while she tutted and swabbed his bites with cotton soaked in stinging, freezing alcohol.

After that night most of their time together was spent in bed. They didn't have much of it—another thing to get used to. By now Sara was completely nocturnal. Her office let her modify her workday, but that meant much of her waking time was spent hunched over her laptop. Jack's office was less understanding, which left him red-eyed and surly most days. Eventually Vernon suggested—gently—that they make an effort to get out more, see people instead of spending every night holed up together.

They took to going out with another couple from their counseling group on alternate Saturday nights. Deni was tiny, with down-to-her-ass long hair. She would have been rather plain if she had been taller and her eyes less bright. She had changed over about the same time Sara had, and she had a quality Jack could only think of as fervor. She kept asking if Jack wasn't so much happier now, if things weren't just so wonderful now. He told her yes and in five minutes she would ask him again.

Evan was blandly good-looking and never said much. Jack couldn't figure whether he had been changed or not, but he didn't ask—that could be a major faux pas. Evan never drank when they were out, but neither did he partake of the expensive herbal cigarettes that bars and restaurants now made available to those customers who no longer required food or drink. Deni chain-smoked these, chattering away and gesturing with her lighter.

Deni's passion for her new life had also—apparently—made her a terrible flirt. Or perhaps she just had a thing for Jack. She was constantly touching his hand, complimenting him on his hair and clothes, telling him what a lucky girl Sara was. Sara seemed amused by this. Sometimes she actually egged Deni on, which surprised Jack a little. She, like him, had always been on the jealous side.

"I wish you wouldn't do that," Jack told her later. Places on his skin where Deni had touched him burned slightly, as though her fingertips had been coated with some acidic substance.

"Maybe I should give you to her to use for a night," Sara teased. "Deni's pretty wild, you know. Very passionate. Eat you up."

"And what? You'd go off with Evan?" Sara laughed at that, and in a moment he joined her. The idea was ridiculous. Evan wasn't Sara's type at all.

But the idea of being given to Deni lingered in his mind. It surprised him a little, because the pamphlets suggested that the addictive quality of being used was linked to a particular partner. He had had the vague idea that now he wouldn't ever want anyone else to use him. Evidently he was wrong.

He kept conjuring images of himself in bed with Sara, but Sara's body would immediately dwindle, her hair lengthening, and then it was Deni's little hands fighting to hold him steady, her lips pursing and mumbling as they came at him. When his vision got that strange metallic sheen and his cock felt swollen and endlessly capable, it was Deni doing that to him.

He had to jerk off after thinking about those things. He wasn't crazy about that.

On his way over to Sara's one night he saw a girl, barefoot in a too-large pair of jeans, playing with a kitten in a doorway. Her hair was straight and stiff and seemed a little too black. Her lips were a bruised-plum color, so were her nails. When she saw him looking, she turned the kitten upside down and made as if to take a bite out of it. Her fangs looked stained.

"Don't!" He was a little too loud.

"I wasn't going to really," the girl sneered. She turned the struggling kitten right-side up and kissed it before setting it down. It sneezed and wobbled stiff-leggedly off.

The girl dusted off her hands. "Have you heard the good news?" she asked, not looking up. They always asked you stuff like that. It was a nice ironic way of finding out if you were hip.

Jack remembered one of the sappier books Sara had brought home, a collection of "inspirational" writings. "When we sleep," one verse said, "we are beautiful. We harm none. We live in undying pleasure and sensuality. When we rise, it is like a white flame." You'd never know how intense it all was, reading that kind of crap.

"A little," he said, and smiled, and started walking.

"Is someone using you?"

He stopped and said, "Maybe. Why? Do you want me?" He didn't know why he stopped or said anything. She looked so young. Of course, she would still look this way thirty years from now, or three hundred. He got a funny feeling thinking that. He wouldn't be around in three hundred years, no matter who was using him.

She touched a finger to the point of one fang. "Maybe."

"Hell. You don't even know me."

"It's okay. You look cool. You'd like me, I bet. We'd play."

She got up and he realized she was almost as small as Deni. Her jeans looked huge on her, ridiculous; less like clothing than some weird furniture designed to support her body in a permanent upright slouch. She cocked her head and smiled and began speaking at him in a quick, soft rush. "Wanna? Right now? Want me to suck you? Suck you good, yeah you do. You want that. Come on. Let's do it."

The thought of this girl using him excited him and frightened him. It occurred to him that he could just start walking again and then he thought, *You could run.*

"Suck me. Use me, you mean?"

"Sure. That's the least of what I'll do, baby, the very least. I'll get'cha here, see, and . . . right here." On the first *here,* her fingernail pressed a dent in his throat. She got his crotch on the second. It all happened before he could jump back.

"C'mon." She leaned out and slid an arm around his ass and just like that, he was caught. He wasn't going to Sara. At least not immediately.

It wasn't Deni. He was stepping out on Sara, but not with Deni. The thought made him feel exultant, not guilty at all. It was like he was escaping something. It left him free to gloat over the coming pleasures.

They stepped through the doorway into a tiny apartment. White floor and walls. Not much furniture—a shabby couch with pink throw pillows and a toy cat bleeding stuffing, a coffee table with a dirty ashtray and a half-empty wine bottle on it. Something on the wall caught Jack's eye, a small statue of a girl carved in black stone. The girl had outspread bat-wings and an open mouth with tiny ivory fangs. Her eyes were crumbs of ruby.

Jack recognized the little statue as a not particularly good reproduction of Gorecki's *The New Christ.* These days, you couldn't get away from the damned thing. Sara had one on order from a place in Milan. Deni had three of them.

The girl shut the door behind them and carefully locked it. She was already half naked. Her nipples were the same dark purple as her lips, but her breasts were barely there. She stepped out of the ridiculous jeans and kicked them aside.

"Listen. Before we start. It's going to be five hundred. Okay?" She sounded nervous now, almost apologetic.

Jack's fingers froze on his tie. "What?"

She folded her arms over her breasts. "Four," she said, almost whispering.

Jack let his hands drop to his sides. "You're joking."

He had heard about girls like this. The papers did stories on them. The Center distributed pamphlets warning its counselees about them. The cognoscenti sneered at them. Jack felt like he should be sneering himself, but now he couldn't look away from the girl.

"Jesus. What are those in your mouth? Implants? How much did they cost you?" On an impulse he licked his thumb, and pulled the girl's arm down. He rubbed at her nipple and she hissed a little, her shoulders rising. His thumb came away shaded purple. She'd used wine, he thought.

The girl's face twisted up—for a moment Jack thought she might break into tears. "Come on! You knew! Don't play that with me, man, you fucking knew!"

Jack shook his head. "No. I didn't." Then he was reaching for his wallet, opening it and flipping through the bills inside.

"I've got eighty," he told her.

She calmed down. Her eyes followed his fingers. "Serious? You still want to?"

"If you'll take eighty." If she didn't, there was an ATM on the corner.

"Eighty's cool. Eighty's good, yeah. So you do like me, huh?" She stepped warily up to him, took the money from his hand and darted back to squat by her discarded clothes.

"You do," she said, more confidently, folding the bills into a pocket of her jeans. Open-mouthed smile, showing off her fangs. "You like me. How do you want it? I've got a bed. With handcuffs. You like that? This one guy? He likes to pretend he's like being sacrificed to me . . ."

Jack said "No." He got on the floor and crept over to her. He took her foot and rubbed the soft gritty sole over his face, followed a trail with his nose from her ankle up to her thigh. He kept thinking, She hasn't washed, she hasn't had a shower, she smells, Jesus.

Her voice turned breathy. "Oh. That's what you want." She sounded pleased. Bare feet with their painted purple toenails slid out on the floor, slowly, one moving left, the other to the right. "You want my little pussy? Want to suck my little pussy?"

She likes saying that, he thought. My little pussy, she likes that. He touched her there. It was wet. Pink gleaming inside black. He touched his fingers to his nose, then his lips, and shut his eyes. He had never thought of this taste as delicious before, even while he was missing it on Sara. He wanted more. He crept forward and got his face between her legs. She spread herself for him with her fingers, saying, *He likes that, yeah.*

He did. His tongue was clumsy at first, then it sought out the place where her clit was, eased it out of hiding, washed it carefully. He wished it was larger, so he could feel it stiffen.

His neck ached, and his shoulders, but he wouldn't get up. He wasn't going to stop, no way in hell. The girl was mumbling, legs and hips flexing on the floor, saying Shit honey, you're good, you don't know, Jesus, you're doing it to me. She said that over and over, patting his head, now and then digging her nails into his scalp.

Sara would be awake by now, Jack thought, booting up her laptop, watching the evening news or talking to Deni on the phone: those were images that usually warmed him.

Blood rang in his ears as he fed, his heart beat a clamor inside him. After this he would go to Sara, but he wouldn't tell her where he had been. He would sit back in the couch and accept her welcome, her caresses and kisses and eventually her fangs. She might smell this girl on him. He would deny nothing. There was no telling what she might do then.

In Service Immortal

Paige Roberts

I was kneeling, trembling at her feet the first time she touched me. I was fifteen. Having been raised as a servant in the royal palace after my parents died when I was eight, I had seen the queen many times, from a distance, always beautiful and unchanging. That day, the queen's normal attendant was ill, and there were several demanding foreign dignitaries staying in the palace. Everyone was overworked and distracted, but the queen called for her tea, and someone had to bring it to her. A harried looking cook shoved a silver platter in my hand and told me to bring it to the queen in the throne room. It was a simple task even a skinny, awkward boy like me could manage.

I stared fixedly at her beautiful feet in their satin open-toed slippers while holding the tray up in shaking hands. Her delicate toenails were painted shiny scarlet, like fresh blood. Her long shapely legs were almost completely bared by the short ornate skirt of dark silken layers she wore, and her pale skin was framed by the layers of black silk in the long train. Scarlet silk embroidery that matched her toenails traced intricate flowing designs in the darkness. I had never seen anything so beautiful as her feet and legs up close, but I was too terrified to look any higher.

It was just the lightest brush of her fingertips with those long, perfect scarlet nails on my cheek, but it brought my head up immediately, and I met her eyes. She looked so human up close, aside from her eyes, incredibly beautiful with her long shimmering black hair, and unusual dusky pale skin, but human. Her nose was even a shade crooked as if it had been broken sometime in the distant mists of the past. But her yellow cat eyes could make a person think that she had never been human. And looking into those eyes, my already terrified boyhood self nearly fainted with fear. They were the eyes of a predator, and they made me feel very small and very vulnerable.

"Do not fear me, child," she said, in a voice like silk and fur. "I take only the willing."

"Yes, my queen," I said, not knowing what else to say. I could not have moved to save my life, trapped by her predator's eyes, as she assured me she would not strike.

She looked away after an endless moment, and I was freed.

I dropped the tray with little grace, and a rattle of dishes ten times older than I was, on the small table at her elbow, and withdrew as quickly as possible, hands shaking as if I had a fever. But, that night, I dreamed of her. I dreamed of being the willing sacrifice at the annual ceremony where she took blood and life from one man, so that she could live on and rule wisely as she had done for a thousand years. I dreamed of the feel of her fingertips on my cheek. I dreamed of giving up my life to her, and when I woke, my bed was wet with the dark pleasure the dream had given me.

After that day, I made sure it was known that I had served the queen, and she had found me acceptable. Any time any duties were required near her, I volunteered.

When I turned twenty, her normal attendant retired. He had served her for fifty-three years—since he was twenty—and now his health was failing. I had served more than once, as often as I could manage, as his substitute, and it came as no surprise when she chose me to be his replacement. No surprise, but a great honor, nonetheless. I had done nothing but plan and train and hope for that day every waking moment of the previous five years. I dreamed of her nearly every night as well, but I told no one of my shameful desires.

That first year as her personal servant, I began to learn her moods, her subtle expressions. I had to in order to anticipate her needs as a good servant should. I came to almost know her thoughts by the tiniest shifts in her posture and expression. And again, she chose me to be the single attendant to prepare her for the annual Ceremony of Blood. She had been growing tired more and more easily the last few months. Her color was not good and her beautiful hair had lost its luster. I thought she would be looking forward to the ceremony, but as I helped her to prepare, she was unusually silent and reluctant in her movements, as if she were going to some unpleasant duty.

I knew that she chose among the many volunteers for the ceremony, at least partially by beauty. The men she chose did not merely die, she took them to her bed and had pleasure of them, and, it was said, gave them great pleasure in return, before taking their blood to feed her long life. Yet, she did not look like a woman anticipating a night of pleasure.

I knew the palace better than anyone, having played hide and seek there as a child. I knew of secret ways behind the walls, where nearly every room in the palace could be accessed, or at least peeked into.

Though I am shamed to admit it, that first time, I watched.

I watched her take the willing sacrifice, a tall, muscular blond man that dwarfed her slender dark form. She stripped him and bound him with black silk cords to her bed. I watched her kiss him and touch his body. I watched as she took his manhood in her mouth and stroked him to full erection. She teased him, touching every inch of his skin with her hands and mouth, and her long bright nails. She gave him every pleasure of the senses imaginable and brought him to the edge of sexual explosion again and again, until he was fighting the ropes madly, wanting to touch her, wanting that final release, begging for it.

Then, she mounted him, and rode him, crying out her own pleasure. His body bucked beneath her as she finally permitted him the release he desired. As his body shuddered, she took a fistful of his blond hair and pulled, and arching his neck, sank her fangs into his throat.

The blond man screamed with the pain and the pleasure mixed, and begged again, this time, to live. "I changed my mind. No! Please!" He begged and fought the ropes, as she drank from his throat, his body still inside her, still writhing with both pleasure and pain. He begged her for mercy, and my queen, who I had always seen rule with great compassion, and gentle love, killed him anyway. "I don't want to die," was the last thing he said, whispered rather than shouted as the strength in his blood flowed out of him and into her.

She pulled her mouth away from his throat at the last. "I know," she said softly, and embraced him, cradling his head against her chest like you would a child in need of comfort. She stayed with him like that as the last breath left his body, and longer, holding him tightly as if she could hold in the spirit that was gone.

I watched and was aroused and fascinated, horrified and saddened by turns. I did not sleep that night, haunted by what I had seen.

The next day, the queen's hair was lustrous and her skin vibrant with life. She had energy, and was determined to do everything at once, it seemed.

I, having slept not at all the night before, was hard pressed to keep up with her.

I never watched after that first time. I knew what would happen to the beautiful men who went willingly to her chamber. And I found, in spite of it all, that I envied them.

I still dreamed of the touch of her slender hands, the feel of the fall of that silken curtain of dark hair on my body. I even dreamed of giving up my life to her.

I lived to serve my queen. Dying to serve her just seemed fitting somehow, and I could not imagine a finer way to end my life.

One night, a few days after the ceremony, I went to attend my queen in her chamber. She stood naked in the darkness by the open window, with the wind blowing in over her skin. I could see only the glory of the curves of her silhouette, but it was enough to tighten my body painfully. I took care to hide my response from her sharp night vision. The queen often dispensed with the burden of clothing once out of the public eye. It was something I had to learn to deal with as her servant.

Her yellow eyes reflected slightly in the dim starlight as she stared out from her high tower over the sparkling lights of the capitol city, like stars spread out below us.

I knew her well enough by then to know her moods, even in the dark. I knew her better than any other human, yet the touch of her skin against mine was beyond my reach.

"Tell me," she said, not looking at me, still looking at the city. "Did I handle that negotiation with the trade unions well today?"

"Of course, my queen," I said without thinking.

"I want truth from you, dear boy, not flattery," she said, a hint of irritation in her voice. "If you were ruler, would you have handled it differently?"

I genuinely thought about it then. "If I were ruler . . . I think perhaps I would have given them more short-term concessions, and fewer long-term."

"Why?" she asked, looking at me now, with those yellow predator eyes.

I had to swallow before I could speak, but I was pleased to hear my voice steady and sensible. "People want tangible results. It's fine to give them something that will benefit their children or grandchildren, but people just don't think that far ahead most of the time. If you had given them some short-term gains, such as a small tax on imported luxury goods that can be made here, they would have been far more willing to accept your long-term cuts to their trade subsidies."

Her eyes released me, and looked back at the city. "I have forgotten what it was like to think in such short spaces of time," she said softly. My eyes adjusted to the darkness enough to see her features in the starlight. Her brow was drawn together in deep thought. Then I saw her lips tighten, and I knew she had come to a decision. "You will attend me when I complete the negotiations tomorrow."

"Yes, my queen."

From that day on, I attended her almost constantly, and she asked my advice frequently. She had an attendant assigned to serve my needs, so I had fewer reasons to leave her side—a strange concept to me, to have someone else serve me. It was awkward at first, but as my queen demanded more and more of me, I found I was grateful for the help.

But no matter how tired I was, I was always the one to attend my queen in the evening. I would permit no one else to take the simple pleasure from me of removing her slippers and jewelry at night, or brushing her hair.

I was also always the one who prepared her for the sacrifice ceremony every year. She would accept no other attendant.

There was one year when she seemed particularly reluctant. I dressed her in her most beautiful garments and jewels, as if she were a bride about to be wed, but she acted more as if she were going to the funeral of a loved one. She was plainly suffering in anticipation of what she would have to do.

There was no solace I could offer her. "I am sorry, my queen," I said, ashamed of my helplessness in the face of her need.

"You have nothing to be sorry for," she said softly. "You do not kill to live."

"But you only take the willing," I offered her. "There are always many volunteers for you to choose from."

Her yellow eyes looked at me. "I have heard your footsteps outside the door, dear boy. You know many of them are not willing to give up their lives to me, though they say they are. Why do they volunteer to die when they still cling to life so strongly?"

I considered the possible motivations for a man in the prime of life to volunteer to sacrifice it. I found I could understand them very well. "They are tempted by your beauty, I think. They delude themselves into thinking that just this once, for them, you will make an exception."

Her eyes closed and when she opened them, she looked into the far distance, into a place I could not see. "Is my life worth the deaths of so many?"

"You have ruled wisely for a thousand years. Because you are immortal, our society prospers and is stable. War is a thing our children learn about in history class. One man a year dies, and thousands who might die in wars and riots and the chaos of an unstable society live in peace and prosperity."

"If the one life that had to be sacrificed were your own, would you still feel that way, I wonder?" she said, more to herself than to me.

"Yes, my queen," I said softly, visions of my secret dreams of being the one she took in my head. "I would."

Her uncanny eyes focused on mine, then, and she searched my face, seeking truth. Whatever she found seemed to give her what she needed.

She went into the crowd of witnesses for the ceremony, head high, striding with the same serene confidence I had seen since I was a child.

I saw eight of the annual blood ceremonies before the night I saw my queen weep. It was two days after a blood ceremony, and it was very late. As usual my queen had nearly run me ragged with her newfound energy, but even so, her eyes had been far more shadowed than usual. I had heard the man's screams for mercy the night of the sacrifice clearly even through the thick mahogany door to her chamber.

She was sitting in the darkness in her chamber as I came to attend her. She often took refuge in darkness when something troubled her. Her bright eyes allowed her to see as if it were daylight in the dimmest of lights, but made the brightness of sunshine a painful torture. I had become accustomed to tending her regardless of light.

I knelt at her feet to remove her satin slippers, and a drop of moisture fell on my cheek. I looked up, and her eyes reflected back at me the dim light from the window, and a sparkle of moisture glistened on the dark outline of her cheek.

"My queen?" I asked. "What troubles you?"

She closed her luminous eyes and became nothing but a darker shape in the dark room. She was silent for a time, and I fetched the brush, knowing its location by touch. She owed me no explanation for her tears, and in truth, I needed none. I had heard the man's screams two nights before, and I knew my queen's compassionate nature.

I brushed her hair gently, taking extra care not to cause her the slightest pain. Then I laid the brush aside and turned down her bed, as if nothing were out of the ordinary.

She did not move to climb into bed, however. She stayed sitting there, a silent, still silhouette. She made no sound, but I knew somehow that tears still flowed down her cheeks.

I was at a loss. I wanted to offer her comfort. If she had been an ordinary woman of my own station, I would have held her while she wept, but no one touches the queen, not even me. In all the years I had served her, I had only that one brush of fingertips on my cheek and the silken texture of her hair as I brushed it. I took great care not even to touch the soles of her feet as I held her shoes for her.

"A thousand years is a long time to be alone," she said, and her velvet voice broke with her pain.

I fought my way past a lifetime of training to do the unthinkable. I touched the back of her hand where it lay on her lap. It was just the lightest of brushes with my fingertips, but it was enough to send a shock of awareness throughout my body. "You are not alone," I said, not knowing where such boldness came from. She was my immortal queen. I lived to serve her. She was no mere woman to be touched.

Her bright predator's eyes locked with mine in the darkness, and my breath came more quickly, and my body froze in place like a rabbit under the eye of a wolf. She looked at me with a hunger that was not human, a hunger that only my death would satisfy.

She blinked, and I broke free of the paralysis. I bowed then, properly, and retreated as quickly as I could from her room.

Her eyes followed me, but she said nothing.

My hands trembled with reaction as I went back to my room. I feared that she would have me dismissed for my breach of propriety. What would I do without my queen to serve?

I passed the night without sleep, in an agony of fear, and, to be honest, excitement. My fingers long remembered the texture of her dusky skin.

The next day, she was filled with energy again, and she made the usual demands of me. It was as if that touch in the darkness had never happened.

I supposed simply that it mattered far less to her than it had to me.

I served her from that day forward, with great care to maintain the boundaries of propriety. I did not wish her to think that I would take such liberties again.

She continued to seek my advice in matters of state, and I was honored to see that she frequently acted on that advice. She began giving me assignments that had nothing to do with my servant's duties. She would send me to deal with visiting dignitaries, when she could not. She sent me as her representative on several occasions to attend to minor duties of state.

I found myself serving my queen in ways I never would have imagined. I did not remember the queen's previous assistant doing any of this, but he had been quite old, even when I joined the palace household as a child. I found myself worrying about diplomacy and political wrangling. Trying to see through the doubletalk of politicians to see who was truly my queen's ally and who only pretended to be, and how I could bend even the pretenders to doing my queen's will.

I heard what my sheltered life had never allowed me to hear before—criticism of my queen's rule. There were many who said that she was out of touch with the reality of living as a normal human. There were many who said that our society, which I had always thought of as rich with tradition, was stagnant and choking on its ancient roots. Other countries were progressing far faster, and it was becoming a threat to our security and success as a society. These criticisms at first offended me deeply, but the more I heard them, the more I remembered my queen's words, that she had forgotten what it was like to think in such short spaces of time.

My queen was wise and had ruled long. She gave me these responsibilities, and asked for my counsel, because she accepted the reality of her position. I came to understand, slowly, that I was her bridge to ordinary humanity. That was my new position. And I strove to do it well.

The greater my responsibilities, the more it wore on me physically, trying to attend to my queen and to the extra duties she assigned me as well. I was plagued for some time with blinding headaches, but I did not mention them. I was working hard, but there was not one moment of it that I would give up. I found I truly enjoyed my new responsibilities as much as I had enjoyed my previous ones.

Five years later, I was serving tea to my queen, between speaking to an ambassador of a small country seeking protection from an aggressive neighbor and writing a speech for my queen to deliver the next day. I was trying to tell her about the advantages and disadvantages of allying ourselves with the ambassador's people, and thinking about her speech, and one of the headaches hit hard until I could think of nothing, and spots of light flashed before my eyes. My words faltered to a halt, and worst of all, I broke the antique cup that my queen had drunk her tea from all my life.

I was mortified, and dropped to my knees immediately, in spite of the spots still dancing in my head. "Forgive me, my queen." I blinked and blinked, staring down at her feet, trying to clear my vision, but the pain and the spots remained.

Her fingertips brushed my cheek as they had so many years

before, and I looked up at her, squinting slightly, so I could focus on her face. It was a testimony to the intensity of the pain I was in that her rare touch did not cause a reaction in me.

"You are not well, dear boy. Go to a physician. You are excused of all duties for the next three days, at least."

"But, my queen, your speech, and the ambassador is waiting for an answer."

"Then I shall answer him," she said. "Go. I do not wish to see you again for three days." Her voice was not loud, but it held the snap of command.

"Yes, my queen," I said, and left her to seek a physician, as ordered.

That was three weeks before the next sacrifice ceremony.

After I left the physician, my pain dulled with medicines, I went to my quarters and spent most of the three days resting and thinking. My attendant brought me food and tended to my other needs.

Each night, I wondered who was substituting for me. Who was brushing her beautiful hair? I did not inquire. I really did not want to know who would most likely take my place at her side.

When my three days of exile were up, I presented myself to her as usual.

"How are you feeling, dear boy?" she asked.

"Better, my queen. Thank you."

"Good. I have missed your counsel," she said with a small smile. And she outlined what I had missed, politically.

I resumed my duties again, doing all that I had done before, but with an odd sense of detachment, a feeling of unreality, or perhaps, simply uncaring. What had seemed so important to me before now seemed trivial.

Only one thing remained important, the time I spent with her each evening discussing the day's events, and lovingly stroking the tangles from her raven black hair.

The day of the ceremony came, and I helped her to dress in her finest. This time it was I who was reluctant, moving as if my limbs were filled with lead, as my mind struggled and argued with itself. My desires and my training did battle, and it was uncertain which would win. But the battle made me sluggish, and reluctant, unconsciously fighting for more time to think.

"Have you changed your mind, dear boy?" she asked.

And I looked at her startled and guilty. Had she read my thoughts? I knew from long association that she did not have that ability, but for a moment, it seemed that she knew what was going on in my most secret heart.

"Changed my mind, my queen?" I asked.

"You once told me that you believed the price of my immortality was worth it. You said that even if it were your own life on the line, you would still believe that. Have you changed your mind?"

"No, my queen," I said, and took a deep breath. I had delayed as long as I could. The moment of decision was at hand. I had to speak my thoughts to her, or give up any chance of ever living my dream. "In fact . . ." I took a deep breath, and plunged in. "I know I have no right, but I ask that you choose me for the sacrifice this year."

"You?" she asked, and her voice betrayed utter surprise, something I had never heard in her before. "But you serve me. Your death would rob me of . . . my most able assistant." She hesitated a moment before saying the last, and I wondered what she had been about to say.

"I will die anyway, and this way my death will have meaning." And for one night, she would touch me as I longed to be touched, and I would touch her. Before I died, I would give and receive pleasure from the woman I had loved since I was a child.

"But you are yet young. I have not lost track of time so completely. You have many years to live."

"It is unlikely that I will live to see the next Ceremony of Blood. There is a tumor in my head, and the physicians can do nothing but ease the pain."

"Oh," she said, and sat down in a chair as if suddenly overcome with the fatigue that sometimes hits her when she is near the time of the Ceremony of Blood.

I knelt beside her knee. "Take the strength that I have left. I know I am not as beautiful as the men you choose, but my life has always been yours. Take it now, I beg you."

"Dear boy," she said softly. She touched my cheek, and a tear traced its way down hers. "I could not bear it."

"I am truly willing, my queen. I want this, with all my heart." I could see her considering it. I knew the subtle shifts in her face better than I knew my own. "I will not change my mind in the end like the others," I said, looking into her predator's eyes without fear. I saw when she came to a decision, and the soft lines of her mouth firmed.

"No. I don't imagine that you will," she said, and wiped the tears from her face, careful not to smudge her makeup. "Go then. Go and wait with the other volunteers. Send in the law minister before you go. I would speak with him before the ceremony."

"Yes, my queen," I said, elation lifting me until I practically floated. At the time, I did not think to wonder why she suddenly needed to speak with the minister of law. I was going to live my most secret desire. I was going to spend my last night on earth in the arms of the woman I worshipped.

I stood, waiting with the others who hoped as I did, for what seemed like forever. The crowd of witnesses that had gathered became restless as the queen delayed her appearance for nearly an hour past the usual time.

I began to wonder if I should go to her, see if she needed anything, but I had been ordered to stand with the others. So I stood, in an agony of anticipation and excitement and dread.

Finally, the queen appeared, walking head high and serene as if nothing could touch her.

She chanted the names of all of the men who had given their lives to her over the centuries, and we waited, listening, knowing that one of us would have our names added to the list, and remembered always.

At the end of the ceremony, at the time of choosing, she walked to me just as I had dreamed so many times, and it was real this time. She didn't even glance at the other volunteers. She walked straight to me, pointed to me, and spoke the words I had heard each year of my life. This time, the words made goosebumps stand up on my body.

"Do you offer your life willingly, that your country might never falter, that your people always be led by one apart, one who will put the good of the people who give their lives above all else?"

"I offer my life willingly," I said, and my voice shook with emotion. "That my queen will live, and my country will stand immortal and strong as she does."

"Then come. And know my gratitude, and the gratitude of our people. Your sacrifice will be remembered."

She turned and walked back into the palace, and I followed on her heels all the way to her chamber, with the thunderous applause of the witnesses following me, praising me for the sacrifice they believed I was making for them. As she closed the door, I remembered the other men I had seen follow her in and the attendants at dawn, carrying out their empty bodies to be buried with honor. Tomorrow morning, it would be my body they carried out, and tomorrow night, someone else would brush her hair. I felt a moment of sadness and regret wash over me.

Tomorrow I would be gone, but tonight. Tonight. I looked at my queen as she turned back around to face me, and her beauty was overwhelming. Tonight, she would touch me, as I had once seen her touch another. Tonight was the whole rest of my life, and it was all that mattered.

Her predator's eyes locked with mine, and I trembled with reaction. I was truly her prey this time. And I found that fear was still there, but I wanted her so badly that fear was only a pale counterpoint to desire.

She touched my face, and I closed my eyes and turned into her hand.

"Do you regret your decision, dear boy?" she asked, fear in her own eyes.

I don't know what she would have done if I had said yes. "No. Never. I have dreamed of this all my life."

She came closer, reassured.

I stood still, torn between an instinctive desire to run for my life, and an even more primitive desire to run to her. She was death, but a death so beautiful and seductive that I longed to embrace it.

She grasped my wrists and held up my trembling hands, looking at the palms as if they were something new and wonderful. She placed gentle kisses on my palms one by one, and I shuddered.

"Touch me," she whispered, and there was a need in her face that I had never seen before. A thousand years is a long time to be alone.

She pulled my hands up to her face, and I touched her. Her skin was the faded dark olive color of a race that had died out before my birth. She had the skin of a race that was meant to live in the sun, but she had avoided the sun's blinding rays for centuries due to her sensitive eyes. Her skin was like the petals of a cocoa and cream rose, so soft that I was timid about touching too hard.

But this rose was made of steel.

Her grip on my wrists tightened and she pulled my hands more firmly to her skin, and guided them down along her long neck, across her collarbone, and down to her breasts.

She threw her head back and exulted in the pleasure as my hands stroked and caressed her. She released my wrists to let me do as I would.

She had not permitted the blond giant I watched her with years before such liberties. But me, she gave all of herself to, and all but sobbed with pleasure as I touched her.

She arched her back, pushing her soft flesh into my palms. My knees trembled from the intensity of the moment. I was touching her, touching my queen's rose petal skin. I knelt before her, fearing my knees would disgrace me by failing if I did not. I looked up at her inhuman beauty, my hands still caressing her, and it was right. It was the place that I belonged. Tears flowed down my cheeks.

My queen brushed my cheek with her fingertips and looked down into my eyes. I could see that she again feared that I regretted my decision.

"My queen." It was true. She was mine, to worship, to love, to serve, to live for, and to die for.

She saw in my eyes and heard in my voice all that I had never said to her. She brought her fingertips to her lips to taste my tears.

"My dear boy," she whispered, and I understood with a shock, that there were many things that she, too, had not said.

I buried my face against the silk of her dress, not caring that I stained the fine fabric with my tears.

She held me there for an endless time, her fingers stroking my hair.

It was perfect, and she, with the patience of centuries, might have let me just hold her for hours, but I could still feel the softness of her breasts in my hands. The scent of jasmine, vanilla, and musk from my favorite of her perfumes mixed with her own warm scent and filled my head till I wanted to devour her, rather than the other way round. The heat of passion chased on the heels of the warm moment.

Fire filled me. My hands kneaded her breasts, then went round her waist, pulling her closer to me. I kissed and licked the thin silk over her belly and down to her hips and between.

She shuddered in my arms, and her hand turned to a fist in my hair, pulling me against her harder.

Through her dress, my tongue caressed her sex, wetting the silk and making it conform to her shape. She writhed her body sensuously, rubbing against my face.

She took her hands out of my hair long enough to unfasten her dress at the neck, letting the stained silk slide down her body to lie in a dark pool at her lovely feet.

My hands followed the silk down her body, across her ribs, belly, hips, legs, clear to her slim ankles. I bent and did what had been in my mind every time I took her slippers off. I kissed her lovely toes with the shiny scarlet nails.

She leaned back against the door and lifted her foot for me.

I licked between her delicate toes and sucked them one by one into my mouth.

She moaned with pleasure and her fingernails scored grooves in the mahogany door.

I caressed the arch of her foot with my lips and tongue, and kissed my way up the inner surface of her ankle to her calf. I traced circles on the backs of her knees with my fingertips. My mouth kissed and nibbled gently the soft flesh of her smooth thigh.

My queen's velvet-over-steel body that could break me in half trembled beneath my kisses. Her legs opened to me, inviting me to taste delights forbidden to even consider before that night.

She was slick and hot already, and she cried out when I touched her tentatively with the tip of my tongue.

Her hands gripped a fistful of my hair on either side of my head and pulled me in hard until I was smothered in the fine dark curls at the joining of her legs.

I licked her again, no tentative teasing touch, but a strong caress.

My queen groaned her pleasure and loosened her grip on my hair.

Encouraged, I did all that I could to bring her pleasure. I

caressed and licked her inner thighs and her sex, and sucked hard on her swollen clitoris.

My queen's cries of pleasure rose in pitch until I knew she was near her crucial moment. Gently, I used the edge of my teeth on her most sensitive bud.

She cried out loud enough to be heard outside the chamber, and shuddered hard in my arms.

I licked and licked as she shuddered and moaned, prolonging her pleasure as long as I could. When her body finally stilled, I looked up into her face. I expected to see peace and contentment. I saw hunger.

Her bright cat eyes, half-closed, looked at me as if I were the only thing of importance in the universe.

Her lips were parted to let her panting breaths through, and her fangs were bare and sharp to my eyes.

Adrenaline coursed through my body as if I were suddenly in deadly danger, but it brought blood pounding between my legs until my desire was agonizing. I suspect my eyes were as filled with wild hunger as hers.

She took hold of the front of my shirt and lifted me to my feet by it. She covered my mouth with hers and kissed me deep and hard.

My mouth filled with her tongue, my lips bruised against her fangs, I moaned in a mix of passion and pain, pleasure, and fear, and my legs again trembled with weakness, threatening to fail me.

But my queen would not let me fall. Her arms went round me. One hand cupped my buttock while the other supported my lower back and forced my manhood hard against her.

She walked to the bed, half-pushing, half-carrying me with her. It was as if we danced, but I floated more than followed, a helpless toy for her to play with. When I felt the edge of the bed against the backs of my knees, she stopped and released me for a moment. She took hold of the front of my shirt again with both hands and pulled until the sturdy fabric strained and finally tore beneath her relentless desire to bare my body.

I stood trembling as she ripped off my clothes, leaving me naked before her. Never had I stood so exposed and vulnerable before my queen, and I was afraid that she would not find me pleasing.

But her hungry cat eyes scorched my skin with the heat of her desire. She pulled me into a hard embrace. One hand in my hair tilted my head to the side so she could taste my throat.

I braced for death, with my only regret being that it was over so soon. But her fangs did not sink into my flesh. Her lips and tongue traced lines of fire along my jaw and neck and down to my collarbone.

She wasn't ready to kill. She sought even more pleasure from me.

Her hands, starved so long for touch, explored my body, touching me everywhere at once it seemed. Her lips and tongue and occasional nips and brushes from her teeth brought my skin alive to an incredible level of sensitivity.

Long before her lips touched my straining shaft, I feared I would lose control. Just feeling her kisses trail down my belly and her hands tight on my buttocks holding me firmly in place, just knowing that any moment I would feel her most intimate kiss was enough to test the limits of my self-control. But she seemed to know when I was near the end of my ability to hold back, and she would slow down for me, allow me to catch my breath before beginning again to drive me to the edge of insanity.

Her patience and skill allowed me to hold onto that edge even as she took me in her mouth and engulfed me with wet heat. I leaned back against the bed to steady myself. I buried my hands in the warm thick satin of her hair, holding it back for her as she swallowed me down, and glorying in the freedom to touch that forbidden silk all that I wanted, as much as in the heat of her mouth. Her tongue caressed the tip of my shaft as she drew back and I made a soft sound of pleasure so exquisite I couldn't contain it.

The sound seemed to drive her past her own patient control. She stood suddenly, and pulled me onto the bed. Her legs wrapped around my waist. Her arms held me so tightly I could barely breathe. Her mouth kissed me so hard, her fang nicked my lip. The taste of my blood made her moan into my mouth.

She rolled onto her back, pulling me on top of her. Her hands, still gripping my backside, pulled me into her hot open body in one powerful stroke.

I shuddered and bit my tongue, determined to hold back for her. I wanted to hear again the way her voice went high, and her body shuddered when I brought her. I thrust into her harder, rocking my hips to grind my body against her where it would give her the most intense pleasure.

She rocked her hips to meet my every thrust. I slammed into her as hard and fast as I could as her voice rose higher and higher in pitch.

I knew she was close. Her half-closed eyes glowed with joy and dark hunger. Her hand closed once more into a fist in my hair.

Now. Now she will take me. And the last sounds I hear will be the sounds of her ecstasy. Oh, yes.

I arched my neck to the side as I felt her shudder beneath me. Her cry of joy was near an animal scream and her body spasmed hard around my manhood, stealing my breath with the intensity.

Her bare fangs touched my throat and I closed my eyes and tensed my body, waiting for the pain. But she pulled back again as her body's spasms of ecstasy faded. She held me tightly, trembling with the effort to control her hunger.

I made a small whimpering sound of disappointment.

She pulled back and looked at me, her predator's eyes no longer held any terror for me. I craved the sweet end she offered.

"Please, my queen. Take what you need from me. I want you to."

Her eyes darkened with pain and she said nothing, but held me tight again for a moment.

Then she rolled again, until I was beneath her, our bodies still joined.

She picked up one of the black silk ropes attached to the bedposts.

I held my hand out to her, so she could slide the loop around my wrist. I would not fight her, but the binding was part of the ritual. Both wrists and then my ankles she bound tightly to the solid mahogany frame of her bed.

I was truly helpless, lying naked and bound beneath her. I could do nothing but watch and wait for her to choose the moment of my death.

She stroked my naked sides with her fingernails, and I shivered in reaction. She leaned down and kissed me, tenderly, and her hair fell like a silken dark curtain shutting out the rest of the world and leaving only my queen and me in an intimate world of our own. Her hips rocked over me, and she began to ride my erection in earnest.

I tensed and fought the ropes, trying to keep the pleasure from overwhelming me. I didn't know if I could hold back again. My body was aching with the need for release. I squeezed my eyes tight shut and bit my tongue again.

My queen's long fingernails bit gently into the muscles of my chest. The sudden pain startled me into opening my eyes.

"Don't hold back," she ordered. "I want to feel your seed inside me."

"Then, will you devour me?" I asked.

"Yes."

I groaned at the thought, strangely craving the feel of her fangs in my throat.

I rocked my hips, pushing my manhood as deep into her as I could reach, letting her know how badly I wanted that. She rode me again, and I went with her instead of fighting her. She slow danced with me, gentle, rocking, deep pushes, giving me all I could possibly want. The pleasure was overwhelming, but I didn't fight it. I gloried in it. My thrusts lost their rhythm and became more frenzied, as I neared the edge.

Again, I felt her hand in my hair tilting my head, baring my throat. I could feel the heat of her panting breaths as she fought with hunger as I had fought with passion. "Yes. Please, yes!"

And we both gave in to our desires. I screamed with ecstasy and pain combined until they were indistinguishable. I came inside her, filling her with my seed as her fangs punctured my skin and my blood filled her mouth. Again and again my body spasmed inside her, giving her all that I had until I was drained dry. She sucked hard on my throat, pulling the precious hot fluid of my life into her, until she had taken all that I had to give.

I was left weak and empty and floating on the edge of consciousness with darkness on the edges of my vision. There was no pain, only incredible weakness, and . . . "Cold," I whispered though my body was too weak even to shiver.

My queen laid down next to me and wrapped her arms and legs around me, settling my head on her breast. "I will warm you, dear boy, do not be afraid," she said tenderly.

She gave me something warm and wonderful to drink, and I drank it greedily, welcoming the end of the bone-deep cold. I settled against her wondrous body, and let myself drift. There was no better place in all the world to be.

There was no discomfort, only a feeling of floating and darkness that began to swallow me. And I remember thinking, dying is not so different from falling asleep.

I woke to a dazzling bright morning and a moment of panic. The quality of light made me think it must be near midday. I had overslept. My queen would be wondering where I was.

I started to get up quickly, but my hands came up short when I moved them. Black silk ropes still bound me to the bed.

I remembered where I was and why, and all I could think of was that I should be dead.

"You are awake?" my queen asked. She was standing next to the bed wearing servant's clothes. Her hair was braided in a long thick rope down her back. A widow's dark, full face-veil was thrown back over her head so I could still see her face.

"I don't understand."

She kissed me long and tenderly. "I gave back most of what I took," she said at last.

"But without my blood, you will not survive until the next ceremony," I said, and tugged uselessly at the sturdy ropes. The mahogany bed creaked in protest.

"I have survived for more than ten centuries. You have reminded me what it means to truly live." Her face was more relaxed and open than I had ever seen it. She stroked the hair back from my forehead lovingly. "What you have given me is enough for a few months. I will treasure every moment of your gift, and then I will die. I have ruled too long as it is."

"But you have always ruled us. Our people will be lost without you. Who could possibly take your place?"

"You will," she said, and kissed my forehead. She walked away while I was struck speechless. She went to the window and opened it to the bright sunshine.

She looked back and saw my consternation. "I have taught you what I know, and for years now, I have been but a conduit for your wisdom, a figurehead. Now you will rule in name as well as truth."

"But . . . but . . . but the law says only an immortal can be ruler."

She smiled just before she lowered the dark veil that hid her distinctive eyes. "Rule well and long, my love."

And she was gone, leaping lightly through the tower window. Any other person, I would have assumed intended suicide, but she would survive the fall. And then, anonymous in the dark veil and ordinary clothing, she would vanish into the city, and I would never see her again.

"No! Wait!" I shouted, and pulled hard on the ropes that held me from her side.

The ropes parted with a snap. I looked at my wrists for a moment in disbelief. I remembered these same ropes holding fast the blond giant my queen took that first ceremony, while he fought and struggled, veins swollen on his great muscles. The ropes and the massive mahogany pillars of the bed frame had held fast without even showing a sign of strain.

I didn't have time to wonder why my queen used inferior ropes on me. I just yanked loose my ankles and ran to the window.

I don't know what I could have done even if I saw her, but I was too late. She was gone, vanished into the maze of the city streets.

Even in my shaken state, the beauty of the city held my attention for a moment. It was dazzling. Never had I realized how much light and color the city held, though I had seen this view many times before. And the stars were just as beautiful, shades of red and blue and yellow, where before they had seemed to be mere pinpricks of white.

Stars? But the sun was bright already.

I looked around, seeking its brilliance, and saw instead streaks of vibrant color on the horizon. The sun was not yet up, just beginning to rise. I feared if everything was so bright now that the sun's light would surely blind me when it did rise.

And I was struck by my own words and my queen's enigmatic smile. "Only an immortal can be ruler."

I rushed to the dressing table where I had brushed my queen's hair a hundred times and looked into the mirror. It was still my face, but the eyes, though achingly familiar, were not mine. Bright in the dim light of early dawn, my eyes were the luminous yellow of a cat's.

Grey and Clinton

Patricia Ethelwyn Lang

Grey only felt alive when she danced.

The lights switched on. The tall speakers stood in the shadows in the corners of the rooms, camouflaged by woodwork, clothes, and a vine plant or two. Grey could feel and see the music pulsating from those concealed speakers. *Boom. Boom.* The light fluctuated with the soul, the beat of the music.

Was this done on purpose? She would have to ask . . . Emil?

Fluttering her long blonde eyelashes Grey looked at her dance partner. He was a tall fellow, reminiscent of a startled elk, with his large dark eyes, and pointed ears. She had wanted to ask if he had done any rutting lately, but resisted the impulse. Would he even know the word?

Boom, boom, and *boom*. She closed her eyes and moved her hands down her long legs; she liked to wear a transparent dress with a mad-colored slip on underneath. Tonight the slip was red, and when she strutted into the room, she had seen this fellow, whom she was now dancing with. She had seen him lick his lips and smooth his hair back. It hadn't taken her long to grab hold of his arm and pull his hand down from his hair onto her full breasts. His reaction was what Grey had expected—he had gasped and she watched his cock rise in his pants.

She smiled at that, and for the first time that day felt happy.

They slithered on the dance floor becoming one snake, her undulating hips marking time with the beat of his hard cock against her soft crotch. There was sex in the air. *Boom.*

The couples nearby moved just as slowly, now. And they talked.

One such couple, a pharmacist and his wife, were comparing notes on the trade of the day as they bobbed on the dance floor.

"What the hell," Grey wondered, but not for long. Sliding her fingers down her partner's crack, she held onto his waist as he thrust his cock between her legs. She had helped him unhook his fly. He was almost blind drunk with the heat he was feeling. The alcohol didn't help either. And the music quickened its beat. Grey felt her legs tremble.

She could tell that he was about to come.

He grabbed her tits. And it was then that she bit him on the throat. She hung on while the blood spurted. His eyes glazed and his orgasm filled her womb. Grey felt her cheeks redden—odd that, since her complexion was usually dead white.

That's what dancing did for her, though, as she left her dancing partner slumped on the nightclub floor. Grey found her way through the club to the outside door.

Moonlight and the glitter of the piercing on a young lad's eyelid attracted Grey's attention. She smiled, adjusted her dress and the bloke blew her a kiss before he disappeared into the club.

He had such fat lips; she thought, and licked her own.

She would keep this flush for a few days, before the blood ran dry and she disappeared into the shadows once more. Walking slowly, her stiletto heels click-click-clicking on the pavement, Grey found her way home.

Clinton growled when Barry called him early in the morning. "Sod off," he said, "get someone else." But the lieutenant insisted.

The dance floor wasn't very large. The large speakers, plants and bar took up most of the room. Narrowing his eyes, Clinton gently kicked Barry out of the way. The fat cop muttered some oath that Clinton politely chose not to hear. As long as he moved . . .

Bending down, Clinton put on his rubber gloves and turned the body over. "Bullocks," he exclaimed, unconsciously clutching at his own balls, a reaction he had had once before to these bloodsucker murders. It wasn't the fact that a vampire was on the loose and blood was being spilled too much to suit Clinton's liking. No, it was the fact that—and Clinton gingerly picked up the corpse's jugglies—the bloke's pecker was always out of his pants, a deflated hard-on. It was almost like the prick had withered a hundred years.

"Sucked the juice right out of him," Barry cackled, standing close to where Clinton crouched.

"Eh," Clinton nodded, absent-mindedly. Gently laying the corpse back on the floor, Clinton reached up to the man's face. "Come on," he breathed.

No go. No matter how hard he pulled at those eyelids, the dead man would not close his eyes.

"Jesus, look at the grin on 'im," chortled another copper who just entered the room to take pictures of the victim and the crime scene.

Eh, but it wasn't just the grin. Balanced, on his toes, Clinton lay his hand on the floor. The look on this clown's face was like the other victims. The corpse's eyes were glittering. Clinton would swear to that.

Was the fuck really worth dying for?

"I guess so," Clinton said out loud. Rising to his feet, Clinton adjusted his pants to make room for his own hard-on.

The music wasn't right. Perhaps it was because Grey had strayed from her usual territory. No place like home, eh? Unfortunately, pickings were growing slimmer in the Bayswater area. If she wanted to stay free, and feed, she had to find fresh meat in other towns.

Looking up at the revolving mirror ball, Grey sighed, and raised her hands up over her head. She felt the lights go into her hands, a thousand mirrors.

She was in the fun house looking for her soul in the back of each reflective hard surface.

But Grey couldn't see herself. There was no reflection.

She opened her fragile eyes when the music turned into the slow dirge. Placing her long cold fingers on the face of her partner for this night, she drew close to him, putting one of her legs between his legs, her second leg outside one of his thighs. Grey began to hump him.

Oh, her crotch was wet and his skin hot.

"Blimey," she heard him say as he put his hands on her hands. His cock was pressed against her stomach.

Grey vaguely heard the hum of the other contestants. Well wasn't life a game and the dance the tryout?

Did one of them say, "Look at the tall bird, she's wrapped herself around that bloke?" Maybe, maybe not. His breath was filled with something that turned her stomach.

Garlic?

Grey screamed in time with the music. Dropping to her knees she took his fat cock out of his trousers and plunged her mouth down.

"Bloody hell, girl," he said, putting his fingers into her light blonde hair. The lights made it look transparent. And he put his legs around her body.

She shouldn't be seen doing this. Oh lord, she must stop. But when he curled his body over hers, Grey groaned and dove in for the ride. His cock rose in her mouth. And when he came, Grey bit him, hard. His scream matched the tempo of the music. Dropping to the floor, he steered his cock into her crotch. Bleeding, yes. And he punched the back of her head. Grey stiffened and bit his nipples in response.

He breathed his last thoughts into her hair. The blood and his bewildered Second Coming filled her mind.

Staggering to her feet, Grey quickly left by the side door.

Outside, she looked up at the sky, but the moon was covered this night. "Good," she murmured. Pulling her coat up around her shoulders she hurried into the City Park.

It was a rum go trying to walk through the parks at night since the officials always closed the gate at sundown. However, Grey knew how to slip through the fence.

She felt at home in-between the trees. Listening to the sound of the owl and the night crickets, Grey touched her own cheeks. She was warm-blooded once again.

His name had been Oliver, Ollie for short. Grey listened to his thoughts drifting through her mind as she danced her way home.

• • •

Clinton snorted when he went into the bar. This was beneath her, him, whoever the killer was. Honky-tonk music, and bit of oompah accordion?

"Get stuffed," the owner of the Swill and Swine pleasantly said, "We catered to our clientele. They like a touch of American Redneck, so . . ."

The owner was a large man, his shoulders twice the width of Clinton's slim physique.

Odd to see such a man embarrassed.

Clinton waited.

"We specialize . . ." the owner finished, and then pointed at the walls where handcuffs and ankle restraints hung—in just the right places (height).

In the corner of the rooms where the speakers usually were, (Well, weren't these clubs generally the same? Clinton thought) could be found whips, and chains.

Picking up a long black one, Clinton ran his fingers down the smooth leather. It reminded him of a snake.

He held the whip in his hands as he walked back over to where the newest victim lay.

Lord. Clinton raised the dead man's broken penis. The man was sucked dry and then some.

Clinton glanced at the torn shirt where the scratches and teeth marks were visible. Were there any DNA samplings here?

Why the change? Clinton walked past the other patrolmen who were busy dusting for fingerprints and talking to the still-alive clientele. That, at least, was the same. No one saw a thing.

It was as if they were drugged.

The sunlight hurt his eyes. Putting his sunglasses on, Clinton caressed the whip and his dick hardened.

Maybe, if they paid attention to the clues . . . maybe he could figure out where she (or he) would hit, next.

A cloud drifted over the face of the pale moon. Grey stood next to a tree, which leaned over the stream.

She called the body of water Long Pond.

The wind was brisk. Holding the clasp of her long black cape, Grey pulled her head down against the wool trying to stay warm. The light from the moon briefly escaped the veil of the cloud and caressed her face. If anyone had seen that face they would have known from the lines in her forehead, they would have known from her small pensive frown and sad eyes, that Grey was unhappy.

The faraway sound of music made her raise her head. Oh, she wanted to dance, but she dared not go near the clubs, for at least a week, maybe longer.

But the sound was palatable and the wind took up the beat. Closing her fragile eyelids, Grey swayed in the grass, bumping her slender hips against the tree.

"Heh, sweetcakes, looking for a little juice?"

Grey kept moving. Her feet moved in-between the grass blades. She stood on her toes like a ballet dancer.

She heard something splash in the water. There was a rustle, bang, thump. Did she hear feathers drifting in the wind? Who fed whom tonight?

Her breathing deepened as she raised her chest. For a pale woman she did have ample breasts.

She heard him. His footsteps heavy, he moved like a thug, a brutish boar, snuffling.

"What's matter, cat got your tongue?"

His hands were on her waist.

"Sweet thing, what are you doing out here?" he breathed in her ear, the knife in his belt brushing against her.

Grey opened her eyes. He sucked in his breath.

Blimey, she had gray eyes—no, black . . . And the would-be mugger felt a momentary doubt.

Grey stood on her tiptoes pressing her breasts against his chest. His eyes widened and she felt his cock harden, right next to the knife in its sheath.

"I'm looking to die," she breathed and licked his broken nose. Going down the front of his wide body, Grey nibbled at his clothed cock, her body still swaying with the wind and that faraway music.

"Bullocks," the man hoarsely squealed as he struggled to unhook his fly. When his freed cock finally sprang up, Grey, too, leaped up into the air. Almost like a ballerina doing a split, she landed on his weapon of choice.

Her slim womb fit him like a glove. And the would-be assassin fell back onto the ground.

Grey, his knife now in one of her hands, continued to fuck him. His hands were grabbing at her tits as she moved over his trembling flesh like an ardent wind. He tore at her dress, which was like the moonbeam dispersing in the rain. When he came, she stood up, bending her chest down to catch the pearl necklace over her breasts. When she slit his throat, he barely noticed since at the time she was also licking and sucking on his blood and come. And the way her fingers caressed him . . .

Later, Grey had to struggle to break free from his hands. His blood and his sperm covered her face.

"Goodnight sweet prince," Grey murmured, her face red and her fingers dancing as she kissed his eyelids.

Getting home was a wee bit difficult since her clothes were half gone, but Grey managed. When she wanted not to be seen . . . she wasn't.

"He shouldn't have been in the park at night," she said, absentmindedly, dropping his bloodstained knife on the sidewalk.

"Goddam shame the city's finest has to shack up in this dump," Patrolman Barry grumbled.

Slamming his pudgy palms up against the window frame, he tried, once more, to open up the window to get some needed air into the room. Failing at that, he picked up a cudgel and slammed it against the rickety radiator. In a cluttered room of desks, files, and don't forget the occasional teapot, a faulty radiator was a grand excuse for murder.

Finally, the hissing steam gurgled, choked, and mercifully stopped.

"Yeahhhh!" In response to the applause, Barry bowed.

"Anytime," he chortled.

"Barry get back here," Clinton growled. And the short, wide cop scuttled over to his desk, which was next to a large bulletin board. A map of the city had been nailed to it, marking the sites of the recent serial killings.

"Does anyone see what I see?" Clinton asked, poking at the board with such violence that the papers describing each scene in vivid, gory detail fluttered. Each spot where there had been a murder was marked with a red pin.

Clinton pushed against the board again, looking around the room.

"Does anybody see it?" His voice rose.

Barry had taken off his shoes, and was feeling underneath his big toes. Clinton wrinkled his nose and pushed his own long black hair back out of his eyes.

Time for a haircut, he thought, absent-mindedly, and then looked around the room. The other Panda man and the one woman cop looked equally mussed up, and tired.

No wonder the foot patrolmen were messed up. The bad boys upstairs didn't like crime sprees. They didn't like serial anything. Whenever anything like that went down in this city, the cop shops never closed. And Barry, mardy bugger that he was, had blisters under his toes from all the walking he had done. Clinton eyed the woman, a square-jawed thing, who looked back at him belligerently, and folded her arms across her chest.

Small wonder she reacted like that, he thought. With all the rumors going around about this perp being a sexual maniac, an insane woman or a man with a very twisted sex drive . . . anyway, the men stayed clear of this cop. Woman or not, she'd take them all down if they dared to twit her about the fairer, weaker sex.

They were tired. Clinton knew that. He also knew that whenever the crime was warped in certain ways, they always called him in, however much they resented doing it. Once a policeman like the rest of them, Clinton had left the service to set up his own private detective firm. For some reason the Pandas saw that as betrayal. Therefore, they hated it even more when this traitor was once more in their midst leading an investigation.

Clinton sighed, and scratched his head. Definitely needed a haircut.

"Look," he erupted, and pointed at the red tacks. He followed the red tacks in with his finger and explained out loud as he did so that chronologically the dirty deeds had been going in a geographical spiral, leading up to one point.

And as Clinton pointed, he pounded in the middle of the circle of red tacks on a white space, and the symbol of a specific building.

Barry looked up at the map and groaned.

"The Cock & Bull," he said grimly.

There were other mutterings in the room. Not that snake pit! No purebred true blue patrolman ever wanted to go near that building. Too many Pandas had just . . . disappeared.

Clinton, his finger still on that white spot, nodded, as if to himself, but was really nodding to the group.

"Dinna werry," he said, lightly, "I'll do it."

And he knew that was exactly why they called him in on this case. He was willing to do what no other self-respecting law officer would do in order to catch the guilty ones.

Grey never opened the blinds in her apartment because the morning sunlight burned her delicate white skin. Plus she didn't like being taken by surprise. However, that particular morning, she woke with a start.

"What, what," she gasped, her hands on her throat. Sheer like spider webs, the blankets on her bed fell to the floor with a graceful sigh. Grey glanced at the dresser table and at her desk. She had learned not to look in the mirror between those two pieces of furniture.

She really needed to get rid of that damn mirror.

However, today, she couldn't be bothered with such insignificant stuff, her mind filled with darker possibilities.

A knife? There couldn't have been a knife! Blood? What?

Staggering from the bed, Grey tripped across the thin throw rug. She went into the bathroom on her toes. Grey never walked, anywhere, deliberately.

The light from the bathroom lamp blinded her. Throwing up her arms, Grey tugged at the switch seeking merciful darkness.

She then looked at her face in the mirror—it was a blur.

Why did she look?

Clinging to the edge of washbasin, Grey could feel the blood in her arms disappearing. It was like the sighing of dead doves.

She dabbed eyes with the cool wet flannel.

She needed to go to the nightclub again. This always happened when she stayed away too long.

Grey then frowned. A knife? Going into the living room, she pulled out the Yellow Pages from underneath the phone, and started leafing through them.

What nightclub had she not been to for a while?

Grey sat back on the settee with the fat yellow book in her slight lap.

The front room curtains mercifully blocked out that offensive morning sunlight.

"Well fuck me," Barry said almost cheerfully as he crouched down on the wet grass near the long river.

The woman cop with the large tits stood behind Barry, with her arms around her chest as she balanced the notebook in her fingers. Was her name Jane?

"Doesn't follow, eh, gov," she said.

Clinton had dropped the victim back on the ground, the water splashing across his immaculate blue pants.

"No, it doesn't," he responded, answering Jane. He walked away from the river, and left the details to Barry and the woman.

He walked up towards the road, his eyes crossed. Why the deviation? Why was the throat cut? Standing near the large billowy trees where the wind let the flowers loose on the birds and ignorant humans, Clinton looked up towards the line of apartments across the street.

Where was she? he wondered. His cock stiffened as the wind sent the petals against his dark trousers. He looked back towards the crime scene.

Why was the throat cut?

"She's getting desperate," Clinton said, softly. Eh, he still didn't know for sure, if the slayer was a man or a woman . . . but then again, he did.

Grey tried on a new outfit.

"Does it suit, Madame?" the store clerk purred.

The walls of this store were made of gray silk with shades of red at the seams. Or was it blood? Fire?

Grey looked at the woman with her fat tits and her powder-puff blond hair. And Grey smiled, pulling the thin red straps of the skin-tight dress up a notch.

"Oh, it could use a little altering," she breathed. The woman clerk simpered, placing her hand on Grey's shoulder.

"If Madame is willing," she said, and they went to the back of the store.

This one, Grey didn't need to kill; a flesh meal and an altered dress were more than enough to get her blood racing, especially . . .

Grey left the store with her bags hanging from her arm, the dress and new cloak neatly folded. Grey left the fat blond in a dead faint in the dressing room.

When her fellow employees and her boss revived her later, the store clerk couldn't remember a thing.

Didn't matter to the boss, when there was an extra 100 pounds in the cash register.

Clinton had put a floor-length mirror in his bedroom. Eh, he knew not to tell *that* to the lads at the precinct. For that matter, he wouldn't let on what he did behind closed doors to anyone.

That night Clinton stood in front of that mirror. The one window in his bedroom was opened. Out of the corner of his eye, he watched the curtains undulate in the night breeze.

For some reason they moved in slow motion, making him remember . . . remember . . .

He was starkers. Holding the whip across his crotch, he stared at himself in that floor-length mirror, the lights from the street being more than enough illumination. Even so, he moved in and out of shadows without even having to breathe. Bless the night air.

And the hookers in the street howled their displeasure at another john beating them out of their spare change. The party-goers were clicking down the sidewalks while the cars went *whoosh whoosh sweeeeee.* Good city workers finally off for the night were going home for a well-deserved rest.

So what was he? Clinton stared at his reflection. His face was fleshy, pale, and with the haircut his scalp was clearly visible. He had a head any sculptor would weep to mold. As for his cock . . .

Whoa, who said that? Clinton frowned at his reflection, and curled the whip around his hand and then his balls. He drew his breath in and moved the leather up, touching his cock which sprang up quite nicely, following his lead.

And when he held his breath, he could feel the blood pulsating in his neck. When Clinton touched his cock, again, he came—gasping slightly, but standing up, sternly. He slashed at the floor with the tip of the whip as his cock jerked and spit all over his stomach.

Come dripped down upon his scrotum. He stared at the white semen. Then he put the whip down on the bed, and went into the bathroom to get a flannel. His tight buns never deviated an inch while he moved.

The Cock & Bull pulsated when the night got going.

Literally.

The walls would move back and forth with the music, and the sound of breathing, and the chains—which rattled and the screams were muffled. That's not even counting the sound of fat, juicy cocks sliding in and out of whatever orifice a young woman would offer up for the sacrifice.

Maybe it was the snakes on the wall. Grey glanced at the undulating snakes drawn to resemble kings and queens of old. They grinned, these snakes, and were painted all the colors of the rainbow. They wore jewelry, and they were wrapped around each other, the buttocks firm and pressing down into whatever . . .

It was like the walls were fucking in time to the music.

A man dressed in a red nylon shirt, which showed off his tight nipples and the hairs on his chest, walked by. His hands were curled around the chain, which he used to tug the beast that crawled on the floor beside him. She was a young girl, and her blue eyes were wide, her buttocks open and inviting, buck-naked. Only the size of her tits, and the teeth marks on her flesh intimated she was . . . old enough.

And her smile grew even wider when she glanced up at Grey. The man, who wore sunglasses and a leather cap, sneered.

"Wanna play?" he simpered, rattling the chain of his puppy.

Grey shook her head, and ran her hands down her buttocks, curving her fingers into her crotch. Yes, she was already wet, but . . .

"Not today, big boy," she whispered and licked her lips. "Later."

He nodded and the dog howled her discontent. Using the end of his chain to whack her small buttocks, the nylon man and his date disappeared into the anonymous crowd.

The music changed. The beat intensified. Grey licked her lips once more and touched her crotch. She felt her head buzzing. It was time to get busy.

"Not tonight princess."

Woosh.

Grey felt leather curl around her neck.

"What the," she snarled in astonishment and then fear as she felt herself dragged across the dance floor. Finally, the embracing whip stopped moving, and Grey was able to breathe a little more easily. Except . . . she was face to face with Clinton. He stood so close that an envelope couldn't get between them.

Eyes wide, Grey automatically put her hands on his shoulders as he smiled and pushed his hips against hers.

His hard-on made her eyes fill up. When he grabbed her tits, moving the whip down around her waist, Grey felt her face go flush.

"Let's dance," Clinton whispered, tightening his hold on the leather strap.

Booming, cascading bass beat filled Grey's ears as she and this tight-assed stranger oozed across the dance floor. His jeans brushed against her light, filmy dress. Grey instinctively rubbed her tits against his hand. She saw him half-close his eyes—blue eyes on a dark-haired man. His head was shaved but the black hair was unmistakable. His lips were full. Grey wanted to bite the lower one.

Her mind swirled. She felt the weakness in her loins.

"No, no," she whispered, and opened her eyes wide when this stranger, instead, bit down on her lower lip!

"Yes," Clinton murmured, his cock screaming in his pants as he savagely pushed his hips against her soft mound of gray silk and pussy hair.

The sex was so hot that he could smell her.

"Don't give in to the intoxication," he commanded himself, inwardly. He bit her lower lip, again, hard. His fingers traveled inside her blouse where he explored until he found her tits. The nipples were hard as tacks, her breasts swollen. He knew she had to be pregnant in some way, and he bit her lip again.

Grey groaned as she felt the blood leaving her mouth.

"What's happening?" she whimpered. She felt the ghost hovering over her, the evil spirit beating his wings against her legs.

The nearby dancers were swaying with the wicked beat, the *boom boom boom* of the fuck-me-now. They were the chorus of the night, such as the thin young woman with the dog collar on, biting the cock of her master. He kept slapping her back with the chain, until she gave in and sucked him hard. And there was a man and woman, fat flesh-peaches, their juice and their spit moving down their arms and her breasts. Was the bird was really preggers? The man sucked and spilled milk all over her chest. The couple nearest them happily joined in talk about a happy meal.

Clinton saw them out of the corner of his eye as he lapped the blood on Grey's lip, his hands on her tits, the whip curled around her waist. She had pulled his trousers off, but he stopped her from going further.

Clenching her breasts he said, "No."

And then he speared her, his come rising. The explosion almost took Grey's head off.

"Agggghhhhh!" she screamed, as the monster beat his wings, his claws going up her spine. She fell into this stranger's arms as he took control of her neck, licking the blood, which made his cock harden once more.

"I'm taking you home, Queen," he said, lifting Grey up in his arms. When they left the Cock & Bull the startled snakes ran from the walls.

And Grey, digging her fingers into Clinton's neck, looked into his large eyes, which looked like blue sky with night stars in it.

"Who are you?" she asked.

"Your soul," he replied, holding her tight against his chest.

And the crazy killings stopped, although no one knew why or how, and knew not to ask.

Barry and the fat policewoman, whose name was really Charlotte, went over the files, writing in the details of what they knew. Barry looked up at mousy Charlotte who had taken off her glasses and folded her arms over her chest.

"Heard from him?" she asked, conversationally.

Barry shook his head and closed the files.

"He'll turn up again, when we need him," he said.

As they went down the hall, Barry slipped his arm around Charlotte's shoulders. She looked up at her partner and smiled.

"Like death and taxes," she said.

Barry nodded and laughed, "Clinton can be counted on."

Blue-Blood Moon

Nancy Kilpatrick

In the immaculate attic of her nondescript home, against the wall, stands a tall armoire.

She sets one tapered, colorless candle in the silver holder on the windowsill next to the armoire, and the other candle on the iron Rococo table nearby.

The mahogany of the armoire is stained a color like rusted blood, similar to the natural grain. Shellac allows the clean patterns in the wood and the detail of the intricately carved pictorial panels to show through. At the peaked top, scrollwork meets at a stylized oval. She bought this ornate piece of furniture because it is French Régence and dates back to the eighteenth century—she fantasizes that it could have belonged to the Marquis de Sade.

She grasps the elaborate iron handles of both doors and pulls them toward her. The clean wood scent, enclosed for weeks, wafts out; she closes her eyes to savor it.

The right side of the armoire holds two items of clothing, hanging neatly, both the precise distance from the other as each is from either end of the bar. The left side is composed of three shelves, and a large drawer at the bottom. One year ago, she added full-length mirrors to the insides of the doors.

She adjusts the doors until the angle allows her to admire herself from the front and side, as well as in the enormous asymmetrical cheval glass against the wall opposite the armoire. In the large mirror she can see her back, from head to heel.

Slowly she slips off her shoulders the nubby white terry cloth robe she put on after her bath. The fabric falls down her body to pile around her feet. Her eyes are fixed to the mirror that reflects her full-face.

Wavy blonde hair cascades over creamy shoulders, stopping short of her breasts. The part is on the left, the hairstyle held precisely in place. Her skin is pallid, as though the effort of living day to day has drained the life out of her. Only a hint of pink blushes her cheeks, and that is artificial color. She glances at her feet; her eyes take in the perfect shape of calves and thighs. Her legs pressed firmly together cause the triangle of curly platinum hair to protrude. She looks to the left; the image in the mirror on the other door shows her slim right hip, the profile of her behind. The mirror against the wall reflects perfect, round cheeks, high and full; she thinks there is something yearning about them.

The mirror-on-mirror permits her to scan the small of her back, her backbone, her shoulders. She turns her head slightly and is looking full-face again.

Innocent sapphire eyes stare back, reflecting a chastity she detests, a coldness she counts on, qualities many find attractive. A small pert nose, high-sculpted cheekbones, full defined lips that never quite close but seem to have a small hole pierced in the center between them, as though she is constantly surprised. But she knows only too well that her life is predictable; she is rarely surprised. Or engaged. Except once a month, when the moon is full. And this month twice. Tonight is a blue moon.

Her face is slightly but artfully painted. She thinks she resembles a cameo. Others have suggested this. Her features are delicate, fragile, receptive. People treat her with kid gloves. She has used their fantasies to advantage for nearly thirty years. They have brought her quick corporate success: A series of dully considerate lovers whom she manipulates too easily and avoids sexually. They have kept her safe. Bored.

She sighs theatrically. Downstairs, the antique clock strikes eleven times.

The sigh leaves her breasts quivering firm mounds, the areolas pale, the nipples soft and pink, expectant. She wants to touch them, to take each nipple between her forefinger and thumb and squeeze. The pleasure that would course through her nearly causes her to yield to this desire. Even the thought firms these desperate nipples. She can barely restrain herself.

She drags her eyes away, down her flat stomach, back to the curly hairs. The candlelight is dim but she thinks she can see the beginning of the opening to the dark land of mystery she explores only a dozen times a year. But this year she will visit thirteen times. A chill ripples through her muscles and skin. The clock strikes the quarter hour. She has been lost in a dream. She must not be late.

From the top shelf of the armoire she takes the only item there, a pair of white French panties, and steps into them. The silk drifts coolly, luxuriously over the skin of her thighs and stomach. The crotch sits high against her slit, and at the back the panties ride up, exposing the swell of cheeks and fringing the pale globes with even paler lace.

Her bra, from the second shelf, matches. It is low cut, and through the lace decorating the top of the cups she can see the tops of her areolas. The straps are thin and wide apart; they rest near the edges of her shoulders, making the cups look like just that—cups, the contents about to brim over.

From the third shelf, she picks up the thigh-high white stockings. She gathers one to the foot, lifts her leg, and slips it over her toes, the nails painted with pearly polish, as are her fingernails. The lacy elastic at the top holds the stocking to her thigh. She does the same with the other stocking and, as she bends forward, notices her nipples swell and become visible through the bra's lace.

She lifts the white taffeta and antique lace dress from one of the hangers, and steps into it. The bodice is low, the sleeves long; layers of ruffles flow nearly to the floor. The wedding dress clings to her form, tightly at the waist, flaring over the hips. She stares in the mirror and sees a pretty package, and wonders who will open it.

From the bottom of the armoire she removes the white-leather Victorian-style boots. She laces them through the eyes carefully. They make her ankles appear very slim, and the hobnails add height.

The white choker with the silver cross dangling from the middle is from the drawer. It is imbedded with seed pearls that match the earrings she affixes to her lobes. Long snowy gloves button to above the elbow.

She turns slowly, her eyes a camera, snapping her image: front, side, back, side. She is a princess. The belle of the ball. Virginal. Delicate. To be admired from afar. It is a look she has endured all her life. A look that has kept her shielded from life. This special costume, bought to honor the blue moon, accentuates that look, and she is pleased by the result.

The only other item in the armoire is the ivory cape. She drapes it around her shoulders carefully, fastens the butterfly hook at her throat, and lifts the satin-lined hood. The few items she needs to take with her are already stuffed into the Victorian white satin bag, attached to the lining of the cape.

Outside, the second moon of this unusual month is sharp and flat, a two-dimensional disc. Its frosty face reminds her of her own. Pale. Hungry. Needy.

The air is frigid tonight, the streets deathly quiet. She walks along the pavement of this residential neighborhood, through dying leaves, heels snapping at concrete. Above, barren branches hover, twisting and turning, whipping wildly against the night sky, controlled by the north wind. She pulls the cloak tightly around her throat. On a night like this, she yearns to be warmed.

When she reaches the main street, she hails a taxi and gives the address. The driver, a worn foreign man, sneaks glances of her in his rearview mirror. She guesses he is from some Eastern European country, and that both her beauty and her outfit enthrall him, even while they unnerve him.

"You got boyfriend? Husband?" he finally manages to ask.

She meets his gaze in the rearview with a withering smile. He says nothing more.

When they arrive at the downtown address, she pays the fare, and the taxi pulls away quickly.

The building is old, red brick, turn of the century, identical to those surrounding it. Despite the chill in the air, the streets here are crowded. Her outfit draws many glances.

She strides confidently to the end of the building, turns the corner, and descends the stone steps, careful to lift her cape and skirt, determined to avoid touching her white glove to the rusted iron railing.

Above the black door is a sign, made of wood, the letters of the words all but invisible in this dark stairwell, but she knows them well:

V-S Club.

She knocks once. The slot in the door opens. An eye peers at her for a moment. The slot closes and the door opens, only enough for her to enter.

"Queen of the Night" by the industrial-gothic German band Dracul pulses through the air from all directions. The entrance is dark. Because she comes here once a month, she knows which way to go.

She hears the door bolted behind her but does not turn as she moves swiftly down the hallway. Off to each side are small rooms, dimly lit. Chatter, glasses clinking, smoke clotting the air. Faces turn toward her as she floats past like an apparition.

At the end of the hallway is a corridor, the walls, floor and ceiling a découpage of posters and lobby cards from vampire films, illuminated by black light. There are also black and white glossies of Gloria Holden as Dracula's Daughter; Delphine Seyrig in *Daughters of Darkness;* Lugosi, Lee and Oldman as Dracula; Tom Cruise as Lestat. She stops to examine the Nosferatu poster, with Klaus Kinski playing Count Orlock. His pallor reminds her of her own.

At the end of this corridor, the light stops abruptly. There is, she knows from experience, another door. Above it is a small scroll which she read once, with the aid of a lighter:

Enter Freely, and of Your Own Will.

She hesitates then knocks three times. The door opens slowly, downward, like a drawbridge. She enters a large room. The walls are a facade, built of glass facing that resembles opaque brick-work. One wall contains an enormous tank of piranahs. Opposite is a walk-in fireplace, and the mantel surrounding it is shiny metal which she knows must be scalding. Coats of arms formed of Plexiglas, tapestries and etched hangings in silver adorn these glass walls that reach up into the darkness of the high ceiling. A raven perched on a metal stand screeches once.

Two dozen people mill about, all wearing clothing that makes intent clear. Black is the preferred color, red the second most popular. All faces turned toward her as she entered, and now she feels the eyes linger, on her white cape and dress, her pallid face. She is not permitted to look at them, but knows that assessments are underway; decisions are being made.

She moves slowly into the room and stands in the center on a round metallic plate that revolves slowly, offering herself like a prize. She stares straight at the fire, heart pounding, catching bits of reflections in the steely mantel—black, white, red, features blurred by the metal. Dracul's signature song is playing, "Dracul." The singer growls, sneers, cries like a tortured demon.

This part always unnerves her. What if no one chooses her? She was rejected once, the first night she came to the club. That night no one found her worthy. She had been sent home, unceremoniously, pride wounded, hunger unabated. That hunger drove her back here, despite the humiliation. But from that moment on, she has always been wary, on guard. Excited.

Gradually, the others congregate around her, moving in like birds of prey, scavengers sniffing carrion. The flames in the fire rise high, and the sweet cedar mingles with the heavy frankincense thickening the air.

"Delightful!" she hears the one named Nightshade say.

The female called Midnight sucks air in between her teeth, a long hiss.

Another voice, one too familiar, declares, "I may have her." It is Sanguine. Her heart sinks. She prays silently that he will lose interest. He chose her at the beginning of this month. He is patient, gentle. She does not need to come here for that. Her spirit deflates.

Another voice rises. At first she does not recognize this one, but the rigid tone causes her heart to soar for an instant, then throb in fear and anticipation.

"Come to me!"

She turns at the sound, trying not to appear eager, trying not to display reticence. Slowly she glides across the room to a large polished iron chair, with a high, severe back and heavy arms.

Seated on the woven metal seat, long legs apart, one extended, is Morpheus. She is not permitted to look at him directly, but sees all this through her lashes. Morpheus has never chosen her. She does not know what he is capable of. The thought that he might select her, that he might reject her, causes her nipples to ache.

Silently he lifts a hand, which she does glance at. He is wearing a black leather shirt and chain mail vest. There are metallic arm guards on his forearms. His fingers are adorned with many large and heavy rings, and she notices one, a skull with fangs on the index finger, which is now turned down toward his crotch. The nail is long, filed to a point, painted black. Intimidating. The thought of it dragging along her skin sends a shiver through her body.

She lifts her skirt and cape enough that she can kneel before him, head bowed. Long moments pass. She becomes fearful that he will reconsider and turn her away. Instead, he unzips the fly of his tight leather pants.

He leans forward, pushes back the hood of her cape, exposing her face, then undoes the clasp and pulls the cape aside. His hands are strong but the fingers that pick up the cross around her neck are slender. Savagely he snaps it off the choker and pitches it across the room.

"Are you stupid or insolent?" he says. His voice is cool, controlled, denying her maneuverability. It was Morpheus who rejected her the first time she came here. He did not choose her then. He sent her home. She knows he might not choose her now. But whether or not he selects her, he will humiliate her before the others, who have gathered around, phantoms creating shadows that press in. All these thoughts excite and terrify her.

She inches forward on her knees, between his spread legs, and stops only when his thighs press against her arms.

His cock stands straight up. The head is uncircumcised. She has never seen an uncircumcised penis before. The look is primitive. Not neat and orderly but fleshy and excessive. Less sanitized. The length and circumference of his phallus are formidable, a bit alarming. She has no idea what such a large organ will taste like, what it can do to her. She is both intrigued and repulsed. She trembles in terror that he will again find her lacking.

She bends down, feeling her nipples peek up through the lace. With the tip of her tongue, she licks her lips, then forms them into an *O,* a bit wider than she estimates his penis to be. Slowly she bends further until the hooded head of his cock pokes between her lips. The tip of her tongue darts out to taste this unusual organ. It is warm and fleshy; salty and moist. She closes her lips around him and lowers her mouth. Has he tensed? She cannot be certain.

And if so, what does that mean? Has she done the right thing, or the wrong thing?

Unlike the others here, both male and female, Morpheus gives no indication. She assures herself, though, that she is pleasing him, otherwise he would stop her.

The flesh on the shaft slides and rolls as she works her lips up and down, taking all of him in. His length forces her to open her throat, and adjust her neck until she thinks she must resemble a swan.

She licks and sucks and pulls on him, working his cock to full firmness. She feels the extra skin around the head stretch, and the veins along the shaft plump, straining.

Her lips perform fast and hard, enjoying the nasty deliciousness of him, hoping that he will reward her with a gush of semen. She wants to hold his juice in her mouth and swallow it slowly, only when she has to, against her will. She wants to carry some part of him with her in some orifice, and this one will do.

Around them, she senses the others, bending, moving in close to watch. She should be embarrassed. But worries of humiliation and rejection are overridden by hunger for his flesh. If there is nothing more tonight, this chance to enjoy him in this way, to sip from him, will be enough. Her speed increases as she feels him primed for release.

Suddenly, it is as if she can read his body where she cannot read his thoughts. They are finely tuned, and she is the one adjusting the dials. She turns up the volume.

In that instant, he shoves her hard. She lands on her ass, then falls onto her back. Morpheus kneels above her face. His pulsing cock shoots into the air, the come splashing down onto her face. The thick liquid puddles on her forehead, on her closed eyelid, her cheek. Desperate, she tries to lick some, but her tongue cannot reach that far.

Around her, the others laugh at this debasement. Hot tears well in her eyes. A sob catches in her throat and then escapes.

The semen cools quickly, but the drops and gobs of stickiness might as well be scalding—they burn her already flaming face.

Morpheus, still above, looks down at her. Through her tears she can see his cruel features. The perfectly applied makeup: cheekbones highlighted to appear sunken; lashes dark and long; eyes circled in black; irises crimson, from the contact lenses. His mane of matte black hair is fringed blood red at the front and sides, like wisps of fire. His look is sardonic.

"How many tears can she cry?" he asks.

She does not answer, of course. It is not acceptable to answer. The tears are under control, but she is busy struggling to hold herself together emotionally.

"Perhaps we can empty her of tears," he says.

He stands. She hears the heels of his high black-leather boots slam against the black stone floor as he walks away. He calls out, "Bring her!"

Morpheus has chosen her! She can hardly believe this. She must have satisfied him in some way. He, rumored to be the cruelest of those who frequent the Vampire-Sex Club, will use her tonight, as he sees fit.

Fear and longing battle inside her as strong hands haul her to her feet. She sees Morpheus's broad back, his slim hips, as he disappears through the door that leads to the place that is the reason why she comes here.

She is dragged across the room, through the door and down the narrow stone steps in darkness. At the bottom, a corridor leads back, beneath the front of the club. It is damp down here, and reeks of mildew and urine. The rough walls are hot and moist; she brushes against them and shivers in anticipation.

They pass two dungeons, both of which she has visited before, several times. She is led further, to the dungeon at the front, the one she has never seen. It is larger than the others and, at a glance, more fully equipped. She is shoved through an arched opening and falls at Morpheus's feet. Behind, the wrought-iron gate is slammed shut. The others gather there, murmuring.

Morpheus crouches down. She trembles, suddenly afraid of him. But he only holds a large silver key before her face. "Crawl on your belly to the gate and lock it!" he demands, his voice glacial. She knows that if she is to leave, it must be now, otherwise she is committed to what will follow. She also senses that if she goes, she may never return. Her dull, restricted days will close in and swallow any life that remains.

She takes the key from him, slithers to the gate and locks it. The click seals her fate. On the other side of the grating are dozens of faces bathed in darkness, faces eager to watch her mastered. She feels their breath on her hand like living creatures of the night.

She crawls back and hands Morpheus the key. In the moment it takes him to hang the key on a high hook, far too high for her to reach, she glances up quickly. Silver sconces along the wall burn muted electric light into the darkness. The floor is black earth, and she knows her white clothing is already irrevocably soiled. The thought annoys her and thrills her and she sticks out her tongue to taste the dirt. It is sweet and tart. Gritty. But before she can swallow it, a sharp but low voice commands, "Stand!"

She climbs to her feet. Inadvertently, her eyes meet Morpheus's. His face is harshly gorgeous, his eyes dangerous. He looks almost human. She has only a fraction of a second to identify his emotion: Fury. He slaps her hard across the face, nearly knocking her off balance, shocking her, filling her eyes with instant tears. Her ear rings; she lifts a trembling hand to her wounded cheek.

"Never look at me, unless I give you permission. Is that clear?"

"Yes," she says, adding quickly, "Master Morpheus." He had not told her what to call him, and she is fearful this is the wrong form of address and she will suffer again. Apparently, though, she has selected an acceptable title.

He rips the choker from her neck and throws it across the room. His arm snakes her waist and his hand yanks her hair, forcing her head back and to the side. Exposing her throat.

She trembles at the violence, desperate to flee. But she is thrilled by this closeness, her body pressed against his. And she craves more. She is not disappointed.

His teeth are at her throat. The sharp points drag down her vulnerable flesh, forcing her to cry out. His are the type of incisors that curve slightly inward, that can easily and quickly pierce skin. Her body trembles. She knows she is making a mistake, but cannot hold back. "Bite me, Master Morpheus! Please, bite me!"

The teeth pause. The points stay just pressed against the skin, making her flesh itch. He shoves her away.

She is so foolish! Why did she speak? Silently she berates herself for this faux pas. She has disobeyed twice. Now he will send her away again.

Instantly she falls to her knees, sobbing. "Master Morpheus, forgive me! Please!" Panic makes her say more than she intends to say. "You can bite me when and if you choose. Now, later, never . . ."

"Silence!"

His voice rings through the hollow cavelike room. The ones on the other side of the gate are quiet as the dead. Trembling, she forces her lips to clamp shut.

"You are here to submit, not to dominate. Don't waste my precious few waking hours!"

"Yes, Master Morpheus," she whispers.

"One more unrequested word, one more act of disobedience, and I walk."

The thought of being abandoned by him overwhelms her. Sobbing, she falls at his feet, kisses his boots, throws her arms around his ankles.

"Since you like crosses, get on that one!"

She freezes. She has come here expecting this, or something like it, and she knows she deserves what will follow. But now that the time has arrived, and so early, she is terrified. Hesitation will be misconstrued as disobedience. On shaking legs, she stands and crosses the room to the large *X* in one corner.

"Take off the dress," he says.

She begins to turn.

He rushes forward, grabs her hair hard and twists. "Did I tell you to turn?"

Her head is back, her mouth open. Tears gather at the corners of her eyes from the pain of her hair being pulled. "No, Master Morpheus," she gasps.

He releases her and moves away. With her back facing him, she unzips the dress and eases it down her body slowly. When she has stepped out of it, she holds it to her chest, not knowing what to do with it, afraid of relinquishing this symbol of her persona. She looks down. The white has been tainted. This shocks her.

He snatches the dress from her and flings it away. She did not hear him approach this time, and is so unnerved that he moves like a phantom.

"Onto the cross!" he says, in a voice that permits no excuses.

She steps up onto the low platform. There are grooves for feet at the bottom of each bar of this black Plexiglas cross, and her booted feet step into them. At the top of the *X* are two spikes. She reaches up and grabs hold. Her body is upright, stretched, spread-eagled.

Suddenly he is up against her, behind her. His hands ride up from beneath her breasts, driving the nipples until they swell over the top of the bra. He fingers both nipples at once, pulling them away from one another, until they are hard sensitive knobs, and until her body rocks and undulates. His hands force the French panties to ride higher up her cheeks and she hears fabric tear. He reaches between her legs, grabs the crotch of her panties and rips it away. Moisture seeps between her legs, and her body feels weak. She begins to pant. Her head falls back onto his chest and her bottom squirms against his cock.

She feels like a slut, rubbing and grinding into him while his fingers play a lascivious tune she cannot help but dance to. He toys with her a long time, rubbing, squeezing, pinching flesh, again and again, until she is dizzy, until the room blurs, until her mouth is dry and her opening sopping. And then he moves away.

She hangs onto the cross, her body tingling. She is as hot and moist as the walls in the corridor leading to this dungeon. Her exposed nipples thrust forward wantonly, hungry for a mouth to eat the pink, ripe fruits. Her exposed bottom thrusts back and forth eagerly, a puppy wanting petting.

Suddenly leather smacks her ass. Hard. Pain jerks her awake. The instant the gasp is out of her mouth, he straps her again.

The shock of this sharp burn makes her pull her hands from the spikes and cover her bottom.

Angrily, he jumps onto the platform and yanks her hands back up to the spikes. "You will suffer willingly, or get out!"

He jumps down and within seconds the strap cracks against her flesh again. Soon the rawhide falls into a rhythm. Fast. Severe. Relentless.

The leather feels wide; it seems to cover most of her bottom with each strike. Her cheeks soon tremble from the pain, and try to avoid the hard leather. But that is impossible. As the pain intensifies, her body twists and buckles wildly, desperate to escape, causing the leather to strike her tender hips and thighs instead of her sore bottom, and she does not know which is worse.

Tears flow freely. She wants to beg for mercy, but is afraid to speak. And she senses his only reply will be more of the strap he so skillfully wields. Blisters must be forming on her behind, but he does not stop. The word that will end it all is on her tongue, but she cannot utter it. Instead, she screams. But her screams do not impress him any more than her charms. She hates him for this. She wonders if she is falling in love with him.

He finishes far past the time she would have wanted him to stop. Her ass flames; her vagina is a fiery cauldron. She sobs as relentlessly as he whipped. And now, when she feels him press against her—his hooded cock hard, demanding, lowering to push between her flailed cheeks, probing her hole—she becomes delirious. She stands on her toes, thrusting her burning behind back, tilting those scalding cheeks up, giving him the best angle. She bites her tongue to keep from screaming, "Fuck me!"

She expects fast and hard, but he enters slowly. His cock is a thick spear, directed. Her walls close around him inch by inch, like a mouth starving for solid food. She throbs inside, and struggles to hang on. But she cannot. Her vagina contracts around him when he is halfway in. Her hips buckle. Her hot bottom pumps back, desperate for him to impale her deeper, to fuck her. He pauses, waiting for her to finish, pinching and twisting her swollen nipples until her climax subsides.

With the spasms, juice floods her dark cave and bathes his cock. She feels the flesh of him, so powerful, so determined—so intimate—and is left limp.

She falls forward, against the cross, gasping. She is still on her toes, her behind still tilted back, hoping to keep him inside. From the gate she hears sighs, and realizes how silent they have been. Or she has failed to notice them. Embarrassment swells within her. They have seen her whipped. They have seen her lust.

He toys with her nipples still. The firm tits are so sensitive, almost unbearably so, but she does not want him to stop. His fingers pull and pinch and twist until the nipples are sore and she is moaning, and then he takes them beyond sore, to another rung of pain and finally to another level of pleasure. All the while his rock-hard cock pierces her with only half its length, and she is humiliated at how little effort he makes and she is mastered, a bitch in heat.

Her swollen walls begin to tingle from the prolonged penetration. Hot firm flesh against hot moist flesh. His cock half-buried in this cave that is usually dry and empty. He has opened her, whipping his way in, and joy soars through her, knowing he will enjoy her as long as he chooses. This security feels like power.

Suddenly, he withdraws.

Her body chills instantly. Her abandoned nipples pulse, like hungry little animals. Her protruding bottom begs to be tended to, she is a hollow cave where the winds of winter blow. A low, torturous moan escapes her lips from this new pain.

Within seconds his hands reach around her body. He grasps her left breast tightly and squeezes the nipple until it is prominent and the areola pressed back. She glances down at the metal and has only a second to react before its teeth bite into her.

She cries out. Her body buckles. Tears gush from her eyes. The teeth hurt, and the nipple throbs with a pain she can hardly bear. He waits, allowing her time to enjoy the torture. And when the pain subsides, and she has suffered it, he grasps the other breast.

Knowing what is to come forces a shriek from her lips even before the clamp locks on. She cries uncontrollably, pleading without words for mercy. The throbbing lasts a long time, and nearly sends her over the brink. She nearly bolts. She nearly utters the word that will free her.

Eventually, numbness sets in. Now she can feel only the pressure of the weights pulling on her breasts, and there is something delicious about this.

She turns her head slightly. Out of the corner of her eye, through strands of hair like golden prison bars, she sees him standing. He is naked, except for his boots; his broad shoulders and muscled form are sexy. His enormous cock makes her spasm. His arms are folded across his chest. His face is so cold, unreadable, and this, too, she finds erotic. He is watching her. Just watching.

His immobility is unnerving. She has no idea what he is waiting for. At the gate, she hears one of the others whisper, "He wants her riper!"

She feels Morpheus up against her again, his firm, strong body pressing at her left side. Gently, he moves the hairs from her neck, exposing it. He nuzzles her neck, kissing the flesh with cool lips, licking it, nipping just a little with his pointed incisors. Her body quivers.

Something sharp—or rough, irritating—moves back and forth across her hot bottom cheeks. The pain of the whipping is resurrected. The muscles of her ass contract, but that doesn't help. The glove he wears is imbedded with tiny spikes. And when he rounds each cheek again and again, lifting them one at a time, her bottom twitches and struggles to shift away from this sensation. She presses close to the cross, but the gloved hand then presses harder, trapping her. Her behind is becoming excruciatingly sore. Sore in a different way than the strap left her flesh.

"Drink in the pain," he says, his lips at her ear, the sound filling her head. His tongue slowly rounds her outer ear then thrusts into the opening.

A shiver races through her body and ends at her crying ass. She hears herself pleading, although she does not want to do this. "Please! Master Morpheus! Have mercy!"

"You did not come here for mercy."

She knows it is true.

He twists the left clamp.

Sharp pain slices through her breast. She screams. Tears gush from her eyes. He pulls her hair, forcing her face around, and laps up the tears, swallowing them as fast as they come.

All the while the horrible spiked glove continues rubbing her raw. Her bottom feels swollen to twice its size. He starts to spank her, at first gently, but soon harder, alternating cheeks. It is like tiny teeth piercing her flesh. The spanks are slow, painfully slow, allowing her an eternity to feel each one before the next bite.

Her left hand begins to slip from the spike she is grasping, but his hand covers hers, forcing her to hold on. Her mind and body swirl, driving her down into the earth. The spiral blazes, the fires of hell. Her body is slick with scalding sweat. The muscles of her arms and legs ache and ripple from the strain. With each smack of the glove, pleasure surges through her. Her mouth is dry and she imagines his long penis forcing its way in there, feeding her liquid thick as blood.

The moment she realizes she cannot escape this agony, she plunges into a pit of sweltering passion. Control snaps; her body convulses. She howls like an animal bombarded by hormones; release will only be at the hands of another; she is at his mercy, and he is merciless.

When she gives up control, he grabs her hips and pulls her flaming behind back. He thrusts up inside her hard, lifting her off her feet, leaving her breathless. As he does everything, the thrusts are relentless. His powerful cock impales her so deeply she thought he may tear her apart, but she no longer cares. Pain and pleasure rocket through her, pain from the beating she took, pleasure from the fucking she is taking.

She responds like an animal to this fierceness. She wants him to take her roughly. She wants him to use her again and again, and, in this use, she wants to serve up to him all that she is capable of offering.

He unsnaps the clips. Blood rushes to her nipples. The pins and needles sensation makes each breath a strangled cry.

He grabs her hair, entwining his fingers in it, forcing her head to the side again, exposing the throat to his teeth. The incisors rake the skin. Her starved body swells and works with his.

"Name me!" he demands.

The word that until this moment would have closed him down is now the word that will assure her liberation.

"Vampire!" she screams.

The razor points of the eye teeth dig into her flesh. Deeper. She gushes scalding juice. His lips clamp to her throat and he sucks hard, drinking her blood.

Her body spasms wildly, ecstatically. His cock pulses, shooting hot lava into her parched desert. She gives herself over to him, now, forever, in joyous release.

The armoire stands open. Before the mirrors, she strips off the dirty clothes. Her pretty satin French panties are in tatters, the lacy bra shredded, the virginal dress filthy. Runs have ruined the pure white stockings. Each item goes into the green garbage bag. The choker. The gloves. She saves only the cloak and the boots, thinking she might dye them scarlet for the next full moon.

In the glass she examines her face—skin flushed, eyes bright, alive. Her nipples and the areolas are crimson and swollen—there are still indentations from the clamps, and the sight of them lubricates her opening and makes her shudder. Random strikes of the strap have marked her thighs and hips, but her behind bears the brunt of the hard leather, and the nasty spikes of the vampire glove. Her bottom is a purple canvas, an abstract painting of dark weals and painful blisters. The skin is too stunned to be much more than numb now, but she knows that as she sits at her desk tomorrow, this week, the following week, she will be more than uncomfortable. Each pulse of pain will remind her of being under the control of her vampire lover. She tilts her head and runs a hand down her throat. The bite marks no longer seep blood where he pierced her and drank. She will wear high collars, and scarves again, disguising his dark kiss that defines her passion.

Dirt stains her body, but she cannot bear to wash it away just yet. She closes the doors of the armoire, no longer needing to see herself from the outside.

In her bedroom, she slips between the pastel satin sheets and pulls the down comforter over her wounded body, a body she has come home to live in, and will live in, for days, even weeks. A body that will throb and ache and pulse with desire, until the world slowly numbs her again. Until the next full moon. If only, she thinks, there were a blue moon every month.

Contributors Notes

A bonafide pervert, **Maria Alexander** has been publishing stories since December 2000. Two of her stories appeared simultaneously on the Preliminary Ballot for the 2001 Bram Stoker Award in Short Fiction. Since then, she's garnered a number of Honorable Mentions in the *Year's Best Fantasy and Horror* anthologies, as well as more Preliminary Ballot showings. She was a Finalist in the 2003 Moondance Competition in Short Fiction sponsored by Coppola, Oprah, and *Variety Magazine.* "Veil of Skin" was originally a birthday present for friend Neil Gaiman. *(Merci mille fois, Monsieur Owl.)* Another of her perverted tales will appear in *A Walk on the Darkside,* the next installment of the award-winning anthology series from ROC Books.

Caroline Aubrey is a Cherokee/Muskogee/Choctaw Indian from California. An award-winning poet, she is also a journalist and playwright, and lives in Southern California with her husband and children. She can be reached at carolineaubrey@hotmail.com.

B.K. Bilicki has been crafting his odd little scribbles for nearly a decade. Some say he spies on other realities and reports on what he sees there. Others suspect his mind shattered from the combination of solder fumes and caffeine he regularly feeds it. Whatever the case, he now spends most of his time evading rabid fans who demand that he get published and become quite disgustingly rich. Some of Furor Scribendi's other stories can be found at www.execpc.com/~grmouser.

Michelle Blaid is an aspiring writer currently working toward her first novel publication. Interests and hobbies include gaming, crafts, writing (of course), music, and theatre. She loves cats and has one of her own, who is a love and a joy despite her very few brain cells and her tendency toward shredding styrofoam. Michelle is local to the New England area, and enjoys a hectic starving artist lifestyle.

Kathleen Bradean lives in Southern California. She writes science fiction and fantasy, but always with an erotic twist. Her stories have been featured in the *Best Women's Erotica 2004,* Logical Lust's e-anthology *Eternally Erotic,* and the Erotica Readers and Writer's Association website (www.erotica-readers.org).

Renée M. Charles' erotic fiction has appeared in many Circlet Press, Cleis Press, and Black Lace anthologies since 1995, including *Blood Kiss, Dark Angels, Women Who Run With the Werewolves, Fetish Fantastic, Wicked Ways,* as well as the magazines *Blue Food* and *Bad Attitude* in the US, and *Forum* and *For Women* in the UK. She lives in the Midwest in a big pink and white Queen Anne house with all her cat-children.

Genevieve Iseult Eldredge is a shy and retiring fantasy author. A virgin to the publishing world, she lists among her influences David Eddings and Kia Asamiya. Her interests include opera, voodoo, and the martial arts.

Award-winning author **Nancy Kilpatrick** has published 14 novels, about 200 short stories, and has edited eight anthologies. Her most recent works are the non-fiction *The goth Bible: A Compendium for the Darkly Inclined* (St. Martin's Press, October 2004), and the dark fantasy *Outsiders: An Anthology of Misfits,* co-edited with Nancy Holder (Roc/NAL, October 2005). Under the *nom de plume* Amarantha Knight, Nancy has published seven erotic horror novels in the critically acclaimed *The Darker Passions* series, which Circlet Press is reprinting. She has also edited five anthologies under that pen name. Check her website for updates: www.nancykilpatrick.com

Patricia Ethelwyn Lang, having written and been published for over twenty years, stumbled into the creative genre of eroticism a few years ago. Here, she felt like she discovered her true niche. To be able to express the human experience in such intimate, vulnerable details is a thrill she never thought possible—especially S & M. "I'll never get it right," she says—at least 'right' in her eyes—" but the fun is in the effort. I'll never give up the pursuit of the Muse!"

Allison Lonsdale translates Engineer into English for a large corporation. Her short fiction has appeared at CleanSheets.com, ScarletLetters.com, and in the anthology *Best Transgender Erotica.* In her spare time, she performs her "geeky music for geeky people" in coffeehouses, works on science fiction conventions, invents new genders, and rehabilitates domesticated memes for release into the wild.

Catherine Lundoff lives in Minneapolis with her wonderful partner. Her stories have appeared in such anthologies as *The Big Book of Hot Women's Erotica 2004, Shameless, Best Lesbian Erotica 2001, Clean Sheets, Electric 2,* and *That's Amore!*

Paige Roberts is a Texas lifestyle dominant who divides her time between writing down her fantasies and living them by surrounding herself with fascinating, sexy people. A mild mannered computer programmer by day, by night, she is the kind of girl your mother warned you about. This is her first published work of fiction. She would like to dedicate this story to her inspiration and copy editor, Rain, who told her so, and to the best husband in the universe, Joe, who helped her pick a better title and bought her roses.

Thomas S. Roche's short stories and articles have been published under various names in over 500 magazines, anthologies and websites. His erotic fiction has appeared multiple times in the *Best*

American Erotica series, the *Best New Erotica* series and the *Best Gay Erotica series,* and his editing projects have included three volumes of the *Noirotica* series and four anthologies of horror and fantasy fiction. In 2004, Roche took up fetish photography; his work (literary and visual) is showcased at www.skidroche.com. After a lucky 13 years to the day in San Francisco, he recently relocated to Los Angeles.

Jason Rubis lives in Washington, DC. His fiction has appeared in *Leg Show, Aberrations,* and a number of anthologies, including *Desires, Guilty Pleasures, Sacred Exchange, Swing! Best S/M Erotica 2,* and *Erotic Fantastic.*

Diane Whiteside's day job involves lots of techie talk about computers. To escape this, she's written at night three books published by Ellora's Cave and a western published by Brava. Plus, Berkley has plans to bring out a trilogy of her Texas vampires in 2006. Please visit www.dianewhiteside.com for more information.

About The Editor

Cecilia Tan is the founder of Circlet Press, Inc., for whom she has edited over forty anthologies of erotic fantasy and science fiction, including *Blood Kiss, Erotica Vampirica, Erotic Fantastic, Sextopia,* and many others. Her own erotic short stories have been featured in *Best American Erotica, Best Lesbian Erotica, Penthouse, Ms. Magazine,* and *Isaac Asimov's Science Fiction Magazine.* A collection of her erotic fantasies was published in 1998 by HarperCollins under the title *Black Feathers*. She continues to write about her many passions, including food, sex, and baseball, from her home in the Boston area. www.ceciliatan.com

Acknowledgments

"Blue-Blood Moon" first appeared online at gothic.net in 1998.

"La Paloma Blanca" was first published in "The Hunter's Prey: Tales of Texas Vampires" by Diane Whiteside, Ellora's Cave Publishing, Inc. Copyright © 2001, 2002.

"The Permanent" was first published in *Big Book of Hot Women's Erotica 2004,* edited by Marilyn Jaye Lewis, A Venus Book Club Exclusive, 2004.

NOW AVAILABLE

My Secret Life
Anonymous

Over two million copies sold!

Perhaps the most infamous of all underground Victorian erotica, *My Secret Life* is the sexual memoir of a well-to-do gentleman, who began at an early age to keep a diary of his erotic behavior. He continues this record for over forty years, creating in the process a unique social and psychological document. Its complete and detailed description of the hidden side of British and European life in the nineteenth century furnishes materials for the understanding of the Victorian Age that cannot be duplicated in any other source.

The Altar of Venus
Anonymous

Our author, a gentleman of wealth and privilege, is introduced to desire's delights at a tender age, and then and there commits himself to a life-long sensual expedition. As he enters manhood, he progresses from schoolgirls' charms to older women's enticements, especially those of acquaintances' mothers and wives. Later, he moves beyond common London brothels to sophisticated entertainments available only in Paris. Truly, he has become a lord among libertines.

Caning Able
Stan Kent

Caning Able is a modern-day version of the melodramatic tales of Victorian erotica. Full of dastardly villains, regimented discipline, corporal punishment and forbidden sexual liaisons, the novel features the brilliant and beautiful Jasmine, a seemingly helpless heroine who reigns triumphant despite dire peril. By mixing libidinous prose with a changing business world, *Caning Able* gives treasured plots a welcome twist: women who are definitely not the weaker sex.